THE HAUNTING OF
FURY FALLS INN

FURY FALLS INN · BOOK 1

BETTY BOLTÉ

www.MysticOwlPublishing.com

Dear Reader,

This story begins a new series of six supernatural historical fiction stories set in 1821 northern Alabama. I'm not originally from Alabama, but enjoy living in its friendly northern realm. I've learned a lot about the history and the people of the state in the process of researching for this series. As an outsider looking in, the view has been interesting and intriguing to say the least. If you're interested in tidbits of history I came across while researching for the series, follow my blog, Betty Bolté's Musings, at www.bettybolte.net.

I'd like to thank my beta readers—authors Leslie Scott, Crystal Lee, Jennifer Caraballo, and daughter Danielle Bolté—who read the original version of *The Haunting of Fury Falls Inn* and provided invaluable feedback. I appreciate your time, observations, and suggestions for improving the story!

I'd also like to thank readers like you who continue to inspire me to write stories with joy and passion. I always enjoy hearing from my readers, so please drop me a line at betty@bettybolte.com any time.

If you enjoy this book, please subscribe to my newsletter via www.bettybolte.com to be informed of the release of the rest of the books in the series. You can also learn more about me, my other books, and read excerpts of each book at my website.

Again, thanks for reading! I hope you enjoy *The Haunting of Fury Falls Inn*.

Betty

Also by Betty Bolté

Secrets of Roseville

Undying Love

Haunted Melody

The Touchstone of Raven Hollow

Veiled Visions of Love

Charmed Against All Odds

A More Perfect Union

Elizabeth's Hope

Emily's Vow

Amy's Choice

Samantha's Secret

Evelyn's Promise

Hometown Heroines
True Stories of Bravery, Daring, and Adventure

Chapter One

Cassandra Fairhope's bubble of happiness evaporated from her heart like fog assaulted by the summer sun as Fury Falls Inn came into view. She faced her virtual prison with grim reluctance as the team of matched bay geldings dragged the bouncing coach closer to the circular carriageway, the harness jangling with each stride. For most folks, the elegant inn represented an escape from their daily drudge. To her mind it represented a beautiful yet elaborate prison.

"Sit up straight, Cassie. I'll not have you slouching." Her mother, Mercy, arranged her pale yellow poplin skirts over her knees with a practiced twitch of her hands. "It's good to be home. I've missed your father more than I thought possible."

"I'm sure he'll be eager to greet you." She stared glumly out the window of the closed coach at the welcoming, confining sight. "I guess it's back to a normal routine again."

Her pa, Reggie Fairhope, worked hard to run an efficient roadside inn where people could refresh themselves before continuing the difficult journey along the Winchester Road. Also for those who ventured out into the wilderness to soak in the hot mineral springs in search of relief from one ailment or another. Two two-story structures stood joined together by a dogtrot and wide front porch. The bigger side on the left housed the inn's extensive dining room and guest bedrooms as well as an immense kitchen. The smaller structure to the right was for the exclusive use of the family, with a private dining room, sitting area, and his office. The family bedrooms along with those for key employees were safely tucked upstairs for privacy. She'd grown up amongst strangers and supposed she'd die among them as well.

"I'd think you'd be glad to settle back to your usual chores." Mercy glanced at her with a question in her aqua eyes. "You've always said you enjoy working in the garden and helping Sheridan transform the produce into delicious meals."

"I do, Ma, but I relished the faster pace of Nashville." She gripped the edge of her seat to avoid bouncing off after a particularly nasty jolt. "I'll miss the boutiques and restaurants with all their variety. The excitement and energy."

Road improvements had been made to the lane leading to the inn. Including widening the winding trail to six feet, but weather often turned the dusty, hard-packed dirt road into a boot-swallowing, wheel-snaring quagmire. Add in the low mountains and difficult terrain where horses and oxen had difficulty traversing the roads between the town of Huntsville, Alabama, and the more established city of Winchester, Tennessee, to its northeast. Reggie had dragged the family away from Montgomery in central Alabama several years before statehood was granted. He wanted to take advantage of the prospective growth in the northern part of the territory and so they'd moved. But, oh, how she wished they'd stayed in the bigger city where she had friends and opportunities. Instead of being buried out in the wilds of the state for the past six years. Visiting the fancy boutiques and salons in Nashville only deepened her need to escape.

For years she'd searched her mind for viable means of leaving like her brothers. Finding some way which her parents would approve for her to provide for herself. Her pa's standing in the community meant she had few options. Indeed, her ma had informed her of the one and only acceptable answer. She chewed her bottom lip for a moment, turning away so her ma didn't see. She had no other choice for the time being but to slip back into the mindless repetition. She swiveled her head around to address her ma. "I'll be ready to pitch in after I take my purchases up to my room. Don't fret."

Mercy nodded as she looked past Cassie out the open window. Cassie also turned to stare out the window. Horses stood hitched and dozing, tails gently swishing, at the rail in front of the inn. The dogs lay curled under the shade trees. Chickens pecked in the dusty grass. Cows grazed in the distance. The air shimmered above the dusty carriageway, the summer beginning with another heat wave. How very pastoral. She sighed silently so as not to reveal even a hint of her dissatisfaction to her ma.

Mercy gathered her purse from the seat between them. "I understand, but we must make the best of the situation. Pa will expect us to support his decisions whether we agree or not. I'll not hear of any complaining, you hear me?"

"Yes'm." Cassie retrieved her flower print reticule and clutched the soft fabric between both hands on her lap.

The driver, a silent and brooding middle-aged man with a thick beard and mustache, halted the carriage in front of the stone steps leading up to the immense porch jutting from the front of the inn.

The four hunting dogs announced their arrival, trotting out from the shade and circling the dusty carriage, barking and sniffing. The snuffling and woofing brought a grin to her tense mouth. Two black retrievers, Beau and Pickles, cozied up to the horses. Red, a golden retriever, came to the side door to wag his tale at Cassie. Cocoa, the smaller tawny-and-white spaniel, stayed a few yards away from the creaking coach, tongue lolling and long silky ears alert. She couldn't wait to be able to pet them again. She smiled at them and then let her gaze travel over the front of the building with its glass windows flanked by shutters and brick walls.

A pair of pinewood rocking chairs with dark green cushions flanked a round table to the left of the double doors leading into the inn, an inviting and cozy place to sit and watch the continuous foot and vehicle traffic flow past the inn. Or perhaps to sew. Or read as time permitted. A favorite, if rare, pastime.

The driver jumped to the dusty ground and opened the creaky door to hand the two ladies down out of the vehicle. The footman was a young clean-shaven fool who tipped the brim of his floppy hat and grinned at her at every turn. He dropped the several hat and dress boxes along with a number of string-tied parcels to the driver, who carried them on bowed legs to the porch and piled them up. She cringed, hoping her pa didn't stumble over the collection. He'd berate the men for putting the coveted boxes where guests could trip over them. Cassie watched the two men finish their task and then cluck to the horses to urge them into a walk toward the stable.

"Would you look at that." Mercy huffed out a frustrated blast of air through her nostrils. "I've told him to turn out the pigs to fend for themselves. Lazy, good-for-nothing boy."

A half-dozen milk cows grazed in a post-and-rail-fenced paddock nestled between the back of the good-sized barn and the towering primeval forest surrounding the clearing. A pair of milk goats kept the cows company. Next to the corral, a sturdy pig sty provided shelter for the herd of swine, the ones who usually roamed freely in search of food as well as mud to keep cool and protected from biting flies. A couple of men worked at replacing a wagon wheel within the shade of the carriage house. The boy in question, a thirteen-year-old tow-headed neighbor kid with a tendency to disappear when needed, poked his head out of the stable, blinked his eyes at the newly arrived coach, and then promptly ducked back inside.

Mercy muttered something under her breath. Shaking her head, she shooed Cassie toward the steps. "Go on in, girl, while I have a word with that idiot." Mercy gathered her skirts in one fist and marched toward the stable.

"Better him than me," Cassie muttered.

She snatched up a couple of parcels and sashayed through the open heavy wood and glass door into the cooler interior. Her pa likely kept busy in the inn side of the structure. He'd want to know they'd returned. She scanned the foyer, wiped her damp forehead with the back of her hand, all while noting with relief the glistening tables boasting lanterns with glass globes waiting to be lit at dusk. Cheery daffodils and jonquils greeted her in vases on either side of the foyer, adding a touch of floral scent to the air. Hannah, an often overly flirty server and all around helper, had thankfully taken on Cassie's chores while she'd been away picking and choosing new clothes. She stacked her boxes, filled with lovely dresses, flattering undergarments, and fashionable hats, at the right side of the foyer by the door leading to the family's side.

"Pa?" Cassie moved toward the dining room, where voices murmured over their noon meals.

She hesitated in the wide doorway, searching for Pa's short-cropped, black hair and salt-and-pepper beard. Several groups of men along with a family occupied various white-clothed square tables, applying spoons to large bowls of either soup or stew, depending on cook Sheridan Drake's mood and the available ingredients. But no sign of her father. She crossed to the kitchen and pushed open the swinging door to hurry inside.

The large room remained her favorite of all the spaces in the inn. She inhaled the mouth-watering aroma of baking bread and smiled with pleasure. Her pa had built the kitchen specially with stone floors and walls to reduce the chance of fire destroying the entire building. An immense cooking fireplace allowed for multiple hanging pots and kettles to simmer at the same time. A hinged spit had been cleverly hung to one side so that Sheridan could spit a piece of meat and then hook it up to a device which slowly rotated near the heat of the fire, cooking the meat evenly on all sides as it spun beside the open flames. Bunches of dried herbs hung on strings stretching from the window to the corner of the room, waiting to be included in the cook's recipes.

Two older women, the Marple sisters, chopped and stirred at a table along the left wall, glancing at her with a nod of acknowledgement before turning back to their tasks. She spotted Sheridan laboring over a plucked chicken on a wooden board on the sturdy work table in the center of the room.

Of medium height with strong, sinewy arms, the black man made her smile with pleasure. She often wondered where he came from but he kept his personal life strictly to himself. He constantly hummed or sang while he worked, some folksy tunes as well as spirituals, giving the kitchen a feeling of humor and happiness the rest of the inn missed out on.

"Sheridan, where's Pa?" She glanced around the bustling kitchen, the heart of the inn, where the freeman performed some kind of magic to produce the variety of meats and stews and desserts that drew customers from miles around.

"He's gone, miss." His golden eyes glanced at her and then focused on the fowl he was dressing for the spit. "Went off to Savannah or somewhere."

A chill swept through Cassie at the news. Her beloved father was a fixture of the inn, one of the supporting pillars. He wouldn't leave unless some emergency forced him to. "Why?"

Sheridan shrugged and continued seasoning the bird. "Can't say. He didn't entrust me with such im-por-tant information."

Cassie speared him with a pointed stare. His tone revealed hurt feelings. He rarely reacted to her father's actions and decisions but this one seemed to rankle. What had been happening during her absence?

She leaned closer, pressing her hands onto the edge of the table. "What's wrong?"

Sheridan shrugged again as he wrapped a string around the hen's legs to tie them together. Then he grabbed a curved metal hook and ran it through the bird. Turning in one fluid motion, he secured it to the spit and set it turning.

The door behind her swung open with the abrupt bang of a palm on the wood door. A shock arced through her frame upon seeing the tall, handsome man. Flint Hamilton, son of her father's best friend James Hamilton, marched in, studying a piece of paper in his hands. Only a few years older than her seventeen years, Flint was good-looking and comfortable in his own skin. Her crush on him had lasted since she was a young girl, a secret she kept from everyone. Something about his easy smile, his loose-hipped stride, and focused attention when he spoke combined to make him irresistible. Still, she remained very much aware of the rumors surrounding him, ones whispered behind hands after he left the room.

"Sheridan, you simply must listen to reason. Adding poached quail eggs and green turtle soup will draw even more customers." He lifted his head and she shivered the moment his bright green eyes spotted her staring at him. "Miss Fairhope. Welcome home."

His auburn hair reflected the sunlight filtering into the bright room as he approached on long legs clad in khaki jeans with a white dress shirt beneath a chocolate brown vest. She'd rarely had the pleasure of seeing him, since he lived miles away in Huntsville. Her ma even more rarely allowed her to go into town for any reason. Unless his parents brought him out to visit, she didn't have any chance to indulge her hope of one day marrying him. Her mother had made it clear that marriage to a good man was her only escape. So be it. As long as he, whoever he might be, took her far away from the stifling effect of her mother.

She gaped at him for a split second before snapping her mouth shut. Then opened it again. "What are you doing here?"

Sheridan huffed as he propped his fists on his hips. "He's the new innkeeper."

She glanced at Sheridan, blinking as his words sank in. "What?"

"Let me explain, Miss Fairhope." Flint laid the paper on the corner of the work table. "Your father had to go to Savannah, Georgia, to oversee the building of the furniture he requested. Apparently, the joiners didn't quite comprehend how to follow his instructions."

"Pa went to Georgia? While Ma and I were away?"

Leaving Flint to share the same living quarters, the same rooms, the same air as her. The realization stole her breath. He'd be around all the time. Her chance of escape had finally come. Maybe. If she could make him notice her not as a girl but as a woman. His words finally broke through her happy fog.

"I'm afraid the matter arose rather urgently." He shrugged lightly as a grin slipped onto his lips. "Your shopping trip lasted a little longer than he'd hoped."

Cassie slowly shook her head and tilted it to one side. "But why are you here?"

"He asked my father if I could manage the inn for him while he's away." Flint rested his fists on the table. "Mr. Fairhope wanted someone with experience, and since my father owns the best hotel in Huntsville, he asked for me to help him out. So here I am."

"Never even asked me," muttered Sheridan as he dropped his hands to start working on his next delectable masterpiece.

Flint shot him a glance and added a half smile. "Your expertise is in your culinary skills, Mr. Drake. Mine lies in ensuring you have what you need when you need it. Please don't be offended."

"Too late, I think." Cassie pressed her lips together. "Ma's not going to like it either."

"Why would she be upset? I'm here to help her as well." Flint lifted the paper and skimmed it. "Sheridan, think about my suggestion to expand the menu. The ingredients are fairly easy to lay hands on and the guests would feel like they're eating in Boston or New York instead of...."

Sheridan grunted and continued his work with a large beef butt roast without further comment.

Cassie studied Flint—he was definitely pleasing to look at—and then sighed as she peered at him. "Come on, Mr. Hamilton. Let's get this over with."

"What?" Flint followed her through the swinging door and into the foyer. "What do you mean?"

"Telling my mother." Cassie halted in the center of the space until her mother looked up from where she was arranging the boxes and parcels for distribution to the family side, the storeroom upstairs, and the pantry in the kitchen. Her long ash-blonde hair was secured in a neat bun at the back of her head. Her pert nose wrinkled as she sorted the packages. Her ankle-length linen dress showed the signs of their recent travels, dusty and spotted. Still, she stood regally, shoulders back and chin even although a slight frown settled onto her brows as she focused on Cassie instead of the boxes.

"Tell me what?" Mercy spotted Flint standing beside Cassie and eased a cautious smile into place. "Well, well. Flint Hamilton. What a nice surprise."

"Mrs. Fairhope." Flint touched his fingers to his forehead in greeting. "I trust you had a pleasant shopping trip to Nashville?"

"We did, thank you." Mercy glanced between Cassie and Flint several times and then arched a brow. "So, what did you want to tell me?"

Cassie cleared her throat, delaying even though she'd been the one to initiate the revelation. Her mother considered herself equal partners with her father, even though her father never treated her as such. Perhaps her mother's way of putting on a brave front? She straightened her back. Nothing for it but to say what had to be said. "Pa had to go to Savannah on business so hired Flint to manage the inn while he's gone."

"Oh…" Mercy started to nod and smile but then suddenly froze, the smile wilting into a straight line. "He's gone to Georgia? Without so much as a by-your-leave?"

"It was an urgent summons, Mrs. Fairhope. He asked me to help you so you wouldn't be unduly burdened with the day-to-day decisions. He also asked me to tell you he'll write to you often."

Mercy spluttered, there was no other word for it. Then stood blinking at Flint as her color changed from alabaster white to pink in her lightly freckled cheeks. Cassie wondered if steam might escape from her mother's ears as her face slowly turned blood red and her brows sank between her eyes. She'd only seen her mother in such a fit of anger once before and dreaded the conclusion of the unfolding scene.

"Mrs. Fairhope, please. I promise to do my best to…"

"Young man, my husband should not have put you in such a spot. Feel free to pack and go home and I'll manage with my daughter's help. You're not needed here."

The light in Flint's expression dimmed as he shook his head. "I'm sorry, ma'am, but Mr. Fairhope made me promise to act on his behalf until his return. I'm a man of my word. I'll have to do as we agreed." Flint swallowed, his Adam's apple sliding quickly up and down in his throat. "As long as he wants me here, that's where I'll stay."

"Well, I never... You have no right to supervise my actions. Do you hear me? You'll wish you'd taken my advice and left." Mercy glared at him with glittering eyes before she hurried through the door onto the dogtrot and across the wooden porch to slam the door to the family's residence.

Cassie stared at the closed door then turned to assess Flint's reaction to her mother's explosive exit. He blinked for several seconds before meeting her gaze.

"I hadn't expected that." Flint rubbed a palm over his chin and then dropped his hand to his side. "I thought that would go more smoothly given your father's urgent request for my presence here."

"Hopefully, she'll get over my pa's lack of trust in her abilities." Cassie tossed a look at the closed door and then shook her head. "But I wouldn't count on it."

The swish of the gingham dress brushing her ankles echoed in the quiet upstairs passageway. Cassie hesitated outside her closed bedroom door, listening for any sound from her mother's room next door. Should she check on her? See if she needed anything? She took two steps and then halted. No, best to leave the sleeping bear lie for the moment. She pivoted and hurried downstairs, heading for the bustling kitchen.

"Want some help?" Cassie paused at the end of the large, square worktable to marvel at the surety with which Sheridan peeled apples. The trees had only recently started to yield usable fruit and her mouth watered at the thought of apple butter on cornbread or a fried apple pie. The sweet smell of fresh apples scented the room. "What are you making?"

"I'm always pleased to have your help, Cassie." Sheridan cast a grin her way and then used his paring knife to strip the skin off another apple. Deftly he cored it and sliced it into a large glass dish on the table. "This'll be somethin' called apple snow."

"I've never heard of it." She leaned closer to peer at the apples nestled in a ceramic pot. "What's in it?"

A new recipe meant as much to her as a new dress. And like a dress, recipes could be used again and again. Maybe with an addition here or there, like adding a festive scarf or pretty pin, to make the old outfit look new. Dabbling in the kitchen with Sheridan remained one of her favorite pastimes because the nature of cooking satisfied an inner craving to create.

"After I get these in the dish, we'll give them a goodly quantity of powdered white sugar on top, and then I'll beat up eggs to a froth to pour over it and beat the whole again to make a truly delightful dessert-dish for supper this evening."

"Sounds delicious." Cassie reached for an apron where it hung with several others on a wood peg by the door. "What can I do?"

Sheridan nodded toward the basket of brown chicken eggs. "You can separate the eggs for me. That'll save me time."

She skirted around the table to snare a pair of small bowls from the stack on the sideboard. Then joyfully cracked open an egg, separating the white into one bowl and the yolk into another.

Sheridan eyed her silently as he stripped the skins off the apples, then cored and sliced them into the dish. "So what do you think of Mr. Hamilton as the new innkeeper?"

Cassie gave him a sideways glance as she hefted the shell halves to drop the white into the bowl, then dump the yolk in with the other. "He's manager more than innkeeper. Pa will be home before too long, I dare say."

"Maybe." Sheridan worked for several moments before catching her eye. "Not my place to try to understand your daddy's reasoning, Miss."

"What do you mean by that?" Cassie paused in the act of picking up the next egg, the cool brown shell smooth between her fingers.

He shrugged and slid her a glance. "He told Mr. Hamilton to stay put until he returned but it could be months before he gets back here. Something about needing to directly oversee the construction of the furniture he wants for the inn."

Months? Cassie froze in mid crack of the egg. The white dribbled down the outside until she jerked it over the bowl. Finishing separating the egg, she wiped her hands on the apron. How could her pa have left them under Flint's care for so long? Her ma would be even more difficult to live with if it were to take her pa so long away from home.

Her mother's reputation for a hot temper had forced the woman's sons to flee as soon as they reached an age where they could find work elsewhere. Cassie received an occasional letter from each of them, her oldest brother Giles mostly. The others kept their distance. She didn't blame them for not tolerating their mother's anger over the tiniest offense. She *did* blame them for abandoning her to suffer it alone. Now even her pa had left her to manage her ma's emotional state, which he'd made worse with his silent departure.

"I wish he'd waited until we returned to make such a

long journey." She slid the bowl of egg whites closer to Sheridan's side of the table. "It wouldn't have been necessary to have Flint here at all that way."

"I could have handled things." Sheridan's lower lip pushed out as he grabbed up a wooden spoon and began to beat the egg whites until they formed a frothy confection in the bowl. "If he'd asked."

Without a doubt, the cook sounded like he'd hoped for a promotion. Her pa must have his reasons for not giving him the chance. Not that Cassie knew what they might be. She loved the sturdy, singing black man with her whole heart as a friend and her sounding board. He could do anything, to her mind. Still, Flint's comment made sense. A cook didn't necessarily know how to manage everything that happened at the inn. Far more to consider than the pantry and larder after all. The laundry, the repairs to the inn, the stable, even the property and vehicles ready for guests to rent out for a day's excursion. Not to mention the livestock. Yet, it wasn't right for Sheridan to feel unappreciated.

"I'm sure my pa wanted to give you free rein to satisfy the hungry customers with your delicious offerings." She aimed a smile at him as she wiped her hands on the apron. "Mr. Hamilton will take the pressure off of you in that regard."

"I don't much like him trying to tell me what to do." He huffed and beat the egg whites harder.

He needed to see the benefit of having Flint around. Flint could be good for the inn's business if he proved as decent as his father at the hostelry trade. His father's success at the Hunt's Spring Hotel paved the way for other establishments in the surrounding area, like the Fury Falls Inn, because of the attraction of so many migrants from Georgia and the Carolinas to the rich, fertile soil of the state. A flood of wealthy Virginians arrived to establish cotton plantations, increasing the economy of the entire region. And of course, there remained one other reason why his presence brought a smile to her face.

"I don't mind Mr. Hamilton being here as he's quite handsome." She smirked at Sheridan with a quick lift of one brow. "I think he's a fine addition to the inn."

Sheridan stopped in his whipping of the egg whites to shake his dark head at her, his golden eyes glowing beneath furrowed brows. "Now don't be getting any ideas about Mr. Hamilton, hear? Your daddy told him outright not to be dabbling with your fancy. No way, no how."

Her elation drooped. Why would Pa think about the idea of Flint's attentions? Not that she'd ever even hinted at liking the young man. But Pa didn't know how she felt, how she dreamed of spending time with Flint. Holding his work calloused hand while they took a leisurely stroll up to the falls. Dreaming together and planning their future.

Besides, her pa wasn't in a position to dictate. Especially when he was currently hundreds of miles away. What could a little harmless flirting hurt? Hannah enjoyed dallying with the young men who stopped in for a meal or ale. She had fun and nobody took offense. Cassie would follow her lead.

"But he's such a catch in many ways. Come on, Sheridan, think about what pleasure he and I could have." She batted her eyelashes at him and then chortled at the horrified expression he aimed her way. "He's not all that bad."

Sheridan lowered his voice and leaned closer to her. "I've heard the boy thinks he can see and even communicate with…haints." The last word slipped through his taut lips as a mere whisper. "I'm not wanting to hear of haints around these parts. No, thank you."

Cassie chuckled at his discomfort with the topic of spirits. "I don't think we need worry about any ghosts around the inn, my friend."

For one thing, she didn't believe for one second the man could in fact converse with ghosts. Given ghosts and goblins only existed in fairy tales or myths told to scare people. Children mostly. She'd never fallen for the spooky stories. She had more sense.

The swinging door opened and Hannah bustled into the kitchen. Short and plump, she proved both efficient and friendly. Her nut brown hair was pulled back into a loose bun on top of her head. Her bright blue eyes smiled at the world. Pa had hired her when he first built the inn back in 1815 and she'd made herself indispensable to him over the six years since. Cassie regarded the other woman for a moment and then grinned at her. She'd pay close attention, make some mental notes of how Hannah drew the appreciative looks from the men, and then imitate her.

"I need three bowls of stew, Mr. Drake." Hannah pulled three pretty porcelain bowls from a stack on a sideboard and set them on the work table. "And some hot rolls if you have them."

"Just a moment." Sheridan spun away and grabbed a thick towel to open the bread oven door. The smell of fresh hot baked bread wafted through the room. He peered inside and sniffed, then reached for the flat paddle to slip under the pan of rolls. Setting the hot pan on the heavily scarred work table, he dropped the towel and quickly scooped several rolls into another bowl. "There you go. Fresh out of the oven, too."

"The stew?" Hannah shifted her weight to rest on one hip, and tilted her head a bit to the side. "Pretty please?"

Sheridan chuckled as he grabbed first one and then the next bowls and ladled stew into each. He placed them on a large tray in front of Cassie, the aroma of lamb, onion, potatoes, carrots, and early peas making her anxious for lunch.

Hannah set the bowl of bread on the large tray and then lifted it with a wry grin, backing through the swinging door and disappearing from view.

"That woman…" Cassie shook her head as she pivoted to face Sheridan once more. "She sure is something."

"What's that supposed to mean?" Sheridan regarded Cassie with furrowed brows. "Hannah's very popular."

Cassie bobbed her head and pressed her palms onto the table. "I know and that's why I'm going to pay attention to how she does that."

"You're too young to being acting like Hannah. She's a widow and knows what she's about." Sheridan aimed a wooden spoon at Cassie, shaking it to emphasize his words. "Back to what we were talking about, Cassandra. You keep your mind on your work and not on that boy. You hear me? It's for your own good."

Spoken like a parent who wants to deny their children from having any fun. He didn't use her full given name unless he needed her to pay attention. Was Sheridan a parent? He never spoke of children let alone a wife. She'd always taken him as he presented himself, ever since her pa had paid to free him from the plantation owner who had migrated from Georgia with him several years before. On one condition: Sheridan had to continue working for the inn with his culinary talents for at least two years. Which he'd done and then some.

"What do you have against Flint anyway?" She pondered the lowering frown on the man's face. "Not the ghost thing again. Or is it?"

"Folks shouldn't oughta poke their nose into dark magic. They're sure to find trouble if they do." Sheridan dove the spoon back into the stew kettle and gave it a hard stir. "Mark my words."

Cassie brushed off his superstitious mutterings as she took over beating the apple snow. As she whipped the frothy mixture, she pondered her mother's reaction to Flint's presence. It didn't bode well for any romantic ideas Cassie held toward him. But finding a husband was the only certain way she could have a life of her own. She'd contemplated many other options, but always came back around to finding a man.

Other women might be permitted to find gainful work to support themselves. Not Cassie. Ma would never allow her to venture down a path likely to lead to spinsterhood. A proper marriage to a decent man, who led a sober and godly life, was her future according to her ma. With at least half a dozen children to raise. Ma had expressed her disappointment that she'd only given birth to five, and four of them boys. She'd so wanted to have several girls to help around the house, or inn as the case may be. Not that her ma had ever desired to live in a public roadhouse. Clearly. Probably why she'd turned so hateful over the last several years, which led to her sons finding work in distant states. Abandoning Cassie to her fate.

She finished whipping the dish and glanced at Sheridan as her resolve firmed along with the egg whites. Whether anyone liked it or not, Flint was her best option.

Mercy sat at her vanity table, peering into the beautiful looking glass her son had given her years ago. Staring at the frown she couldn't remove from her expression. Reggie shouldn't have done it. Shouldn't have gone around her, tapping the young upstart boy to run the place. She blinked slowly at herself and then lifted the short note she'd found pinned to her pillow upon her return. A few short, hurried lines trying to explain his sudden actions.

My heart,

I know you'll be upset with me but I have to hurry to Savannah to deal with an impending disaster regarding my order. I know you'll understand and will ultimately see my decision to have Mr. Flint Hamilton manage the inn in my absence is in your best interest as well as the inn's as I may be away for several months.

I will write once I arrive in that city and let you know I'm safe and sound.

Your loving husband,

Reggie

He knew and yet refused to wait a few days, just days, until she could arrive back home. She dragged in a deep breath as she laid the paper on the table. Her dismay, perhaps even a simmering anger, stemmed from knowing he didn't trust her. After all she'd sacrificed for his dream, he didn't see her as a partner but a helper. Someone incapable of serving alongside him.

She didn't question his love. He had proved a doting husband, surprising her with a posy of wildflowers now and again, or a special bar of chocolate, or some other such treat. They shared a passion for each other which expressed itself in their five children. Could she help it if the same fiery passion fueled her emotions in other arenas of her life?

Her gaze drifted of its own accord up to the painting of a house nestled among flowering bushes and towering oaks and elms. A deep blue sky with an explosion of white clouds rising up to the heavens provided a dramatic backdrop. The details of the leaves on the oaks, in particular, encouraged a tiny smile of appreciation. She'd worked especially closely to replicate the delicate nature of the curvy shapes and yet in such a way as to convey the overall fuzzy appearance to the groupings. Her home outside Montgomery hung on the wall, an everlasting reminder. She closed her eyes to blot out the image.

At least he'd left her a note, an attempt to explain and mollify her reaction to his sudden departure. A sign of the depth of understanding he held for her sensibilities. But how would she survive without him for months? The very idea sent a shaft of pain into her midriff, forcing her eyes open.

She wrapped her arms around her waist to try to ease the sudden discomfort. Since their marriage twenty-eight years ago, they'd rarely been separated for more than a couple of weeks when one had to travel to another city for supplies or clothing. Facing the harsh reality of months without him to share a conversation, or a joke, or their bed brought tears to her eyes. Could she survive, emotionally as well as physically, without him? She brushed at the stream of tears and sobbed.

Chapter Two

The midday onslaught of customers seemed even more than usual. The din of deep voiced male conversation, high-pitched female voices, and boisterous laughter grew to an incredible volume for people supposedly gathered to eat, thus keeping their mouths full. Instead the babble apparently made the job of waiting tables even more of a challenge. Hannah and Cassie each had to lean close to hear what the customers mouthed to them. A move the male clients appreciated far more than necessary. Flint straightened from depositing a fresh tankard of ale in front of a rawboned coachman. A rough and rugged mix of working men crowded in the room. Mercy paused at the open doorway before turning away with a stern look and disappearing into the kitchen. He'd done his best to avoid her but really what could she possibly expect him to do? Vanish?

Like the soldier... A chill rattled his shoulders for an instant. Long enough to allow the image of the specter he'd seen sauntering across the carriageway between the stable and the inn to form in his mind. All of the usual animal sounds had stilled. The dogs lay on the porch, their heads resting on front paws as they kept a close eye on the intruder. The cattle stared toward the ghost while the horses pulled their heads inside the barn. The soldier peered at him with questions in his eyes. The ghost appeared to shimmer into a more corporeal form and then turn into smoke as he walked past, his Continental uniform torn and bloody. In some unknowable way, Flint sensed the man would never rest until he'd found a path away from the foothills of the Appalachians and back to where he belonged.

Another shiver flashed across Flint's shoulders. He blinked to erase the impression and then glanced around the dining room again to anchor himself in the present and ensure he hadn't revealed his secret. Nobody else had seemed to notice the lingering spirit hanging around the inn and falls. He'd prefer to keep it that way.

Cassie hurried by bearing a tray of steaming bowls of turtle soup and a metal pitcher and cups. The girl had a fine future ahead of her. She'd surely find some lucky young man to partner with and make beautiful babies. If her mother would let her. He didn't envy the man who tried to take Mercy's only daughter away from her.

"Don't just stand there, Flint. Make yourself useful." Cassie flashed a glance at him as she walked toward a young family seated at the back of the room.

Her smile lingered along with her scent. A combination of something floral and her unique fragrance.

"I'm supervising," Flint called after her with a smirk.

She tossed her head, her long, blonde curls dancing at her waist. Casting a flirtatious wink over her shoulder, she grinned before turning her attention fully to the family eager for their meal.

She might be about marrying age but Flint had bigger and better plans. If he played his strategy right, he hoped to one day have a fine hotel of his own. In a big city. Perhaps Nashville or Knoxville. Maybe even somewhere farther away and even grander. With fine china, eating utensils, a grand fireplace to provide adequate heat for the guests. He envisioned the bedrooms with lavish wallpapered walls, candelabras or better yet oil lamps for lighting. He'd hire the best chef to prepare elaborate fare—maybe even using one of those newfangled cast iron cook stoves he'd heard rumors of—and a barkeep who'd make the fanciest cocktails. He scanned the rustic dining room with its unsophisticated customers with a sense of distaste. He needed to figure out how to make the place better, more refined, more inviting. More…

He'd mailed several letters to establishments in other cities, inquiring as to opportunities and possibilities. He'd asked about apprenticeships or paid positions where he could learn firsthand better and more efficient ways of operating a high-class hostelry. With any luck, by the time Mr. Fairhope returned, he'd have his next position secured in a bigger town.

A group of coopers in worn blue jeans and homespun work shirts rose as one from the front corner table and hustled out the double doors, their scuffed boots thumping across the porch before the doors swung closed. He liked the cheerful and hard-working boys even if they epitomized the uncouth, rough backcountry type of man. They made a point of coming for lunch once a week from the neighboring farm where they built barrels of various sizes. Wanting to support the local economy in their own small way. Their hard coin commerce mattered to him. Even as temporary as he was, having repeat customers meant the business would survive. His reputation would also survive as a matter of course. Making him an even more attractive employee or apprentice for the next step in his master plan.

He crossed the room to begin clearing the table as the front door again swung open. Hannah slipped past him to plunk a basket of cornbread muffins on a nearby table. A liveried black man held the door for a gentleman to lead his wife and daughter inside. At least, given the fine suit of clothing in the new style of trousers—no breeches for this man—black top hat, and polished Hessian boots, Flint assumed the man enjoyed a higher status. The woman seemed tense in her elegant silk gown and frilled bonnet while the girl stood somewhat stooped in a pale green dress and matching bonnet. He motioned to Hannah to clear the table the men had vacated and then made his way to greet the newcomers.

"Howdy, folks. Welcome to the Fury Falls Inn. How may I help you?" Flint held out a hand to the man who clasped it and shook twice.

"I'm Sterling Nelson and this is my wife, Abigail, and daughter, Naomi. I believe you're expecting us?"

Flint quickly recalled as much as he knew about the family huddled inside the now closed front doors. Sterling Nelson worked for a bank in Huntsville, manager of loans if he remembered correctly. Abigail busied herself with helping to feed and clothe the poor in the city when she wasn't fretting over little Naomi's epilepsy. That's why they'd come to Fury Falls for an extended stay, for the mineral springs and their healing waters. They represented the kind of clientele he hoped to attract on Mr. Fairhope's behalf: sophisticated people who also had the cold, hard cash to pay for it. No trade in kind or bartering from this customer. He smiled bigger as he nodded to the man.

"Mr. Nelson, yes, of course." Flint waved them toward the dining room. "You must be hungry after such a long drive."

"Indeed." Sterling urged his charges to follow Flint as he led them to a table. "I'm very glad to be out of the coach after such a bone-rattling experience."

The roads could be as rough as a washer board, rutted and bumpy until people fell off their seats, even off the wagon. Heaven help them if they dared to ride on the roof and fell off on particularly rough patches. Travel proved more an adventure than a pleasure as a result. Rollovers happened so frequently the passengers often measured the distance by how many times the vehicle would turn over. Personally, Flint preferred to ride horseback when he traveled into town for the mail, but was forced to take a wagon when purchasing supplies.

"We'll get you settled in and then you can head out to the hot springs to soothe your weary limbs." Flint held out a chair for Naomi to sit down. The slim girl moved carefully, slowly easing onto the cane-bottom seat. "I hope you'll enjoy your stay. The peace and quiet as well as the springs will surely cure whatever might be troubling you."

"We hope our girl will find relief from the fits she's been experiencing." Abigail glanced up at her husband after he'd helped her to the table. She fixed a small smile on her lips as she nodded to him and then peered at Flint. "Nothing else has helped."

"The minerals and heat may be the thing then." The Lord worked in ways he didn't understand. Sometimes the springs could bring about seeming miracles. Flint motioned to Hannah to come assist the new arrivals. When she sashayed to his side, he grinned at Sterling. "Hannah, here, will get you set up with a hot lunch and cold beverages."

"Thank you for your kindness, sir." Naomi smiled up at him, her dimples deepening as her blue eyes reflected her gratitude.

The young girl would mature into a right pretty woman in a few more years. Some bloke would be fortunate to win her heart and hand when she reached the right age. Not Flint, though. He had no interest in saddling himself with a wife. Not yet. He'd treat everyone equally, with respect and kindness and hope to make a good name for himself so that when he did have his own place, they'd become customers.

He smiled at Naomi and nodded. "You're very welcome, Miss Nelson."

Mercy chose that moment to fling herself into the room and then stop to stare at Flint for two frantic beats of his heart. Then she marched her way between the tables of gawping guests. What now?

"Behave yourself, young man." Mercy rested her fists on her hips and glared at him. "You'll not be flirting with the guests. Not as long as I'm around."

Flint snapped back his head to stare at her, blinking in shock at her accusation. "Mrs. Fairhope, I assure you I was doing no such thing."

"I have eyes, Mr. Hamilton." She shook her finger in his face, nearly bopping his nose with the flailing digit. "Don't think I don't recognize you for what you are. You're out to take advantage of any girl you can lay hands on. I won't allow it. You hear me?"

"Trust me, my dear woman, that is the farthest thing from my mind or my intentions." He took a step back and put up a hand. "Now lay off this harangue in front of our guests."

She scowled at his words. "I shall inform my husband of your insolence." She turned to address Sterling with a softening of her features but not her stance. "My apologies for this man's behavior, sir. I do hope you'll ignore him in future."

Flint seethed at her dismissive tone. Ignore him? He was in charge of the entire operation whether she liked it or not. She hadn't hired him, after all. She wouldn't bear the brunt of Reggie Fairhope's wrath if anything adverse occurred to the business during his absence. Flint had every intention of keeping the inn running smoothly and profitably. Despite her attempts to undermine his every action. He needed an outstanding letter of reference in order to make his dreams a reality.

Sterling slowly rose to stand by the table, the tips of his fingers splayed on the white cloth. "I can assure you, ma'am, Mr. Hamilton has been nothing but polite and welcoming. Which is more than I can say for your offensive attitude."

Mercy lifted her chin and straightened her back until it was ramrod stiff. The smile she'd pasted on disappeared beneath the weight of her surprise. "Well, I never——"

"Perhaps that's the problem." Sterling nodded once and sat back down. "You could learn a lot from this fine young man."

Mercy shot a look filled with virtual daggers, or perhaps even poisoned blow darts, at Flint and then marched from the room, ignoring the shaking heads and murmurs of the other patrons.

"Thanks for your support, sir. I appreciate it." Flint laid a hand on Sterling's shoulder for a second and then moved to let Hannah take their requests.

"One thing, Mr. Hamilton." Sterling caught Flint's attention with a lift of a well-manicured hand. "There's news on the road of some rogues round about these parts who've been robbing folks and brutalizing women. You may want to take precautions."

"I appreciate the advice, but it's unlikely they'd think it profitable to bother us so far out from town." Flint shrugged and tilted his head to one side. He had little cash on hand worth anyone bothering with but the silver plate and candlesticks, the livestock and vehicles, would prove valuable for trade. "I've a means to protect the place should it come to it, but I can't imagine it would be necessary."

"I'm sure you know best." Sterling rested his hands on his lap. "Just keep an eye out in case they surprise you."

"Thank you, sir. I'll be sure to do that." Flint sauntered away from the Nelsons, leaving them to their meal while necessary steps for several precautions floated through his mind.

Cassie brushed past him with an empty tray at her side. He watched her disappear into the kitchen, the hem of her ankle-length gingham dress swishing with each step. She didn't interest him. Not at all. He wouldn't—couldn't—allow it.

The chef knife sliced through the cabbage with a heavy *thunk* on the work table. Cassie sliced the head into smaller wedges which she set aside to boil along with the already chopped carrots and parsnips waiting in a large wooden bowl. She nabbed another cabbage and sliced it as well.

"What kind of meat goes with this again?" Cassie glanced up at Sheridan. "One of the stewing hens?"

"Naw. I've got some fine corned beef that will season these vegetables up nice." Sheridan winked at her as he hefted a butcher knife and cut the reddish-brown loin into chunks. "You've never tasted such a fine dish."

He hefted the platter of meat and carried it to the immense stew pot simmering over the fire. Scraping the meat into the gently boiling water, he let the juices run into the stew before returning to the table. Setting the platter on the table, he laid the knife on it as he studied Cassie.

"Where did you learn to make this? Back in Savannah?" Cassie didn't know much about his past other than the fact he'd been brought to Alabama from Georgia, specifically the bustling port town of Savannah, as a slave. She assumed he worked in the house based on his talents and his refined speech. Her father had bought him at one of those awful auctions she'd witnessed and then freed him so he could continue working for her pa. Why had the previous owner deemed it necessary to put him up for auction rather than a private sale? She didn't know if perhaps the slave had upset or angered the plantation owner. When her pa had bought the trembling man, she'd been very relieved on his behalf to learn of his impending freedom. Sheridan had agreed to work for her pa out of gratitude and because he enjoyed cooking. But what, or who, had he left in Georgia?

"One of my former master's guests requested it one cold day." He shrugged and picked up a fresh head of cabbage. "Everyone seemed to enjoy it, too. So why not introduce it to our guests here?"

She peered at him before adding the latest chopped vegetables to the bowl. "Do you miss Georgia?"

He shook his head with a slight frown that vanished in an instant. "This is a much better place for me. I like it here. If only… But never mind. Let's finish up this bit so you can go out and work in your garden. I know you like doing so more than this."

The rows of vegetables and flowers provided one kind of escape. She could lose herself while working with the soil, encouraging life from the rich dirt. Tending to the flowers. Raking the ground into mounds to plant seeds and bulbs. Pouring water on the new plants poking their green leaves up toward the sun and sky. Dragging the weeds out, roots and all. Cleaning up the debris and minding the tall, wooden-slatted deer fence and gate to keep them strong. With the large herds roaming the mountains and valleys, she'd had to resort to drastic measures to prevent them from eating her harvest.

The tall rail fence surrounding the sixty-foot square of ground had proved itself in keeping the deer on the right side of the fence. She'd had one of the stable hands fit rails tight together at the bottom to deter smaller critters like rabbits and possums from eating on her young plants. Not that they frequently ventured so close to the busy inn with its passel of dogs, but it would only take once to destroy all her hard work and make Sheridan's job much more difficult. The other reason she enjoyed working in the garden stemmed from the fact her ma didn't much cotton to working in the dirt, so Cassie could escape her criticism for a time.

"One day I'm going to have my own place with my own garden. Where I can plant and harvest what I want for my own family." She grabbed a parsnip and began to peel the outer skin off with the paring knife. "A house and garden in town so I can window shop, or visit a museum, or see a play. Perhaps the town will be big enough to have its own library. I love to read but we don't have many books. I get kinda bored reading the same ones over and over."

Sheridan rested his strong hands palms down on the scarred table. "Don't be dreaming too big. Your mother has her own ideas as to what's to happen. Don't be forgetting that."

She rolled her eyes at the reminder. "I know. Trust me. But one day I'm going to find a way to make my life mine. Not Ma's."

"If you think you'll make that happen, then you're really dreaming." He slowly shook his head as his gaze turned inward. His expression grew sad as he remained quiet for several beats. "Some dreams are just too big."

He seemed so sad she hesitated to ask him what he meant. Seemed like prying where she shouldn't. Yet again, perhaps he needed some comfort. She sliced into the cabbage with extra force as she debated what to do. How she might help him, the man who'd become her friend and advisor over the past several years. She glanced up at him from the corner of her eyes. His lips curved down as he cut the shank of corned beef into smaller chunks.

"Sheridan, can I ask you something?" Cassie laid down the knife and nearly chickened out from asking the burning question in her mind. Was if he took offense? Was it too personal? Even between friends? She moistened her lips as she waited for his reply.

"Sure." Sheridan peeked at her and then focused on his actions with the sharp knife.

The moment had arrived. He'd given her permission but he didn't yet know what she'd ask. No going back. "If you could have anything in the world, what would you want?"

His hands froze in midair as he met her gaze, unblinking. "That's easy. I'd want my family to be here with me."

Cassie nodded slowly, considering the revelation she suspected but had never had the nerve to inquire about. "You must miss them. How many are there?"

He sliced into the meat in slow motion. "My wife, Rachel, is still back in Savannah as far as I know. Our sons were sold to two plantations outside New Orleans. I don't expect to ever set eyes on them again. None of them. But I sure wish I could."

Cold horror settled on her shoulders as she peered at Sheridan. His wife back on the coast, hundreds of miles away. Two sons also hundreds of miles in a different direction. To think of never laying eyes on your own children again. Her brothers stayed away, but of their free choice not because they weren't allowed to travel back home. Back to kin. Her pa had journeyed far from home but with every intention of returning in due course. She simply couldn't imagine living at the whims and demands of a master.

"If you could?" Cassie had a sudden determination to find a way to reunite him with his wife at a minimum. Maybe the sons, too. Somehow.

"Surely, that would be a blessing." He peered at her and then shook his head slowly in defeat. "There isn't any hope of such a miracle coming to pass."

Maybe not. Cassie mused over the separation of a man from his spouse and his children all for the sake of somebody else's purse. Seething, she carved the cabbage into pieces. She'd like to do the same to the men responsible for her friend's sadness and pain. Perhaps she should write to her pa and see what he'd have to say on the matter. Maybe he could help. If not, then she'd find a way all on her own.

The peace and quiet seemed strange. Flint nabbed a cloth and rubbed down the bar counter, mopping up the wet rings of ale and whiskey from overzealous pourings. The afternoon lull between dinner and supper customers provided a much appreciated respite from the sound and activity. Chance to catch his breath and focus on what needed to be done before the next rush.

Flint inhaled the lingering pungent scents of whiskey and boiled cabbage as he inspected his cleanup job. Polished to perfection. He flung the cloth over his left shoulder, and then took inventory of the bar. Ensured clean glasses and tankards waited to be filled. He leaned down to check the shelves beneath the counter to determine whether he needed to order more whiskey or rum.

Footsteps alerted him to an approaching customer. Straightening, he exhaled sharply when he espied Mercy's serious countenance peering at him from the other side of the bar.

"May I help you?" He pulled the cloth off his shoulder and pressed it onto the shiny surface of the bar.

"That's your job, isn't it?" Mercy crossed her arms over her waist. "My husband deemed it necessary and I have to accept his decree. But I don't have to like it."

"Mrs. Fairhope, I assure you—"

"How did you manage it, Mr. Hamilton?" She leaned forward, hugging herself until the veins on her arms stood out.

"What exactly?" Flint had no idea where she was going with this line of questioning. He could only hope she had a point soon because he had work to do.

"I go away for a few days…all right, weeks…and my husband hires you to manage everything. Why? What did you do to make him turn his back on me?"

Flint peered at the irritating woman, finally understanding where her animosity originated. "I never asked for this job. I thought I was doing him a favor."

She huffed, her eyes fierce as she studied him. "He could have left Sheridan in charge until my return. He knew I'd be home in short order."

Flint shook his head once, pressing his lips together. "While Sheridan is a fine cook, he's no manager. Mr. Fairhope sent word to my father requesting my help, such as it is."

He'd been thoroughly shocked at the request, truth be told. His experience was limited to the refined establishment in town. Fury Falls Inn felt more like a working farm with lodgings for hire than a hotel of any kind. Sure, he had some idea about how livestock and vehicles are managed but not first-hand experience with either. He could ride and shoot a gun, but those skills were not used in his day-to-day existence in town. Good thing he proved a fast learner.

"What do you mean by that?" Mercy barked out her question.

He shrugged lightly and glanced around the empty dining room. "Just that I've never been in charge of an establishment like this one."

The rough walls and simple furniture reflected the rough location. Out in the wilderness of Alabama, away from civilization. Where savages had roamed amidst the bears and panthers. Where people paused but didn't live, except for the daring few like the Fairhopes. Trying to carve an existence out of the wilds. Mr. Fairhope either had a strong vision of the state's future or a failed dream that would lead to their destruction. Could he help them succeed? His talents and experience gave him a unique set of qualifications. He'd like to try. His resolve hardened as he contemplated improvements.

Mercy followed the direction of his gaze and straightened her spine as she returned her glare to him. "It's a fine establishment."

"Indeed." Flint scanned the sparsely furnished room again, considering the many ways he could improve on the setting and the customers' experience if the owners would permit him. Ideas that would cost money and effort but would pay off in the long run. The place definitely had a good start and had potential under the proper care. Until he secured the kind of employment he desperately craved. A secret best kept under his own counsel. "I will do my best to manage the inn efficiently."

She dropped her hands to press her palms on the counter. He could feel static emanating from her as she snaked her head toward him, eyes glittering. What had he said to incite such a response? All he'd done was declare he'd do his best.

"Listen to me, young man." Mercy pinned him with her glare. "I don't trust you. Pure and simple as maple syrup."

Surprised by the heat in her expression, Flint took a step back. "That's uncalled for. I've done nothing to warrant your distrust."

She lifted one brow as she stared at him for two beats. "You may think this place is beneath your attention, but you can just keep that opinion to yourself."

"But I—"

"Hush. I'm speaking to you." Mercy pushed off the bar and folded her shaking hands in front of her. "Reggie wants you here and so here you are. Do the job he hired you to do and nothing more. Understood?"

He nodded, unsure how to respond. He'd been doing what Reggie had requested and she'd given him nothing but grievances. One thing certainly had been made plain:

Mercy Fairhope tolerated his presence but not with any sense of grace.

"Mrs. Fairhope, I will do all in my power to ensure the continued smooth operation of the inn on behalf of your husband." He swallowed a promise to make it even better, not wanting to push the woman too far in her present state of mind. She'd probably think he was horning in where he wasn't wanted. Better to play that music softly. "I've given my word to him and now to you."

She dragged in a breath and let it out on a huff. "Very well." She turned to leave only to swing back around, shaking a finger at him. "One more thing."

"Yes?"

"I've heard tell you claim to see spirits." She shook both her head and her forefinger at him. "Don't be spouting off about seeing any around here. The Fury Falls Inn is not haunted. You hear me?"

He could only blink at her for several seconds. He'd hoped to keep his secret but apparently it was no longer his to hide. Did she fear ghosts or merely the reputation the inn would garner if rumored to be haunted?

"I would never suggest such a thing about the inn." Even though it was already true. He could interact with a ghost and one haunted the property. But she didn't want to hear such news. On the other hand, he couldn't lie without impugning his own reputation. He had no other choice. "Unless, of course, the inn actually is haunted."

Late afternoon sunshine filtered into Cassie's bedchamber to light upon the pink stationery and the letter she'd finished scrawling to her oldest brother. Far off in Mobile, Giles had built up a respectable import/export business. He kept in touch with her far more frequently than Abram, Daniel, and Silas, providing a sounding board for her over the years. They all kept their distance from their mother and her sharp tongue and barbs. Which left Cassie feeling alone and abandoned by her brothers. At least he wrote to her once in a while. She shifted her gaze to his most recent note, picking it up to peruse again, ensuring she'd answered his questions thoroughly.

Mobile, AL May 28, 1821

Dear Sis,

I hope these few lines find you well and happy. You crossed my mind this morning so I thought I'd check in and see how things are with you and our parents. Is mother any happier with her lot in life? How is father managing? I do miss your smiling welcome but you know very well why I cannot live in the same house or even the same area.

My business is flourishing and demanding most of my time. I did acquire some help a couple of months ago which has taken some of the burden from my shoulders. Although, the business has grown along with the additional staff, so I don't see much of a difference in the number of hours I must work each day.

I must end as I'm being summoned. Your devoted brother,
Giles

Folding the letter, she laid it aside. She'd tried to honestly answer his questions about their parents, but feared she'd hedged around the actual truth.

She picked up the letter to Giles and skimmed its contents. Pleased, she laid down the nub of a pencil she had scrounged from her pa's desk. The thought of him so far away in addition to her brothers weighed heavily on her mind. Stuck at the inn with her ma, with only Sheridan to provide any kind of buffer, seemed a life sentence in her practical prison. Flint proved no help whatsoever given her ma's disgust with his presence. Disgust which became detestation and bitterness even more deeply felt than ever before. Living with the woman had become nigh impossible.

Her ma had her faults, always had. She could be overly protective, for instance. Keeping Cassie from venturing away from arm's reach or having any friends. And of course appearances mattered more than substance. Clean, fine dresses and hats and hair in a pretty coiffure were hallmarks of presentation. The very reason why they'd spent two weeks visiting every fashionable boutique available in Nashville. Even though they lived in the middle of nowhere her ma insisted they dress appropriately. Meaning quality fabrics and flashy hats in case someone of any importance happened to stop in for a bowl of stew. Like that would happen.

Cassie folded the letter and sealed it closed with a blot of warm wax. She'd asked one of the coachmen to carry it to the post office on their way into Huntsville but he wouldn't be leaving for another hour. She stood and paced to the open window to gaze out over the prospect behind the inn. Her favorite view as it encompassed the forest and the falls in the distance. The foothills provided a lovely vista even as they secluded her from everything she wanted to experience. Still, there were worse places to live than along the frontier.

A commotion drew her attention back to the clearing immediately behind the inn. Several small buildings spanned the area: an outhouse, a laundry with its set of clothes lines behind it, a smokehouse, and the chicken coop. At the far right end stood her sixty-square-foot garden surrounded by the specially designed fence to prevent invasion by the wild critters. Only, the gate hung open and Flint ran about frantically inside trying to chase out several does. She froze at the sight of the deer in her garden then spun and raced out of her room.

She clattered down the steps, uncaring and desperate to reach her safe haven which had been invaded. She hurried across the sitting room and onto the dogtrot and then turned and bolted toward the backyard, her skirts lifted in both hands as her feet flew over the boards and down the steps. Flint's shouts boded ill as he scared the does even more with the racket he made. As she crossed the slick grassy lawn she saw him, arms waving up and down, trying to herd the animals out the gate.

The frightened deer bounded this way and that but didn't pass him to exit through the open gate. Instead they attempted to leap over the fence, one after the other. Crashing into the rails and shifting them from the post holes they rested in until the rails clattered to the ground. The deer leapt over the cascade of rails and bounded toward the forest. Flint burst through the gate and stood with his hands on his knees, panting from exertion.

Cassie practically skidded to a halt beside him as she gauged the damage to the garden. Not only had two sides of the fence come down, but the deer had enjoyed quite a feast on her collards and turnip greens. Hoof prints pocked the ground around the immature corn stalks and bean poles supporting climbing stems. Her heart vibrated her chest as she wiped her damp palms on her skirts. How dare he? What was he thinking? She propped her fists on her hips to keep from taking a swing at Flint.

"What did you do?" Cassie clenched her fists as she stared at him.

"Me? I tried to get them out." Flint straightened and brushed his hair back from his forehead.

"And destroyed the fence in the process." Cassie sighed with disgust and annoyance. "How'd they get in there?"

Flint shrugged and shook his head as he glanced to the point where the deer had disappeared into the woods. "I don't know. I saw the gate open and them inside. I tried to get them out because I knew you'd be upset."

"Naturally. They've done quite a lot of damage to my garden." Cassie scanned the rows of vegetables and herbs as well as the medicinal plants nearly ready for harvesting. Seething at the mess laid out before her, she crossed her arms and glanced at Flint. "Who left the gate open?"

Flint splayed his hands with another shrug. "No idea."

"Then what *do* you know?" His flippant attitude irked her. He hadn't spent weeks nurturing the plants and encouraging them to grow thick and strong. "For goodness sake, Flint."

He speared her with a quizzical smirk. "Forgive me for trying to help."

"Help?" She huffed as she tread slowly into the garden to begin straightening the disarray. She lifted a pole covered in green fuzzy bean pods and propped it against a corn stalk. "You made it worse not better."

She'd need to have the stable hands rebuild the fence, replacing the broken rails with new ones. A stronger latch for the gate seemed in order as well. If she ever found out who left the gate open she'd tell him a thing or two about respect and responsibility.

He touched two fingers to his brow in mock apology. "I'm so very sorry for trying to be of service. Please forgive me."

He turned on his heel and marched away, passing her ma who stood silently by the laundry house. He didn't do more than glance at her frowning countenance as he stormed up the steps and inside the inn. Mercy started toward Cassie, urgently picking her way across the uneven terrain.

Cassie sighed as she pivoted to survey the damage more intently. Her safe haven had been breached. Violated. That was how she felt. Exposed and left to weep. She straightened her back and began to set things to rights as best she could. Tears lurked in the corner of her eyes but she refused to let them fall. Especially in front of her mother. Appearances, after all.

The broken and trampled plants mirrored her feelings.

All her hopes and dreams were crushed over and over. Her efforts seemed fruitless. What hope did she truthfully have of finding happiness in her current situation? Her one hope of Flint being her savior didn't hold much water when he refused to look at her let alone think about her as a woman and not a child.

She'd done everything she could think of to attract his attention. Fixed her hair just so. Applied a light rouge to her cheeks. A little eye-black to her lashes. She hung on his every word and laughed at the lamest of his jokes. In response, he regarded her more and more like his little sister. Friendly, polite, aloof. Never seeking her out. Rather, hurrying away from their brief exchanges. Always some urgent task he had to tend to.

"Cassandra, what on earth has happened?"

On the Flint front, nothing. What did she lack that he wouldn't give her the time of day? He laughed and return the flirtation with Hannah. Why did he seem to avoid spending time with her? She feared he thought of her as a child, beneath his attention. Yet he was only a few years older. Frustration mingled with the anger in her chest.

"Deer got in. Somebody left the bloody gate open." She yanked up a broken corn stalk and tossed it onto the compost pile in the corner.

"Watch your language, young lady." Mercy slowly surveyed the garden area and then fixed her gaze on Cassie. "Why were you arguing with Flint?"

Why indeed. He had tried to help, however ineptly. Perhaps that was why she remained aggravated. The manager didn't even have enough sense not to startle the deer while inside the enclosure.

"He made everything worse." Cassie tugged on a trampled vine and it snapped in two, making her totter backwards several steps. Regaining her balance, she sighed. "Why is he here again?"

"He claims to keep things moving smoothly." Mercy crossed her arms over her chest and huffed. "Doesn't look like he's as capable as he imagines."

He needed to let her in. Then she could make changes of her own. Make him see her as a potential wife, for example. Perhaps if she flirted with him even more he'd open his eyes to her presence and the future. She'd studied Hannah's techniques but lacked the confidence to bat her lashes and throw suggestive looks at the customers like the older woman did. But if Cassie had any hope of seeing her escape plan succeed, then she must grow closer to him. Be with him more to have any opportunity of attracting his attention the way she craved, needed, required.

"We'll need to keep a closer eye on what he's doing, I suppose." Cassie brushed the dirt from her hands, small clods dropping onto the grass blades around her feet. "Come on, Ma. I need to get some of the hands to fix this mess. Then I'll see to making some adjustments for the better."

Chapter Three

*D*usk settled over the clearing bringing softer air and a gentle breeze. Flint stretched out his legs where he sat on the front porch of the inn, a dark lantern on the table waiting to be lit. Not yet. He wanted to stay hidden away from the eyes of others. The last day had been a nightmare of his own creation. After he'd helped to destroy the garden fence, Cassie shot pointed looks his way every time they passed each other. Which was quite often. She'd insisted he help fix the damage, so he'd worked alongside one of the barn hands to rebuild the fence, made it taller and stronger than before. Rebuilt the gate with a safety catch so it would naturally swing closed to prevent slip-ups in the future. Still she regarded him with distrust, suspicion even. Somehow he'd make it up to her. He couldn't tolerate the silent rebuke day after day. The tension of her disappointment weighed on his conscience.

Her demeanor had changed to coquettish sweetness when she'd waylaid the coach driver, laying a hand on his arm while she talked to him with a smile on her face. Batting those lovely lashes and tilting her head just so. All to cajole him into carrying her letter to the post office for her. Why hadn't she asked him to take it when he rode into town in a few days for his biweekly mail run? Why did she flirt so outrageously with the driver? What was so urgent in her letter? Who was it addressed to? Most importantly, why on earth did he care so much? Annoyed with himself, he stopped the train of thought to focus on his bigger problem.

Mercy. He held little hope of winning her over. She sidled around him as if he carried the plague on his shoulders. After an initial five minutes of harangue she'd barely spoken to him. But he knew where Cassie had learned to spear someone with a menacing regard. Apparently, Mercy had more to teach her on that point. He shivered as her latest scowl reappeared in his mind. Best he stayed out of their way until they went up to bed. Snatch a few minutes of peace and tranquility, staring out over the grazing cattle and snuffling hogs in their pen. The chickens had been secured in the chicken coop, and the four hunting dogs lay curled up at intervals on the wooden planks of the porch, dozing. He let his eyes drift closed, concentrated on the steady beat of his heart, the sighing of the breeze through the trees.

He pictured the horses in their stalls, most likely settled down for the night. Reggie had made it abundantly clear to Flint that his horses were prize possessions. He had a mix of breeds, some grade horses of no specific breed for pulling the carriages and as saddle horses. But he'd also purchased a pair of Morgan horses, known for their gentle nature, comfortable gaits for riding, and their willingness to please. Alongside those pretty bays, he'd also managed to locate four Florida Ponies, two blacks and two bays, gaited horses known for their smooth "coon rack" walking gait as well as for their speed and agility. Reggie planned to show them off to his customers as well as his friends and neighbors. He was right proud of his stable.

Flint's mount, Buck, stood out among the others. A paint buckskin with white legs and a white star, he was calm and gentle. Friendly, too. Flint loved his Buck and doted on his care like a father over his son. They'd been together for five years and had grown as close as a horse and man could be. Flint merely thought about where he wanted to go and Buck would turn and head in that direction as if he'd read the man's mind. Flint had never owned a horse like the paint buckskin.

He sat alone for several minutes, listening to the night sounds, feeling the cool air flow over his skin. He let his mind wander, let dreams form and coalesce into hopes for his future. He'd received the first issue of a new hostelry magazine, *The Innkeeper*. As soon as he had a few minutes of private time, he planned to scour its contents for potential opportunities. Any chance to better his situation and move up to the next level of management. His secret dream fueled his every decision regarding upgrades to the current task at hand with regards to the Fury Falls Inn. Striving to show the kinds of ideas he could generate for such a mediocre establishment to improve it would be his ticket to working at a high-class hotel.

The nearest dog—Red—shifted, lifted his golden head with a low woof. The others soon followed his lead. Flint opened his eyes and scanned the perimeter, searching for movement or a difference in the scene illuminated only by the stars above. At least it couldn't be the spectral soldier since the dogs reacted protectively not cowed as in previous encounters.

Several horse heads poked out of the stable half-doors, their ears up and eyes alert. Unusual for them to be on edge after dark. Flint slowly shifted to sit upright, lean forward to closely inspect the scene as a growing sense of disquiet filled his chest. The night sounds stopped, the dogs rose to their feet, growling and stalking slowly forward to the edge of the porch. A sudden rush of sound drew Flint's attention to the barn door. Was it moving? He rose to his feet and snatched up the rifle propped by the door, preparing to cross the carriageway and determine what was happening.

He'd never been particularly good at hand-to-hand fighting, nor with shooting a gun, truth be told. More likely to miss than hit a target, but at least he could scare away intruders. They wouldn't know he couldn't shoot straight. Something he'd need to work on so he didn't feel this sense of incompetence hampering his actions. He eased down the steps slowly, not wanting to draw attention to himself. Better to try to surprise the culprits than take them on directly.

Two shadowy figures slipped inside the partially open door. They wore only a headdress with feathers and some kind of leggings. He puzzled over their attire. Something didn't feel quite right about it but he didn't have time to think about it too deeply as the dogs bolted off the porch and raced toward the barn, barking as they ran. Flint sprinted after the dogs, noting the horses pulled their heads inside as the double barn doors flung wide open. He readied his weapon as he approached. Doors banged and dogs barked while men yelled within the dark confines of the building. Flint slowed to cautiously peer around the open door.

Flashes of the reports of the horrific slaughter at Fort Mims eight years previous slowed his movements. Had those men been Creek? He thought the Creeks had all moved farther west, but maybe they'd come back to seek revenge for being forced to abandon their heritage and lands. He didn't want to be scalped in his effort to protect and preserve the property. The savage Creeks had brutalized and killed more than five hundred poor souls at Fort Mims, leaving their bodies to rot all over the enclosed fort. Even children had their heads bashed in, swung by their feet against the wooden fence surrounding the fort. He couldn't imagine such atrocity. Pregnant women violated and killed in ways to horrific to imagine. A shudder rocked his shoulders. Well, perhaps he could at that. On alert, he reached out a hand to wrap around the edge of the door to peek inside.

A shout preceded the men, now mounted bareback, herding a dozen horses out of the barn at a lope, Buck in the middle of the pack. Flint jumped back to avoid being run over, raising his gun as he took several steps backward until he ran into the wall. Horse thieves. They had all the horses, including his beloved buckskin.

"Stop!" Flint recovered his balance and then ran after them. As he raced across the yard, he spotted blond hair beneath the feathers. Indians had dark hair, not blond. These men were not actually savages but men disguised as Indians. Damn. The dogs chased them down the carriageway with Flint hot on their heels. "Thief!"

"What's all the fuss about?" Mercy abruptly appeared on the front porch with a musket in hand. She paused and took aim, fired a shot at the escaping men. Flint waved her off, fearing she'd be injured or killed by the desperate men. Then Reggie would have his hide. He wanted to keep all body parts intact. But she shook her head and started down the steps as he raced past.

One man pivoted and fired a shot at Flint. A searing pain ripped across his upper arm and he stumbled to a halt. Damn. Did he get shot for his trouble? He'd give as good as he received, if at all possible. No time to waste. They were getting away. Lifting his rifle with some difficulty, he fired at the man but his shot went wide. They whooped with glee and disappeared down the road with the prized horses running at full gallop.

Unable to catch them up without a horse, Flint cussed as he grabbed his throbbing arm with his free hand. He spun around and headed toward Mercy. "Why did you distract me like that?"

Mercy stalked toward him, fire shooting from her eyes. "You let them steal our horses."

Stunned, he glared at her. "I didn't let them do anything."

"I saw you, standing there watching them run by. Until it was too late to stop them." She held her gun with both hands across her thighs. "I knew you were worthless."

"I tried to stop them." The woman had lost her mind. He'd done all he could think of to try to prevent the theft. Everything transpired in a matter of minutes. What more could he have done? Nothing. But he could do something about the theft. "I'll get the horses back. All of them. Don't you worry."

"So you recognized the Indians? Know their names and where they live?" She huffed and shook her head at him. "I seriously doubt we'll ever see my husband's prime horseflesh again."

"They took Buck, too. I've got a dog or rather a horse in this fight just like you do." Anger and frustration boiled inside Flint's core making him tense and irritable. Damnation. She was right. He didn't recognize the men, but he did know they weren't Indians. A start toward retrieving their property.

"I'll go to the Sheriff at first light and report the men." Flint glared at the woman shaking her head at him. "Now what?"

"Stephen Neal? He won't do anything. I bet he's scared of them savages."

"First of all, they were white men dressed like Indians. Second, it's his job to do something."

"You'll see."

"Yes, we will. I'll insist he take steps to recover Mr. Fairhope's property forthwith." Flint grunted as he stared down the dark road stretching into the distance. He glanced to the night sky noting the lack of the moon to lessen the darkness surrounding him. Felt the loss of his best friend deep in his soul. "I promise you here and now the thieves won't get away with it."

"You and your promises." She pivoted on one heel and

started marching toward the family's residence. "I didn't expect you could do what you'd said."

"What do you mean?" Flint called after her, making her pause.

She turned to face him and shrugged. "You promised me you'd keep the inn running smoothly. Now we have no carriage horses, no saddle horses. Our lovely Morgans and Florida Ponies are gone." She sniffed harshly. "Because of you."

"It's not my fault." He squared his shoulders and then winced at the pain in his arm. He needed to tend to the bullet wound. Perhaps Hannah, or better yet Cassie with her gentle touch, would help him clean and bandage the scrape. Then again, Hannah would be safer. "I'm going to check on the rest of the animals. Go on inside and go to bed. I'll take care of securing the rest of the buildings."

"Pshaw. You will try, I'm sure." She grabbed her skirts as she stepped up to the porch, hefted the musket with one capable hand, and went inside the residence.

He stared after her for a long moment. He'd compounded matters. First the garden, then the horses stolen right in front of his nose. He'd done his best. Hadn't he? What more could he have done? He froze as he recalled Nelson's warning of rogues, which he'd dismissed as unlikely. He could have done more. Taken more precautions. Set a guard for instance. Steps he'd put into place beginning the next day.

He glanced around the inn's property, noting the silence from the barn where the horses usually rustled in their stalls. The other livestock remained safe and secure and he'd ensure he kept them such. No more slipups on his part. Would it be enough? He wasn't sure. But one thing was certain. All his hopes of building a respectable reputation may have just simply crumbled at his feet.

Before the sun appeared over the top of the foothills behind the inn, Flint was up and dressed. Snagging a roll and mug of coffee, he closed himself into the starkly efficient office and studied *The Innkeeper*. Only for a few minutes, though, to find out whether the pages contained any valuable information while he ate his simple breakfast. Noting two potentially helpful articles, he carefully placed the magazine in a drawer, and then strode out of the office.

He paused on the front porch to scan the awakening inn and stable. Beau loped over to greet him and Flint laid a hand on the dog's silky head for a moment. His plan for the day included walking over to the next plantation and borrowing a horse to ride to the sheriff's office. For the moment, the quiet morning slowly grew in sound and activity. The tow-headed stable lad yawned his way over to open the gate to the hog pen. Milk cows mooed in the distance, a low mournful sound on the warm morning air. A great blue heron flapped its wide wings slowly across the sky, its long neck curved into an S as it glided by. Another day like all the rest except for the fact he had to report a theft to the sheriff.

He wanted to present a professional appearance when he spoke with the officer. He'd chosen khaki trousers, brown polished boots, a white dress shirt with a dark green vest and brown coat. Somber and sincere attire meant to impress upon the good man how serious of a matter Flint brought to his attention. He started for the neighboring plantation two miles down the road. The walk along the lonely dusty road gave him plenty of time to contemplate what he'd say to the man and then what he'd do to the horse thieves if he ever caught up to them. Make that *when* he caught up to them. He wanted his horse back equally to how Reggie Fairhope would feel once he learned of the theft. Which meant he'd need to write a letter telling his boss of the loss. At some point. First, he would try to retrieve the horses.

With each step, he vowed to find all of the horses, but mainly his buckskin. Buck represented more than a means of transportation. He had become a friend over the years they'd been together. The first time Flint saw the paint buckskin standing with a group of other paints and bays, he'd been attracted to his unique coloring. His white legs and star mixed with the white and tan splotches marked him as a rare color indeed. Then he'd recognized the intelligence of the gelding and taught him to respond to a special three-tone whistle. No matter where he might be in the fields or pasture, when Buck heard the whistle he'd come at a gallop.

He turned up the short carriageway leading to an imposing manor house situated along the river. The red brick and tan clapboard house with dark blue shutters at the windows sat at the end of the drive, surrounded by flowering bushes and stately shade trees. Smoke rose lazily from the chimneys into the bright blue sky. A few outbuildings in need of a fresh coat of paint peeked through the trees behind the main house. He could hear the distant chant of slaves working in the cotton fields stretching away from the main buildings. The sound saddened him as he thought about Sheridan and his past life under such conditions and restrictions. Several children, three white and four black, raced around the corner of the building and disappeared behind it, laughing as they seemed to be playing tag or some other game. At least there was some small amount of hope to be found. He smiled at the light-hearted sound and quickened his pace.

As he approached the blue painted front door, it swung open to reveal a man with white hair combed neatly back from his pale brown face. His dark eyes held a question along with a welcome. His spotless dark blue suit, yellow shirt, and blue dotted tie indicated his status as butler of the premises. Briefly Flint wondered whether he was a freeman or a slave but dismissed the thought since it was not his business as to the man's status. He could hope he proved to be free, though.

"Good morning, sir. May I help you?" The butler smiled, a slight lift of the corners of his mouth as he held onto the door to deter the visitor from brushing past him.

"I'm Flint Hamilton, working at the Fury Falls Inn for Mr. Fairhope during his absence. I'm afraid we had a bit of trouble last night. Two men stole our horses so I'd very much appreciate it if I could borrow one to report the theft. I need to speak to the homeowner, if I may."

The butler grimaced ever so slightly. "I'm afraid Master Baker is not at home."

"Is Mrs. Baker available?" He fretted at the delay but without a horse he could not possibly make it to the sheriff's office and back again in one day. Leaving the inn unprotected overnight was not an option after the previous night's violence.

The butler nodded once and opened the door wider. "Please come in and wait here while I inquire if she's receiving guests this morning."

The butler left him in the large foyer of the manor as he quickly disappeared down the hall leading toward the rear of the building. Flint removed his hat and drifted his gaze over the well-lit and welcoming space. The tiled floor gleamed beneath the lit golden candelabra hanging from the ceiling. A marble-topped cherry wood table nestled along the left wall with a large vase of fresh flowers in an array of colors scenting the space. The wallpaper boasted pastoral scenes complete with rivers and flowers. The very air seemed to smell of wealth. He pivoted by degrees until he once more faced down the hall.

The butler returned with smart steps along the tiles. "Mrs. Baker will see you now if you'll follow me."

"Thank you." Flint worked to keep up with the spry

older man as he led the way to a small parlor at the back of the home.

Flint paused at the threshold to take in the entire elegant room with one quick skimming glance. Mrs. Baker sat regally upon one of a pair of chintz settees flanking the fireplace with its small yet merry flames dancing around several logs. Flowered drapes hung at the floor-to-ceiling windows, pulled back to allow the morning light into the room. A silver coffee and tea service waited on a cherry table along with a plate of steaming fruity biscuits.

"Mr. Hamilton, please have a seat." She indicated the opposite settee with a graceful wave of her hand. Several gemstone rings occupied her fingers, glinting in the light. "Coffee or tea?"

"Coffee, if you please." Flint laid his hat on the seat beside him and accepted the hot brew with extreme gratitude. Taking a sip, he swallowed the robust flavor with a smile. "Thank you for seeing me, and for the coffee. I apologize for my unannounced visit especially while your husband is away."

"Mr. Baker will return before noon. He's inspecting the other farms this morning."

"I'm sorry, but I'm new to this region and I do not have the benefit of your names." With heat in his cheeks, Flint sipped to cover his discomfort.

"I'm sorry as well. I did not mean to make you feel uncomfortable nor unwelcome." She smiled ruefully with a light chuckle. "I'm Tabitha Baker and my husband is John. I'm pleased to make your acquaintance."

"As am I, ma'am." Flint glanced around the parlor and then back to his hostess. "You have a fine home, Mrs. Baker."

"We enjoy it. Thank you." She finished sipping her tea and set the china cup on the silver tray. "Mr. Richmond tells me you are in need of a horse to borrow? You had some kind of mishap last evening?"

One way to think of having your herd of horses stolen. "Horse thieves ran off our entire stable. I need to report the theft to Sheriff Neal as soon as possible. Might you be able to help?"

She canted her head slightly to one side as she considered his request. "I understand your predicament but you must realize I do not know you."

He'd worried along those same lines as he'd trekked down the road winding along the low foothills. He'd need to convince her to trust him, but how?

"Mrs. Baker, you're quite right to be cautious with strangers. However, I can assure you I have no desire to harm you or anyone. My father, James Hamilton, is good friends with Mr. Fairhope two miles up the road. Mr. Fairhope requested through my father for me to manage the inn property while he's away on a business trip. You can verify that with Mrs. Fairhope if you feel it necessary." He could only hope Mercy would give him a good reference should Mrs. Baker indeed find it prudent to send a message back to the inn.

What else could he say? He had no printed letter of recommendation or authority from Reggie. An oversight he'd correct with his next employment. Something to verify his credentials and ability to act on his employer's behalf would prove useful. In the meantime, all he could do was wait and hope for the desired outcome. A saddle horse.

Tabitha studied him silently for several minutes. At one point, she refilled her tea, adding a half spoon of sugar and a splash of cream and stirring silently. She laid the spoon on the saucer and then continued to contemplate his features, one by one from forehead to chin and back again. Finally she nodded once to herself.

"I believe you're telling me the truth, young man. Finish your refreshments while I have my butler send word round to the stable."

"I'm in your debt, ma'am." Relief flooded his core as he took a gulp of the hot liquid. "The sooner I can reach the sheriff the sooner I hope to locate the horses and the thieves."

Part of the urgency flowing through his veins stemmed from the thought of the horses being herded out of the state. Perhaps into Tennessee or worse farther west into Indian territory. Any hope of finding them in such an event would be slim to none. But he'd try no matter.

She rang a small bell at her elbow and Richmond appeared as if on silent wings at her side. "Claudius, please have a horse saddled and brought up for Mr. Hamilton. Quickly."

With a hurried thanks and farewell, Flint soon mounted a spirited dapple gray gelding and cantered down Winchester Road toward Huntsville and the sheriff. The sun had flowed higher into the sky during his seemingly lengthy visit at the Baker plantation. As he rode he scanned the surrounding fields and pastures for any hint of the horses. Not that he held out any real hope of the thieves being dumb enough to keep them in plain sight. He heaved a sigh at his own foolishness and urged the horse into a gallop.

Reining to a halt in front of the sheriff's office and jail, Flint flung himself out of the saddle and tied the reins to the hitching rail. Striding inside, he pulled his hat off as he nodded a greeting to the deputy at the large wood desk. A hefty man, probably in his early thirties, with a chip on his shoulder. The angle of his jaw and the distrust in his eyes spoke to his attitude at Flint's sudden appearance. He pushed to his feet and extended his hand.

"Name's Barney Parker, Deputy Parker. What brings you in?"

"Flint Hamilton." He clasped the strong hand for a brief shake. The firm grip reassured him of the deputy's sincerity and integrity. "I'm managing the Fury Falls Inn up

Winchester Road. A dozen horses were stolen last night by two men dressed up like Indians."

"Do you happen to know who they were?" Barney pulled out a small notebook and pencil from his shirt pocket and jotted down some notes.

"No, but they headed south, I think. At least as far as I could see them." He dragged a palm over his smooth chin. "They've got a distinctive buckskin tobiano paint in the herd. The gelding is my personal property and I want him back. Along with Mr. Fairhope's valuable horseflesh. Can you help?"

"We'll do our best to help you locate them, sir." Barney tilted his head, his dark eyes flashing with irritation. "We always do, though some folks around these parts don't believe that."

Like Mercy. She had little faith in the sheriff's abilities and made no bones about the fact. Apparently, the erstwhile deputy had taken the criticism to heart.

"I'm sure you will." Flint extended his hand again and Barney accepted the handshake with a small smile. "I'm going to look on my own also but I'll keep you informed if I find them. I want those men arrested and this thievery stopped."

"I'll send word with anything we find as well." Barney's abrasive demeanor relaxed enough to permit him to drop his shoulders to normal height. "Together I'm sure we'll find them. Don't worry."

"I am worried because my boss entrusted me to care for his property in his absence. Now a significant investment has been stolen. I want it back before he returns from his business trip." Flint pressed his lips together, determined to find Buck and the others.

"Just don't take matters into your own hands, you hear?" Barney rested his knuckles on the desktop. "Those men will fight to keep what they've taken."

While not much of a fighting man, he couldn't help but be tempted. With a bit of practice and help from his dad, the odds would become more even. He'd stop in at the hotel and have a talk with his parents. Get some tips from his dad on handling himself in a fight.

Flint tamped his hat back on his head with a flash of a grin at the deputy. "Maybe we should give them what they want, then."

The spiral steps creaked softly as Mercy hurried up the steps to the small attic above her room. Reggie built it special for her to stow her few secret treasurers away from prying eyes. She glanced down at the closed bedroom door, listening for any approaching footfalls. Silence. She slipped the key into the lock and easily opened the door. She lit the fat candle waiting on its bronze plate on a small shelf. The soft light fell upon a wooden chest, bound with sturdy leather straps, and its heavy lock. Fumbling with the few keys on the chain, she eased closer to the chest.

Sinking onto a chair nearby, she carefully inserted a large silver key into the brass lock. With a sharp click, the lock fell open and she lifted the lid. Inside, neatly tied stacks of letters stared up at her. The distinctive handwriting of her sons chided her for her behavior toward them. More letters from Giles than the others. No surprise. Giles left first, with the younger boys following suit as soon as they could.

Giles, her firstborn and secret favorite of sons. His powerful build and serious eyes always watching, assessing. In many ways, he resembled her beloved Reggie. Not so much in appearance as attitude. Ever since a young boy, Giles acted as part watch dog and part herd dog. Ensuring his younger brothers' and sister's safety at every turn. He'd shocked her when he declared he was moving to Mobile. But that was after... So probably not as much of a shock as a surprise. She probably deserved his desertion after what she'd done. She heaved a heart weary sigh.

Then there was her sweet Abram. She fingered the stack of letters written in his loopy writing. Her dear, reckless son. Off on one adventure after another, he kept Giles on his toes. Until he slipped away to dive into the shallow pond at their previous home and split his nose open. The blood that poured from the wound scared him, sent him shrieking and running across the grassy yard, up the wood steps, and into the safety of the house. Mercy cleaned him up, calmed him down, and cuddled him until he could breathe without hiccupping. The resultant scar across the bulb of his nose plagued him as a reminder and something more. Something he held close to his chest like a gambler's card hand.

She lifted the next stack out of the chest, the writing clear and precise. Her third son, Daniel, and his driving desire to please everyone. To the point he never had time for himself. He'd agree to help in the stable, in the garden, rounding up the cattle, herding the chickens into the coop, driving guests into town on a sight-seeing tour. Then drop exhausted into bed without having accomplished whatever task he'd intended to accomplish on any given day. When she'd brought this tendency to his attention, he'd accused her of being selfish. Of wanting him around to help her or that she didn't care if others needed help. After his rebuff, she kept her opinions to herself. Still, he'd left eventually.

She picked up the small stack of letters from her youngest, Silas. The bookworm. His handwriting revealed how carefully he chose his words. She could almost see the pauses as he contemplated how to phrase each thought. They'd spent many a happy hour reading together, or with him reading a story he'd written. He'd invented tales about talking muskrats and panthers. Reported on the changing seasons, detailing the various colors of the tree leaves and the withering of the plants in the garden, in a melodramatic monotone that made her laugh. His creative nature must have come from her. Yet as much as they'd been alike, perhaps too much so. If she hinted at any kind of suggestion for improvement, dared to offer even the gentlest critique, he withdrew. Stung by her lack of belief in his talents. She saw his potential far more clearly than he, but he wouldn't listen. Thus he fled and rarely even wrote to her anymore.

Her four sons broke her heart with their hasty departures. Not that she blamed them. She'd fought to retain her objective outlook on life after moving to the Fury Falls. Grabbed onto a positive attitude with both weakening hands. Day after day, month after month, she fought until she had no inner strength left to battle. She'd dreamed of so much more for her family. Wanted to give them a better life, not a more difficult one.

She and Reggie had made the decision to move north knowing everyone's life would change. They'd hoped for the better. In fact, Reggie acted as though he believed it had. Mercy could only see the drudge, the never-ending stream of people needing or wanting something from her. From her family. That realization had colored everything with a red brush of irritation and frustration. She knew her sons left because of her souring view on life. Knew Cassie longed to follow in their footsteps. And fought all the harder to keep her daughter with her. She needed her. As an ally. A friend. Someone to love her no matter what.

Most of all, she needed her family. With her husband and sons far away, only Cassie remained to comfort her. Whether she liked it or not.

She laid the packet of letters on top of the others and locked the chest. On a long sigh, she pushed to her feet and blew out the candle. Shoving her feelings aside, she closed and locked the attic door before easing down the spiral staircase. Time to get back to work.

"You have such lovely things, Ma." Cassie swiped a dust rag over the frame of the looking glass on her mother's dressing table. "Where did you get this beautiful mirror?"

"Abram gave it to me several years ago." Mercy glanced at the looking glass with a small smile lingering on her lips. "He said he thought I'd appreciate it."

Cassie studied the elaborately carved mahogany oval frame resting on a polished matching four-footed stand. The reflective surface showed her arched brow and sparkling eyes. She wiped the stand free of dust and then moved on to the table, pondering the significance of the present. Her brother acted mysteriously at times.

She picked up a small silver filigreed bowl containing a key chain with several different sized keys. Wiping the bowl clean with a few swipes of her cloth, she set it back on the table. "Ma, what are these keys to?"

"They're to my treasures." Mercy strode across the room from where she'd been straightening the quilt on her four-post bedstead with a lacy canopy. She lifted the ring and let the keys clink against each other for a short while. "One day you'll inherit them after I pass over."

"Oh, hush, Ma. Let's not talk about you dying." Cassie sidled over to the night table and tackled the collection of small boxes holding bits of ribbon and jewelry. "What treasures do you mean?"

Mercy selected a two-inch long rounded key and glanced at Cassie. "This one opens the attic door upstairs."

Cassie paused in her chore to meet her mother's gaze. She actually smiled at Cassie for a second. "I forgot we had an attic."

"Right up those stairs." Mercy glanced at the staircase in

the corner of the room. Then she dropped the key and chose another. "This silver one opens a chest of papers."

Cassie stared at the shiny key, pondering what kind of papers her mother meant. Perhaps the marriage certificate or property title. Perhaps her sketches she used to do continuously. She didn't ask, sensing a reluctance to share the details. So instead she simply nodded and her mother continued.

"This one opens the chest that contains my wedding trousseau including my gown and veil. One day you may want to wear it for your wedding."

"You kept it all these years? That's remarkable. I'd love to see it." If her wishes came true, she'd need to locate an appropriate dress for a wedding before many more months went by.

She'd dreamed of her wedding day ever since a young girl. Pictured in her mind the special light blue dress with layers of lace. Blue satin slippers to match. She'd carry a bouquet of wildflowers picked fresh the day of the ceremony to perfume the air she'd share with her soon-to-be husband. Inside in the parlor or outdoors under a shady tree? The choice would have to wait until a time of year and day had been selected. Either way, she'd make sure it was a lovely day no matter the weather.

"Perhaps one day." Mercy jingled the keys and then dropped them into the bowl. "We don't have time for a walk through my memories. Come, help me smooth this quilt more evenly, will you?"

Cassie slipped the rag into the waistband of her skirt as she crossed the room to do as asked. "This quilt is beautiful. Didn't Grandma Julia make it for you?"

"A wedding gift, yes." Mercy trailed her fingertips over the tree of life center medallion of the quilt, the bright primary colors on the bird's plumage and surrounding flowers the focal point of the room. "She wanted us to always have warmth in our marriage."

A nice sentiment but how true could it be? Her ma seemed a bit cold toward her pa. Were they always that way? Or had it changed after moving to the north end of the state? Memories of her mother humming as she tended to the flower gardens surrounding the house outside of Montgomery floated through her mind. Something she never did at the inn. Work in the garden or hum. What had changed?

Perhaps her ma really hadn't wanted to journey so far from her family. All of Cassie's grandparents and aunts and uncles remained south, unwilling to move when her pa had decided to uproot his family. Years had passed since she'd seen them, although they did receive a letter now and again to update them on family doings and events.

Or maybe even her ma felt as Cassie. Wanting to live within easy distance of the city if not in the city proper. A thought she'd never associated with her mother but something worth considering. Even though far from family, living closer to Huntsville would at least enable more frequent visits with friends.

"Has Flint returned from his foolish errand?" Mercy interrupted Cassie's musings with a sharp-edged question. "I sure hope Mr. Baker didn't mind lending him a horse for the ride all the way to Huntsville. He can be quite difficult."

"I believe Flint came back a while ago." Cassie regarded her mother's stern expression. "He didn't say what Sheriff Neal said he'd do about the theft."

"Not surprising." Mercy picked up a pale green cotton dress draped over the chair by the window and crossed to the wardrobe to hang it inside. "I told him it was a waste of time. But of course he thinks he knows better."

Flint seemed rather pleased when he'd returned, as if the conversation with the sheriff yielded some happy results. She needn't tell her ma about her observation since she didn't specifically know anything. Best to not ruffle any more of her feathers. With luck, the sheriff would indeed be able to locate the stolen horses and return them forthwith.

"I'm sure he's doing the best he can, Ma." She picked up a figurine her mother had purchased on their trip to Nashville, a lacy-winged fairy sitting on a red dotted toadstool while holding an open book, and carefully wiped it clean. "What more can he do?"

Setting the decoration gently on the table, she picked up a small wooden box with an inset dove carved on the lid. After wiping the table off, she rubbed the box and then returned it to its place.

"Are you about done with the dusting?" Mercy propped her hands on her hips as she abruptly changed the tone of the conversation.

"Yes, ma'am." Cassie perused the room, mentally checking off each piece of furniture and its contents. Her ma obviously preferred not to speak about the man. What a shame. She found him intriguing. And infuriating by turns. Sometimes she didn't know whether she wanted to kiss him or hit him. "I believe I'm finished."

"Very well. Mary and her daughters will be arriving in a little while and I want everything to shine." Mercy clapped her hands twice and motioned toward the door. "Off with you now. We've got more to do with the guest bedrooms."

Cassie let her mother usher her through the door but she cast a quick glance over her shoulder at her mother's room and her sentimental treasures. Who knew her ma could harbor such an emotional attachment to a few objects. Her personal collection of inexpensive yet meaningful items apparently served to keep her connected to her family and friends even during long absences. Sweet memories to offset the bitter reality she lived day to day. Thinking about her ma's exterior attitude, Cassie smiled at the sudden tender insight into her mother. Maybe she had hope for her own future after all.

Chapter Four

*H*annah paused at the open office door, one hand spanning her waist as she cocked a hip. "Mr. Hamilton? Looks like you've got company, sir."

So soon? He'd hoped for more time before the anticipated visit occurred. When he'd talked with his father about defending himself, his mother had been absent on some charity business. He hadn't been able to explain his side of the events of the last few days. But he'd really wanted to have things running along with ease before his mother made her anticipated visit. Not having blundered twice in as many days. He expected Mercy would be quick to relay all his failings. Still, he must face the music.

"Thank you, Hannah." He laid the pen on the ledger, aligning its tip with the right margin, and then pushed back from the desk.

He trailed after the woman, taking his time crossing the room to push the front door open. Striding outside, he inhaled the sweet honeysuckle laden air as he reached the front steps. A coach-and-four deposited his mother and sisters on the carriageway, the footman handing each down with care. Several other carriages rattled past, discharging passengers who scurried inside for their dinner. Saddled and napping horses crowded the hitching rails on either side of the steps leading up to the porch. The dogs milled about the clearing, tails wagging and noses busy. The inn enjoyed a thriving business and he meant to maintain the steady flow of revenue to prove to Mr. Fairhope he hadn't erred in hiring him to stand in for him.

"Flint, my son." Mary Hamilton rustled her way to him, her long brown satin skirts stirring up dusty swirls with each stride. "I've missed you, dear."

She took both his hands in hers and kissed his cheek. She smelled of freesia, her favored perfume, as she smiled up at him. Her bright blue eyes held curiosity and concern in equal measure. She'd pulled her light brown hair up into a soft bun at the nape of her neck, her chocolate satin bonnet edged with a lighter colored lace tied neatly beneath her chin.

"I trust your trip was uneventful?" Flint pasted a smile on his face. He loved her but feared she hadn't journeyed all the way to the Fury Falls Inn for a simple meal and visit with her friend, Mercy. Though she would use her visit as a pretext for the real reason she'd arrived so soon.

"Not precisely but we're here now. Thanks to the extreme efforts of the coach driver. He and the footman had to replace a wheel that had shattered on the rocks. It was awful, let me tell you, standing out in the heat and sun. But we finally made it, thank goodness." She swept her gaze behind her to include his sisters in her declaration. "Girls, come greet your brother properly."

Edith led Wilma closer, clasping hands as they stopped beside Mary. Edith, next in age to Flint, always seemed to take charge of Wilma and even Julian, their younger brother, if given the chance. Edith tipped her face up to grin at him while Wilma stood quietly at her side.

Flint surveyed their appearance, looking for changes since he'd last seen them weeks before. Edith stood erect and ready for anything, her bright blue eyes wide open and aware of her surroundings. Her blonde hair was pulled away from her face but the curls left free to hang about her shoulders. She wore a pretty frock of pale gold with a deep brown bodice and white gloves on her hands. Wilma studied him from pale green eyes rimmed with silver as if she couldn't look away. She'd always been a touch in awe of him, or at least that's the way she made him feel. He gentled his smile as he met her gaze and then skimmed her dark blue ankle-length dress and white gloves. On another girl the somber color might be staid or too mature, but not for her quiet self-assurance.

He pulled Edith to him and planted a light kiss on her forehead. "You're looking lovely as usual."

"Stop flirting with your sister." She tapped him on the chest with a gloved hand. "I have a beau, you know."

He tilted his head to look at her askance. "Since when?"

"Since last Sunday when Ambrose Davis asked Father if he could wait on me." She folded her hands demurely over her stomach.

"Poor guy, he doesn't know what he's in for." He slowly moved his head side to side in an exaggerated show of pity.

"Stop." Edith chuckled at him.

Flint turned his attention to his younger sister. "You're also looking very pretty this afternoon." He kissed her forehead as well before pulling back to smile at her.

"Thank you." Wilma regarded him with adoration in her eyes. "You're kind to say so."

"It's very true." He motioned to the inn's double doors. "So, welcome to the Fury Falls Inn. Come, let's get you settled, shall we? Sheridan has prepared something special for you all."

At that moment, Mercy burst through the doors and hurried across the porch and down the steps, Cassie close behind. "Mary, it's a delight to welcome you."

Cassie hesitated at the top of the steps before easing down to the carriageway. Her pretty blue dress flattered her figure. Her hair was pulled into a chignon that emphasized high cheek bones and bright eyes. Some lucky man waited for her in the future. He could appreciate her fine qualities without risking his heart. Especially when he intended to stay focused on improving his reputation from the recent setbacks. But if the sheriff could indeed discover the identity of the horse thieves, at least then he'd recover from part of his embarrassment. He'd make sure to have a hand in recovering the stolen horses to prove he wasn't a total failure.

Flint took a step sideways to permit Mercy to embrace his mother. The two friends hugged and exclaimed for several moments while he and his sisters watched, exchanging amused glances. Finally, the women broke the embrace but kept a loose grip on each other's hands.

"So, Mother, may I ask why you've chosen to visit?" Flint studied his mother, suspecting the real reason. His father had hinted at certain concerns he harbored with regard to Flint's involvement at the inn. Had he sent her to investigate? Would she confess?

Mary lifted her chin, eyes clouded as she addressed him. "Can't a mother visit her son? And her best friend in all the world? Without being suspected of ulterior motives?"

He arched one brow as a smirk pulled his mouth to one side. "What ulterior motives might you be accused of, do you think?"

She cast about with her eyes, looking for a way out of her verbal corner. Fixing her gaze on his, she smiled. "I have none."

"So, Father didn't ask you to check in on me, hm?"

"He'd have very good reason to worry about the kind of job you're doing here." Mercy shook her head at him before pinning her friend with a sad expression. "He's incompetent. Surely Jim won't want him to take over the hotel like he's always said. Not after what Flint has done."

Mary frowned at Mercy's serious countenance. "What's happened?"

"It's not all my fault that—"

Mercy stopped him with a flash of reproach in her eyes. "Not only did he destroy the garden fence and permit deer to decimate the crops Cassie worked so hard to grow, but he also failed to prevent Indians from stealing all of Reggie's prize horses."

His mother turned disbelieving eyes to him, slowly blinking three times. "What have you to say for yourself, son?"

"I tried to shoo the deer out of the garden but they wanted to go over the fence instead of through the gate." A cold sweat broke out on his back, trickling down between his shoulder blades. "I've never had to deal with a herd of deer in my life."

"If you hadn't been standing between them and the gate, waving your arms all over the place, then perhaps they would have gone through the gate the same way they had come in." Cassie stood with arms firmly crossed beside Mercy, staring at him.

Logically, Flint agreed. After the fact. During the crisis he'd focused on trying to herd them out of the pen any way possible before they did more damage. Quick action had seemed the best course. Which, looking back, he recognized as not necessarily so. "I know that now. I've never had to face hungry deer before. I tried to do what I thought you'd want done."

"Tear down the fence and trample my plants? I don't think so." Cassie slowly shook her head at him, holding his gaze until he had to look away.

He glanced to his mother and shrugged lightly. "What more can I say."

"Tell me about the horses then." Mary gripped her reticule with both hands, fingers digging into the soft fabric.

"Now that's not my fault at all." Flint rubbed a hand across his scalp, glad it remained firmly attached. "I couldn't stop the thieves. They not only took every horse including Buck but they even shot me as they galloped away."

Mary startled and dropped her purse into the dust at her feet as she closed the short distance between them. "Oh lord! Where? Are you all right?"

"It's just a scrape. Hannah patched me up last night." Poured something into the wound that nearly made him cry but he'd kept his composure in front of the woman. Reflexively, he covered the bandage under his long-sleeved shirt with one hand. "I'm fine."

Mary peered at Mercy for a brief moment before a slight frown appeared on her face. "My friend, I think you're being rather hard on Flint. He's still learning and this is a different situation than the hotel in town."

"He doesn't belong here. Reggie shouldn't have done it." Mercy crossed her arms, clutching her elbows.

The defensive posture irked Flint since she'd continued to be so negative about his every breath. What had she to defend against when she did the attacking day in and day out? If anyone should be raising an imaginary protective wall, he should in order to stave off the arrows and barbs she shot at him with every word from her mouth.

Mary moved to put one arm around her friend's shoulders. "I'm sorry he hurt your feelings by asking Jim to send our son out to help. I assumed you knew and agreed. But none of that is Flint's fault. He graciously accepted the responsibility even though his father was against it."

Flint bristled at his mother's revelation. His father had not expressed such reluctance to him. He'd assumed the only hesitancy from his father came from not wanting to manage everything on his own. He needed Flint's help to keep the operation running without a hitch. Yet his mother seemed to contradict his own impression with her comment. Well, just as well he intended to work elsewhere if his father felt he couldn't handle the responsibility. He started building his own imaginary wall, brick by painful brick, at the concept of his father's lack of faith.

"Why did Jim let him come then?" Mercy tilted her head and frowned at Mary as she waited for an answer.

"Because his friend needed help." Mary squeezed Mercy's shoulders and then dropped her arm down to her side.

Cassie stepped forward to retrieve Mary's purse and handed it to her. "Why didn't Mr. Hamilton want Flint to come?"

Mary thanked Cassie with a nod and then smiled. "Purely selfish reasons. He doesn't want Flint to get any ideas about leaving and starting his own place. Jim hopes he'll keep the hotel in Huntsville running after he retires."

His father would simply have to adjust to the reality. His father didn't realize how much Flint desired to strike out for a bigger and grander place to establish his own hotel. His dreams may be just that, but he couldn't let them go. Not until he either achieved them or proved to himself he couldn't. Granted, the last couple days at the inn opened the question of his potential success. But he'd learn from his mistakes and would take steps to prevent a repeat of them. Never did he intend for his father to consider him a disappointment or failure. He'd do all in his power to keep their solid reputation in the hostelry trade.

A flash of movement drew his attention to the edge of the circular drive in front of the inn. He spotted the Continental soldier he'd seen the day he'd arrived at the Fury Falls Inn. Hat askew, blood on the front of his uniform, and wary eyes. He stared at him, wondering why he haunted the inn, why he lingered in this place so far from town. The dogs and horses stilled around him as Flint nodded at the soldier. An eerie quiet seemed to blanket the area even as people continued to move about. The ghost tipped his hat to him and started toward him.

"What are you staring at?" Mercy barked her question.

Startled, Flint blinked and glanced at her, then back to the soldier. Only he'd vanished. Had he imagined the man? "Nothing."

The carriage horses shook their heads, harness jangling as the black manes danced in the breeze. The dogs went back to sniffing around and welcoming the many people coming into the inn, oblivious to the appearance and then disappearance of the phantom behind them. Sound abruptly returned to normal level. The ghost's presence affected everything whether anyone else realized the change or not. He swallowed the unease pushing bile up his throat. He hadn't imagined the ghost then.

Mercy leaned forward, eyes narrowed and mouth pursed as she searched his expression. "Don't be acting like you see any haints, you hear me? I won't tolerate such nonsense."

The woman was hateful. Pure and simple. How could he mollify her attitude toward him? How could he manage to work with her for several more months? Keep his cool and maintain a professional attitude no matter what she did. Like his dad always said about the hotel's customers. He pushed back his shoulders and leveled his chin so she could take no umbrage with his attitude toward her.

"I won't say a word that's not true. You can trust me on that." She'd have to be satisfied with the simple truth of his nature. He never lied.

Ever since a young boy, he'd understood the harsh ramifications of fabricating tales instead of speaking the truth. His mother had swatted his backside on more than one occasion when he'd tried to fib his way out of admitting he'd broken a glass or hurt the housecat. She only employed the switch a handful of times before he vowed to never lie again. The punishment was far worse than simply confessing his childish crimes. The resulting pride and respect he earned from his parents for being honest proved well worth the short-lived embarrassment of admitting to his mistakes.

"Nothing about ghosts." Mercy shook her finger in his face to emphasize each word. "Understood?"

He nodded, unwilling to voice his real opinion of her request. She wished him to deny what he witnessed and experienced. Merely because she refused to entertain the notion she might be wrong about ghosts and hauntings. She may not see them, but he had. More than a couple of times, in fact. If she wanted to ignore the reality, then so be it. He'd keep his own counsel on the matter.

Mary laid a hand on Mercy's raised arm to gently urge her to lower her finger. She glanced between Flint and Mercy and then shrugged. "I'm sure Flint will honor your request. Won't you?" With her question, Mary arched one brow in his direction.

"As you wish." Flint bowed his head briefly and then caught Cassie's questioning gaze.

She studied him in silence for a moment and then smiled as she addressed her mother. "Ma, you know Flint doesn't lie and he's a man of his word. You have nothing to fear if he gives you his word he won't say anything."

"Fine. Enough of this gabbing out here in the sun and heat. Flint, see to their horses and such. Cassie, help me get them inside and ready for their dinner. I'm sure Sheridan is anxious to share the delicious meal he's prepared special for them." With that, Mercy ushered the group of women up the steps and inside, chattering as they left.

Flint stood still for a moment, until the double doors banged shut. Then he slowly pivoted to catch the grinning faces of the coach driver and footman regarding him. He heaved a sigh and then shook his head as he strode to the pair. Nothing for it but return to work and keep his mouth shut. His mother could return home to reveal to his father how badly he'd handled things, which should make him happy seeing as Flint's chances of opening his own tavern or roadhouse let alone a fancy hotel may have recently fallen off a cliff. Going home may end up being his only option.

For the time being, he needed to see a man about some horses. He strode to the stable and saddled up the gray and rode back to Riverwood to negotiate with John Baker for some stand-in horses. The inn had to continue functioning, and the coaches needed horses in order to provide transportation for the guests. Besides, riding away from the painful discussions most likely occurring over dinner inside the inn seemed a much better plan. Gave him time to compose himself before facing the adversarial nature of his boss's wife. He'd poke around as he went to see if he spotted his and the other horses. One day, he silently vowed, he'd find them and bring them home.

Tired from the quick ride to and from Riverwood, but pleased to have come to an agreement with his neighbor, Flint hesitated at the open doorway to the dining room, searching for his mother and sisters. Most every table was full with rough men looking for a hearty meal on their way to do business elsewhere as well as the more refined inn guests who enjoyed the healing springs and the quiet countryside. He nodded to his mother when she glanced his way from her seat by the cold fireplace. Edith and Wilma flanked her while Mercy sat across from her. Enjoying their roasted snipes, calves' feet, duck with green peas, and custard for dessert. His mouth watered as he contemplated his growling stomach. Perhaps Sheridan had reserved some of the special meal for him, but somehow he doubted the man would have considered such a thoughtful gesture on his behalf. He most definitely seemed an outsider.

Cassie hurried past him carrying a tray with several bowls and steins, foamy ale sloshing over the sides with her quick steps. The scent of lavender and vanilla wafted past his nose, making him inhale deeply to preserve the pleasant aroma. Her attire emphasized a sense of style and attention to her personal hygiene which also proved attractive. Her willingness to pitch in impressed him. As the boss's daughter, he'd rather expected she thought herself above serving the guests. Instead she worked as hard as Hannah to ensure everyone had their meals as quickly and efficiently as possible. Where would her pleasing personality and abilities take her?

Mercy glanced his way, her smiling eyes baffling. She turned back to address Mary and then both of them looked his way. What was up with them? Why did they keep looking his way?

"Hey, there. Mr. Hamilton?"

Startled, Flint searched quickly left then right for the man who'd called his name. John Thomas, a pump manufacturer from Winchester, occupied a seat at a crowded table near the bar. Flint sidled between the bustling tables to approach him.

"Good afternoon, Mr. Thomas. How may I be of assistance?"

"Your cook has outdone himself with this meal. I'm curious as to the seasonings used in the chicken and dumplings. Is there any chance he might share his secret with me?" John Thomas angled his head to peer up at Flint.

"Let me get Mr. Sheridan to answer your question." He patted the man's shoulder once and dropped his hand to his side. "I'll be right back."

Flint wove through the customers, returning greetings

with a nod and a smile, until he could poke his head into the kitchen. "Sheridan, do you have a moment to answer a customer's question?"

Sheridan looked up from the haunch of pork he was preparing for the spit. "In a minute, sir."

"That's fine. Come out when you can."

Flint returned to the dining room and held up his forefinger when John Thomas lifted one brow in silent question. His mother cast a glance his way, unsmiling, as she studied him for a brief moment. What were the ladies discussing? Apprehension hunkered in his core. A far too common sensation since arriving to work at the inn.

He forced his gaze away from his family to skim the patrons enjoying their meals. A group of men, one blond head angled toward the other two brown-haired men, dressed in nondescript work clothing huddled at the table closest to him. They exchanged few words but Flint sensed they kept aware of the conversations flowing around them. As if they eavesdropped on the other tables. Not unusual behavior for many of the customers with an active curiosity. Perhaps innocent but he'd keep an eye on them. Mr. Nelson's caution regarding some firebrands echoed in his mind as he gave them one last glance before turning to peruse the rest of the clientele.

Sheridan emerged from the kitchen, wiping his hands on the half-apron tied at his waste. He stopped beside Flint with a low grunt. "What did you need, boss?"

The sarcastic tone of his question rankled as Flint motioned toward John Thomas. "Mr. Thomas would like to ask you about the dumplings."

"What about them? Something the matter?" Sheridan's brows lowered along with his voice.

"No. He wants the recipe, I think." Flint indicated with a lift of his chin for Sheridan to go talk to the man. "It's a compliment."

"Oh, okay." Sheridan grinned as he strode over to chat with the man in a low voice.

Having a fabulous cook on the staff proved essential to attracting loyal customers as well as new ones. The reputation of the cook carried as much weight in the hostelry business as the innkeeper. Reggie Fairhope had been fortunate indeed to locate such a gem as Sheridan Drake. Even if the man had no respect for Flint and only reluctantly adopted the new menu items he'd suggested. But he'd persuaded him to expand his offerings and the customers responded with enthusiastic praise and by coming back for more. Maybe he stood a chance of success despite his missteps.

Sheridan nodded twice to Mr. Thomas and then straightened to head back to work. Cassie brushed past him with her empty tray at her side. Sheridan waited for her to reach his side.

"Where were you this morning, Cassie?" Sheridan fell into step with her. "I thought you were going to help me with the custard."

"Oh, I'm sorry. Ma asked me to help her with her treasure this morning." Cassie winked at him, a smirk flashing onto her lips.

"What treasure are you talking about?" Sheridan stopped in front of Flint, laying a hand briefly on Cassie's forearm to stop her from continuing into the kitchen. "Where?"

"In her bedroom. She asked me to help her clean everything before Mrs. Hamilton and her daughters arrived."

"You hush about such private matters. You hear me?" Sheridan frowned as he darted his gaze around the room. "Best keep it to yourself."

Flint noticed the deep furrows between the black man's eyes as he scanned the people sitting closest to him. His gaze rested on the group of rough men for two beats and then slid away. Flint frowned as the three exchanged glances then drained their mugs. Try as he might, the only thing noteworthy about the three men was how common their attire proved. One man with bright green eyes met his gaze for a flash of a moment, but long enough to send a shiver down Flint's back. He turned back to the conversation between Cassie and Sheridan, uncomfortable with the silent warning from the stranger.

Cassie shrugged as she glanced to the kitchen door and then back to Sheridan. "Do you need anything else from me? Or can I fetch the bread for the family at the table by the window?"

"Go on with you." Sheridan shook his head as a smile bloomed on his lips. "Sassy miss."

Cassie lifted both brows as she chuckled, spun on one heel, and sashayed through the kitchen door. Flint appreciated the diversion of her swinging hips until the door stopped its pendulum swing. He could look just not touch. With a sigh, he dragged his gaze away from where the girl had disappeared.

"Is Mr. Thomas all set?" Flint searched the cook's expression, finding the affection Sheridan felt for the young girl reflected in his eyes. "You answered his question?"

"Yes, sir. He wants his wife to make something similar. Quite a compliment, like you said." Sheridan nodded, eyes shining.

"Indeed." Flint noted the group of men at the nearest table openly listening to his conversation with Sheridan. Again. He searched for any distinguishing characteristics but found little to cite as memorable. Uneasy with their interest, Flint waved Sheridan off. "That's all for now. I'll catch up with you later."

Sheridan nodded once and then strode into the kitchen. Flint scanned the room, purposefully avoiding making eye contact with any of the strangers as he drifted his gaze to the bar where several men sipped whiskey and on to the tables by the rear windows. He inclined his head to his mother when she met his assessing gaze. When he finally looked back at the nearest table, the men were gone. Their vanishing act did nothing to allay the worry in his chest.

"I just don't understand why Reggie would leave before we came home." Mercy stared at her dearest friend as they enjoyed afternoon coffee and tea cakes. Simmering resentment gnawed her innards. "Reggie's note said he might be away for several months."

Mary sipped the dark brew, pursed her lips, and then set her cup on the table between them. "He told Jim the message he'd received from the journeymen indicated they'd completely misunderstood his directions for the new furniture he asked them to build. So he saw no choice but to supervise directly. That's my understanding."

Mercy let her eyes shift to the rolling hills stretching behind the residence of the inn. Fully leafed oaks and maples and other deciduous trees climbed the foothills of the mountain range, the southern end of the Cumberland Plateau. Gray clouds boiled and scudded across the crests, hinting at showers later in the afternoon. She dropped her gaze to strive for calm as she cast an eye over the several small buildings occupying the clearing behind her home. The sturdy outhouse with a crescent moon carved in the door. The smokehouse waiting for the fall slaughter of hogs and steer. The laundry with its door and windows wide open, smoke drifting up from the chimney as the laundress worked over the bubbling cauldron of water inside. The chicken coop, its door open to receive any hens wishing to escape the summer heat. All connected by a worn dirt path winding between the work places. Then her daughter's prized garden, the fence mended and gate securely closed to protect the rows upon rows of vegetables and flowers flourishing inside. Flint had, come to think about it, tried to make amends by helping rebuild and improve the fence and gate. A reluctant note of appreciation for his effort sounded in her chest.

"Mary, believe me, I don't dislike your son." She swiveled her head to peer into her friend's azure eyes. She drew in a deep breath and forced it out again. "I just resent Reggie hiring a manager instead of trusting me."

"Did he know when you'd get home from your shopping trip?" Mary poured cream into her coffee and stirred quietly. She lifted her cup and cradled it in both hands, wisps of steam floating up past her nose. "Delays happen, after all."

"Well, we *were* later returning than originally planned." Mercy nodded to Hannah as the woman arrived with fresh coffee in a silver service. With a wisp of a smile, the server placed the tray on the table and then spun away to hurry back inside. Mercy waited until she'd disappeared before addressing her friend. "But he knew I'd be home in a couple days."

"Flint knows what he's doing. Jim trusts him implicitly." Mary set her cup down on the table and poured fresh coffee. "Give him a chance, my friend."

"I have no choice, do I? He won't leave until Reggie returns or tells him to go." Mercy thumped her palm onto the flat arm of the rocking chair. Mercy lifted her shoulders and let them fall into place. "My concern for Reggie is how far away he is. Traveling is dangerous. Accidents happen. Highwaymen hold up the coaches and rob the people of everything. There's no law enforcement across much of the country."

"I'm certain he took precautions. Reggie is no fool." Setting her empty cup on the table, Mary folded her hands in her lap as she regarded Mercy with kind eyes. "What's really going on with you, my friend?"

How could she put into words her fears and anguish? They swirled and tumbled throughout her thoughts and emotions. Stemming from her husband's decision to move from southern Alabama to the northern climes. To build a fine tavern or roadside inn to establish his reputation in the hostelry trade. She had protested to deaf ears. He'd listened but argued for the move until she'd relented. Which started the irritation growing into aggravation and bitterness. She never wanted to be an innkeeper's wife let alone live so far from civilization. Then to have him turn control over to a young whipper-snapper like Flint behind her back when she had no recourse to the decision but to accept.

"I miss him and I worry about his safety. But you're right." Mercy laid her head against the high back of the chair, hands gripping the armrests. "There's much more upsetting me about this entire situation."

"Want to share?"

"What if he never returns? If I never see him again?" She closed her eyes as a stabbing pain pierced her midriff. His love meant the world to her. They'd made five wonderful children together as a result of their affection for one another. She opened her eyes to look askance at her friend. "I don't know how I manage to breathe without him."

Mary laid a hand on Mercy's nearest clenched hand. "He'll come home. Wait and see."

"My sons didn't after they moved far away." Another stab to her heart made her press a palm to her chest. "My bitterness made them leave. I know. I can't help how I feel. Can I?"

"Perhaps but perhaps not." Mary squeezed her hand and then sighed. "Only you can change your perspective, my dear. Whether you accept your situation or fret and fume is entirely up to you."

Mercy concentrated on her breathing, in and out, in and out, delaying a reply until she could formulate the right one.

"Sometimes I want to scream and rant about how unfair my life is. But then…"

"What?" Mary squinted as she studied Mercy's features. "What happens?"

Mercy shrugged and bit her lower lip. "Cassie does or says something to brighten my entire world. I love her so but it's hard for me to show how I feel, other than my anger. The anger overrides every other emotion I have. I don't know how to change it without changing the situation."

"Then find a way to change the situation." A trace of a smile graced Mary's lips as she patted Mercy's hand. "You'll feel better if you take some control back."

"Ah, that's the rub, isn't it?" Mercy sat up straight and shook her head. "Reggie took away the little bit of control I thought I had. Gave it to Flint. Instructed him to manage the place, a wild place where I don't even want to be."

"See? There's an opportunity for you to make some other changes." Mary patted her hand once more and then settled her hands in her lap.

"What do you mean?" Mercy didn't follow her friend's reasoning. She couldn't make changes to the way the inn was run with Flint in charge. He had lots of ideas, really good ones, he'd suggested and she'd dismissed out of hand. On principle not merit. She would eventually agree, but she wanted him to work for it. Make his case for why the upgrades would benefit the property. If she could put him off until Reggie came back, then she wouldn't need to make the decision. Indeed, she'd be reluctant to assert any kind of authority while her husband remained away and largely out of touch.

"Since Reggie wants Flint to manage the inn, then you have the chance to do something else you'd like to do."

A thought worth contemplating further. If she relinquished any role in the running of the inn, what would she do with her time? Perhaps take up painting again. Her gaze roamed the foothills, imagining how she'd capture the undulating variety of light and dark shades of green, cloud shadows shifted and draped over the landscape in oils. Or she could make the quilt she'd put off for the past six years, the one she intended to give to Cassie on her distant wedding day. Her only daughter neared the age when she'd need a husband, a home of her own where she could raise a family. Perhaps she should begin on the time-consuming sewing project. It may even distract her from the reality of her daughter moving away from home, from her.

She prayed for a fine young man to come a-courting her. Someone who had a respectable job or at least could provide a better life for Cassie than she had at present. No tavern or inn to manage with strangers coming and going constantly. Mercy had the perfect situation before they moved north. A quiet manor on fifty acres of rolling pasture and crop fields. A place where the children could grow up near enough to the city and society to be active at church and school. Not out among the savages and marauders who infested the foothills surrounding the Fury Falls and its inn.

"Soon I'll need to see about a husband for Cassie, but not yet. She's not even eighteen yet. I want her to wait another year before we begin the quest to find a man for her." Mercy peered stoically at Mary's smiling face. "In the meantime, I think I'll take advantage of your observation. I've a quilt I want to make."

"Oh, Mercy, that's a grand idea!" Mary clapped her hands lightly. "I'm pleased I could bring you a bit of peace during my visit today."

"Yes, thank you, my sweet friend." Mercy rose from the chair to invite Mary to stand with her. "But one thing."

Mary accepted the hand Mercy offered and stood up beside her, gazing at her with one brow lifted in question. "What's that?"

"Flint better not let Reggie down or he'll answer to me."
Mercy briefly hugged her friend, then led Mary back inside
to freshen up before dinner. "He'll sorely regret it if he
messes up. Let's be clear on that point."

The afternoon sun angled into the family parlor, creating a
golden trail across the floor. Cocoa lay curled up beside the
chair where Cassie worked on mending a guest's torn dress
shirt. She examined the blind stitching to ensure the neatest
finished repair. The pin money she earned for her efforts
would be secretly and carefully tucked away.

The idea had not been her own. A few years back a
guest's child fell while running around the falls and tore the
knee of his best breeches. The mother had asked if anyone
could mend the tear and Cassie's father had suggested she
could help. Cassie had stitched up the pants and given them
back and the mother was so pleased she paid Cassie with a
few coins. The weight and shine of the pair echoed in her
mind to the present day. That moment proved the beginning
of her planning for her own future. Paying her own way
with her talents and abilities.

Over the years her savings had grown, slowly and in fits
and starts. She kept her stash in a locked box buried in the
clothing in her dresser. Intermittent mending jobs would not
be enough to establish her own household. But it would help
her have some freedom after she married and moved away
from home. She could hope her future husband would not
object to her taking in sewing. Another creative and yet
practical talent. Plus, the sense of accomplishment satisfied
enough to make her want to continue to take on the
occasional mending task.

The front door opened and Flint strode into the room,
bringing a waft of fresh air and sunshine into the dimmer
interior. Of course, his mere presence brightened the room.

She smiled at him when she noticed he carried the mail in his hand. He'd taken to riding to the post office every couple of weeks and thus making sure everyone living at the Fury Falls property received their letters and periodicals.

"Anything interesting?" Cassie set aside the shirt, laying it on the round table at her elbow.

"Something for you." He crossed the room in a few strides and handed her a folded letter. "Looks like it's from one of your brothers."

She peered at the exterior of the letter and nodded. "Giles."

Cocoa rose and went to sniff at the shin of Flint's blue jeans for several seconds. Flint bent to pet the dog's tawny and white head, then straightened to level his gaze on Cassie.

"Did you want me to take her out with me?" Flint motioned to the dog with one hand. "Or leave her in here with you?"

"That's up to her." Cassie glanced from Flint to the letter. "But why don't you see if she'll go with you. She's been inside a while now."

He nodded and then snapped his fingers. Cocoa looked up at him, ears alert. "Come on, girl. Let's leave Cassie to her letter."

He whistled and started for the door, the spaniel trotting at his side. She watched until the door closed behind them and then let her gaze fall to the letter in her hand. Giles' letter came in quick reply to her last one. Or perhaps they crossed in the mail. She broke the wax seal and opened the paper to lie flat in her hands.

June 6, 1821
Mobile, Alabama

My dear sister,
Just a few lines to let you know that I am safe and well before I tell you that I've had an injury. I stepped on a shell on the beach of the

Gulf, slicing my heel. Nothing too serious but it laid me up for a couple of days. I know how you worry and so I wanted to reassure you that I will fully recover. My two helpers were much appreciated for their quick action to get me to a doctor and handle the trade in my absence.

I believe the two men are honest and trustworthy despite their situation. I hope one day to repay them for their quick thinking and care during my recovery. They demonstrate what it means to look out for others and to take care of those who are unable to care for themselves. Which reminds me of my long-time desire to do something similar but on an official level. Would you laugh if I ran for Sheriff instead of being an import/export tradesman? Seriously. I'm curious.

I must return to my current duties and end the daydreaming for now.

As always, your loving brother,
Giles

She folded the letter and laid it on the table, staring out the window at the sun sinking toward the horizon. Activity in the front of the inn had dwindled to a crawl, few horses and even fewer carriages and coaches coming and going. Her thoughts remained with Giles, imagining the pain, the blood. Her strong, vibrant brother laid up without being able to walk properly for several days. Good thing he hired those men to assist him as needed. Both with his personal safety and the business at large. His success as an importer made her proud of him. Would she ever see him again and be able to tell him that?

She didn't hold much hope of him coming home anytime soon. Obviously, his work kept him busy and so he wouldn't have time to make the long journey from the southern edge of the state to the northern. No, letters must suffice.

She considered his private dream of serving as sheriff along the Gulf. Her oldest brother wanted her opinion and feared she'd denounce his ambition. She'd have to write him and contradict his supposition she'd laugh at the idea.

If he felt he could make a difference acting as sheriff in the port city, then he should pursue his desire. Every man should pursue his goals and dreams as best he could.

Flint strode into view, crossing from the south side of the clearing toward the inn. He carried a squawking, flapping chicken in both hands, held straight out and away from his body. She laughed at the sight as she rose and hurried outside. She reached the porch in time to see him dash through the dogtrot toward the chicken coop out back. The man had many talents as well as a caring nature. Wondering if the bird was injured, she hurried after him, pausing at the top step of the back porch.

Flint carried the hen into the coop and let her down on the floor, before spinning and rushing back outside and closing the door. The squawking slowly subsided as he brushed off his hands and walked back to the porch where Cassie stood, smiling at him.

"What was that all about?" She stepped to one side as he climbed to the porch.

"She ventured too close to Beau and almost got eaten for her troubles." Flint grinned down at her as he slowly shook his head. "I decided to put her up for her own safety."

"Kind of you." He always seemed to be thinking of others, looking for ways to brighten someone else's day or make their chore easier. "Thank you."

He tipped a finger to his forehead as if touching an imaginary cap. "Anytime. See you later." He strode back through the dogtrot and turned right once he reached the door into the inn.

She stood still for several minutes, contemplating possibilities. A slow smile spread on her face as a plan took shape in her mind.

Chapter Five

Over the past two days, Cassie had worked up her nerve to act on her intentions. She hesitated outside the stable doors. Peered into the dimness, searching for the man she'd come to find. She eased past the threshold and into the barn aisle. Rows of stalls, their wooden slats marked and stained from years of use, flanked each side of the aisle. The sweet smell of hay fought with the pungent aroma of horse manure. Barn swallows flitted and flashed above her head, chittering and darting through the mote filled air. The dirt aisle showed signs of a recent raking to keep it clean and neat. As clean and neat as a dirt floor can be. As her eyes adjusted to the lower lighting she spotted Flint at the far end, staring into the last stall.

Her best hope. Maybe her only hope. The tall man laughed easily, comfortable with himself and his station in life. She longed to flow his shoulder-length auburn hair through her fingers, if only he'd let her. Longed for his beautiful eyes to see her as a woman and not the daughter of his boss. Surely she could use all of her seventeen years of experience to attract him, to make him notice her the way she wanted. As a woman he'd consider to be his wife, to give him a pleasant home to retire to in the evening. Give him beautiful, loving children to surround him with joyful arms upon his return home. Someplace close to town or even in the city so they could make friends and be part of the hustle and bustle of civilization. Not living out in the wilderness with strangers day after day.

Flint murmured to the bay gelding poking his head over the door in search of an apple or carrot. He ran a hand over the glossy red-brown neck, looked into the soft brown eyes, lifted the black forelock and smoothed it in place. All with gentle motions and soft words. He showed his concern and care for the animal with every movement. Assuring her of her choice for both a husband and a father of her children.

No time like the present. An added bonus was meeting the new arrivals. She didn't often venture into the shadowy barn as the horses sometimes frightened her. Especially the bigger ones. The plate-sized hooves on the bigger draft horses could flatten her feet in one misstep. A bump by a strong haunch could send her sprawling on the hay covered dirt floor. She'd even seen one of the stable boys bitten by a particularly nasty stallion when the boy had moved too abruptly. She squared her shoulders. She would overcome her fears in order to pursue her intent. If only the beasts didn't act up, she'd stay the course.

Flint had arranged with Mr. Baker for four new geldings trained to both saddle and harness to be delivered. On loan until the stolen ones came home. Two bays and two palominos had arrived an hour earlier, compelling Flint to quickly finish what he was doing inside to rush out to the stable. Giving her the chance she'd waited for to be relatively alone with him where she could put action to her desires. Relatively, since the stable hands didn't count to her mind; they weren't her mother and wouldn't care about her being with Flint.

She rubbed damp palms down her prettiest day dress, a coffee-with-cream brown with white cuffs and hem. She'd spritzed on her favorite vanilla lavender perfume and primped her hair into a cascade of curls down her back. She'd practiced smiling coquettishly in her small mirror and even made sure her rather uneven teeth sparkled. She pushed aside the insecurities surrounding her teeth, angled this and that as a result of tumbling down a rocky path as a young girl. She couldn't change them and Flint had already seen them, so no reason to pretend they didn't exist. She'd also practiced what she'd say and how she'd say it, practicing the inflection and pacing. The moment had arrived. And every practiced word fled her mind as she started down the aisle. She'd have to play it by ear.

"There you are." She sashayed toward him, exaggerating her hip swing from side to side with each stride.

Flint turned to glance at her, straightening his shoulders as he pivoted to greet her with a nod. "Is something the matter?"

Not the greeting she'd hoped for as she prepared to increase the intensity of her flirtation with the handsome man. "Why would you think something wrong? I wanted to come meet the new horses."

He flicked his gaze down to encompass her dress and rich brown low boots, and then back up to her face as he grinned. "In such a pretty outfit?"

He'd noticed she'd donned her new day dress, the nicest one she could find during her recent trip to Nashville with her mother. Such attention must mean he had some interest in her. The thought brought a bigger smile to her lips.

"Why not? I want to look nice." For you, she wanted to add, but bit it back. No point in pushing him away by being too forward. "Are you pleased with the new horses?"

"They'll do for now. Until we can recover the others." Flint reached out to run a hand down the inquisitive nose of the nearest bay gelding.

"Do you think the deputy will find them, both the horses

and the men who stole them?" Cassie sidled up next to Flint and trailed her finger tips along the horse's jaw. The horse's lower lip quivered as if trying to speak. Standing so close to Flint she could detect his manly scent over the usual aromas of the barn. She much preferred his scent to the manure and hay blend, but the combination also allured and drew her attention toward the man beside her.

"He told me they would begin the investigation two days ago. I should hear something from them soon." Flint pivoted to inspect the pair of palominos in the stalls across from the bays. One calmly munched on hay, its nose over the stall door with wisps of hay hanging out of either side of his mouth. The other paced slowly back and forth in the stall, never pausing as it moved from point to point. "Your father will be upset if Sheriff Neal and his men don't find them."

"And yours." Cassie moved to stand beside Flint, studying the beautiful golden horses with pale gold manes and bright alert eyes. "Like your buckskin, they were Pa's pride and joy."

"I hope they will be again." Flint shoved his hands into his trouser pockets. "I can't afford to replace such quality animals on my pay."

"He can't blame you for their loss." She touched his arm to draw his attention. "If there's anything I can do…"

He grimaced as he shook his head. "Your mother blames me and I'm sure will be very clear on the point to your father."

"I don't think she's quite as antagonistic toward you as she was." Cassie batted her lashes at him until he smiled a little, the merest hint of his lips curving. "Since your mother visited, Ma has been…quieter about her displeasure with Pa's decision."

"I wonder if my mother said something to her." Flint strode closer to the stall to peer at the palomino pacing to the window and back to the hay mound in the corner. "She even passed me without snarling yesterday."

Cassie chuckled and rested her hands on top of the stall door, bringing her closer to his proximity and allowing her to admire the sleek lines of the horse. "She's softening toward you."

"Or trying to trick me into believing so." Flint glanced at her and then focused on the pacing animal. "This one is nervous. I don't know if he'll suit my needs."

"Give him a chance. He just got here after all." Cassie studied Flint's profile, admiring his sleek lines as well. The firm jaw, straight nose, high cheekbones, and intelligent forehead. He belonged among the Greek gods of lore. More than his appearance, his gentle, caring nature attracted her like dew to the long grass stems in the early morning. "He may settle after he grows accustomed to the place."

"Maybe." Flint turned to drift his gaze around the barn. "The other horses seem content enough. Not that one. I'll give him a day and then decide."

Cassie swallowed her protest in order to understand his reasoning. Flint had been nervous when he first arrived. She'd seen it in his expression when she and her ma had returned. He knew horses better than she did, but surely he could understand how the animal would feel upon arriving at a new barn with so many strange people and horses to adjust to. She couldn't hold her peace. She had to ask.

"You know what it's like to be wary in a new situation." She pinned him with her gaze, willing him to listen. "You were a touch on edge when I first saw you last week."

"It's different for horses who are needed to do their jobs without causing a ruckus." He indicated the pacing horse with a nod of his head. "That one is more likely to resist the harness, for instance, than the others. He might be fine under saddle with an experienced rider."

She studied the gorgeous palomino gelding in silence for

several moments. His coloring matched his neighbor so closely one might think they were twins. A slight dappling of the haunches added an interesting pattern to the glossy gold coat. The swishing and twitching long cream tail and mane contrasted perfectly with the body and legs.

"Which ones will you use for the carriage?" Cassie laid a hand on his arm, perched as lightly as a butterfly on a flower. The muscles tensed under her fingers.

He blinked at her hand and then met her gaze. His grass-green eyes regarded her for a moment before he answered. "I'd hoped the palominos. They're a flashy pair. But it might be more prudent to use the bays instead."

She smiled up at him as she tilted her head to one side and slowly batted her lashes. He stared into her eyes while she held onto his arm. "The bays are beautiful."

How might he respond to her declaration? She held her breath, silently urging him to notice her. Really see her as a young, enticing, perhaps even enthralling woman standing before him. Ready to give herself to him if only he'd venture to ask. She moistened her lips, inviting him to drop his gaze to the flick of her tongue over her lower lip. She held still, hoping. Waiting for his reaction to her overt invitation.

His pupils dilated the longer he looked into her eyes. A vein pulsed in his throat, revealing the rapid beat of his heart. His upper body gravitated toward her, ever so gradually, closer and closer, and then he jerked back to stand upright again. Blinking, he cleared his throat as his eyes narrowed. "Yes, they are. I…need to get back inside and finish updating the…ledgers."

"Right this minute?" He'd been about to kiss her. Really close to following through on his wish to do so. His entire posture indicated his desire to meet her lips with his. Before he broke the spell.

"I hadn't realized the time. I'll see you later." He stepped away, forcing her to drop her hand from his arm.

He put distance between them with each rapid stride away from her and out of the stable. But if only for a moment, he'd shown interest in her. She grinned as she trailed after him out of the barn and across the carriageway. Only a tiny hint of interest, but enough to give her hope.

Halting the jigging dapple gray gelding with a firm grip on the reins, Flint scanned the peaceful vista laid out before him. Blue skies clear of clouds and bright sunshine combined for a beautiful if hot day. He'd arranged to have the day off from regular inn duties to search for the horses. Finding his missing friend remained paramount in his mind. After traipsing up and down the hills and valleys surrounding the inn all morning and half the afternoon, he'd taken to riding up into the mountains to gain a better perspective. From his position at the top of the mountain overlooking the western valley, he could see for miles. Meadows and rolling hills stretched away in all directions, the winding Winchester Road the only mar upon the land. Which meant no herd of horses in sight. No Buck.

If it were him stealing horses... He'd take them away from their home so they wouldn't seek out their familiar stables. Perhaps he searched on the wrong side of the mountains. A surge of hope filled his core as he turned the horse to cross over the ridge of the low mountain and picked and lurched their way along narrow rocky deer trails to a vantage point on the other side. With the sun beginning to set, they would have to head back soon or be caught out in the dark in unfamiliar territory. A shiver of dread coursed down his back. Urging the gray forward, he pushed aside the niggling fear of the dark threatening his calm. Finally locating a place where he could survey the land, he reined up. He searched the hills and valleys before him. The view proved remarkably similar with one important difference.

Off to the left he caught a flash of color amidst the trees where the meadow met the forest. Guiding the gray cautiously along a steep, winding deer trail, they made their way down the mountain.

His pulse increased as they approached a fenced enclosure nearly hidden by the surrounding brush and trees. A whicker floated on the light breeze, his gray pricking its ears at the sound.

"Easy now." Flint kept a loose hand on the reins and a tight grip on his burgeoning excitement.

He slowly scanned the surrounding terrain until he spotted a shack two hundred yards from the enclosure. From that distance he could only see clapboard siding, shaker shingled roof, and a thin column of smoke twisting into the sky from the lone chimney. Somebody was home.

He turned his attention back to the enclosure and located the herd huddled under the shade of the fully leafed trees. He urged his mount closer and around the outside of the fencing. Closer until he could distinguish colors of the horses. Brown, chestnut, black, and...one buckskin paint. He whistled and Buck's head shot up from where he'd been napping. Seeing Flint, he galloped toward the fence, sliding to a stop on the other side so that tiny pebbles rattled against the lower fence rails.

"Hey, big guy." He sidled his jigging horse over to the fence, settling the gray to stand quietly for a moment so he could reach out and stroke the star on Buck's forehead. Joy and relief flooded through him for a sweet moment. Safe and uninjured.

He reached out for the gate latch, eager to release the horses and take them back to where they belonged. Only to realize he couldn't take the horses with him. Not that he wasn't capable of driving them home on his own. He was enough of a horseman to accomplish the task. No, the law needed to be involved in order for justice to be served.

Damn. It broke his heart to have to leave the horses and ride for the sheriff's office. How else could they capture the culprits and bring them to justice other than to catch them with the stolen property in their control? If he rescued the horses, the proof of the crime fell apart. Surely there was some other way. He racked his brain, glancing toward the shack half fearing armed horse thieves would spill out of the building and try to stop him. Sadness and concern replaced the joy of moments before as his heart thundered in his chest at the fateful decision he faced. Torn in two by the desire to rescue his horse and the need to bring justice to the thieves. He only had one choice.

"Stay here, big guy." He patted the gelding's neck and then picked up the reins, the gray responding by shifting its weight from foot to foot in anticipation of an imminent signal to do something, anything. "Help is on the way."

With that, he reined the gray away from the enclosure and set out for Huntsville again. He'd inform the authorities and show them where he'd found the horses. Then the arrest fell to the sheriff. But oh, how he'd love to go nab the thieves himself. Given half a chance, he'd teach them a lesson about stealing. He kicked the gray into a gallop, leaning low over its neck and praying they'd return in time.

The straw broom whisked the coating of dust and dirt off the wide porch with each swing of his arms, a low lying cloud of dust swirling off the wood boards. Flint relished being out of doors for a span early in the morning when the dew still clung to the grass and flowers. He paused in his chore to trail his gaze across the peaceful scene. The hogs in their pen, waiting to be released to forage by the ever slothful stable boy. Flint determined he'd have to have a word or two with the lad, light a fire under his backside. The cattle grazed their way across the pasture. Beau and

Pickles trotted past and disappeared around the end of the residence. So early in the day the carriageway stood clear of vehicles but in a few hours it would be crowded with coaches pulled by teams of horses, heavily laden wagons pulled by oxen and driven by tough men, and saddle horses carrying tradesmen and merchants on their various business dealings. For the moment, he drank in the peace and quiet of a new day, a new week beginning.

He cast a glance down the drive, searching, waiting. He'd shown Deputy Parker where the horses had been kept and then had been told to leave it to them to catch the criminals. That had been two days ago and his patience grew thinner with each passing hour. He wanted to see them coming up the road and soon. Maybe he should have slipped Buck out and brought him home, left the rest for the sheriff to recover. But then he'd feel guilty for leaving his boss's horses behind, subject to being driven off or sold or worse. No, he'd done the right thing. Only the waiting proved bloody hard in spite of knowing he'd done what he must.

Red and Cocoa trotted toward him across the open space, joining him on the porch. He set the broom aside to pet on their heads. One had a burr tucked behind a silky ear, so Flint picked at it, cursed when he pricked his finger on a sharp spine, and then finally pulled it free and flung it aside. A chilly breeze wafted over his cheeks. The dogs stilled for a beat before curling up by the table and flanking chairs, heads on paws but eyes on the carriageway. Flint followed their gaze, unsurprised when the soldier's ghost appeared in the middle of the circular drive.

Flint sucked in a breath as he contemplated the wavering image in silence. The Continental uniform had seen better days. The battered black tricorne hat on his head appeared scuffed and ragged. The navy blue coat with swept back tails and red facing on the lapels also sported red blood dripping over the left breast. His white breeches and knee socks bore dark smudges and his brown leather shoes showed signs of wear and tear. But it was the man's eyes that scored into Flint's soul. Pain and sadness echoed from within the depths of his gaze.

As he regarded the phantom, the wavering form solidified as he strode toward Flint. His pulse quickened with each step the soldier took. He swallowed the lump in his throat, holding his ground with an effort of will. Red whined briefly and then fell silent but remained watchful. The blood on the coat shimmered in the morning light when the soldier halted at the base of the steps.

"Please, sir. Can you help me?" The soldier's voice sounded young and unsure.

Flint peered closer at him. With a jolt, he realized the man was in fact a boy. A teen at most, only a few years younger than Flint. Clearing his throat of the fear lodged there, he studied the boy. "What's your name?"

"Private Louis Johnson." He smiled at Flint, a slight lift of the corners of his mouth.

Flint searched his memory of the history of the American Revolution but couldn't recall any fighting in these parts. Along the eastern coast to the east side of the Appalachians but not on the west. How had he come to be so far west then?

"Where are you from?"

"Charleston, South Carolina." He removed his hat and held it in both hands in front of him. "Can you help me?"

The roving soul must search for something. But what? Could he actually help him? Flint swallowed hard as he nodded twice. "I will try. What do you need?"

"I was separated from my unit and have wandered for so long." He glanced away and then back to meet Flint's gaze.

"Where were you when you got separated?"

"The wilderness in western Georgia. I'm lost and I need

to find my way back to my unit." A tear glistened at the edge of his eye and then trailed down his cheek. "Can you help me?"

"You're a long way from home, I'm afraid." Hundreds of miles separated the inn from the major city. "I can point you in the right direction but it's many days' journey from here."

The boy sighed as another tear followed the first. "Tell me how to get there and I'll find a way. I must go home. My family and fiancé are waiting for me to return."

With the span of time passed since the revolution ended, Flint seriously doubted his family continued to wait for his return. At least, living family. He keyed on the subtle inclusion of the boy's intended and his heart dropped at how long the girl might have waited, futilely, for the lad's coming home. Did she marry someone else or stay true and a spinster? Tragedy for everyone resulted from the missing soldier's failure to find his way back to his home, his heart. Still, if he'd rest easier by returning to his hometown, then Flint would try to help.

He gave him directions for the fastest route home for a man on foot. Perhaps not the most direct but the easiest path. Maybe somehow somebody could give him a ride.

"Thank you kindly, sir." Louis settled his tricorne firmly on his head with a pat. "I'll be on my way."

"One thing before you go." Flint held up a hand to ask him to wait. When he turned back, Flint nodded. "It's not an easy journey, especially on foot. Take care."

Louis nodded once and then strode away toward the road in the distance until he vanished into the morning sunlight. Red and Cocoa rose to their feet and sidled next to Flint, pressing against his legs on either side of him. He dropped a hand onto each head as he blinked at the spot where the ghost had disappeared. The boy had fought and died in the effort to create a new independent country. One with lots of promise despite its problems. Not a perfect country but better than any before, to his way of thinking.

"Well, that was a first." Flint addressed the dogs pressing against his legs, wondering at their reaction to the specter.

"What was?" Cassie stopped at his side, a curious smile tugging on her lips.

Flint jumped back, the dogs dashing down the steps at his sudden movement. "Don't do that."

Cassie looked at him askance as she chuckled. "What's wrong with you?"

"You startled me." At her arched brow, he shrugged. "That's all."

"You look like you've seen a gh—" Her eyes widened as her mouth formed a silent O and then she slowly shook her head. "You didn't, right?"

He swallowed his retort before he said something untrue. But how to respond and keep his word to Mercy? Perhaps a bit of redirection might smooth over the rough patch in the conversation.

"Do you see anything unusual?" He swept one arm out and back, encompassing the entire front of the inn and residence.

"No. Do you?"

"Why do you keep asking?" He had to change the subject. A different topic of conversation would save him. He grabbed the broom and moved to finish his interrupted chore.

She propped her palms on her hips as she stared at him for several moments. Kept his sweeping even and steady despite the weight of her stare on his shoulders. Coughed as the dust cloud churned in a light breeze. He glanced at her frequently as he worked his way down the porch boards. When he reached the end, he spun around to find her grinning at him.

"Now what?" He carried the broom back toward her, intending to keep on going inside the building to find another task waiting for his attention. Anything to not dwell on the unearthly and vaguely unsettling conversation with the young ghost.

"You're avoiding my questions, which tells me you're uncomfortable." She snagged his arm as he neared her. "Is it me that's got you flustered?" She batted her eyelashes at him as she flashed him a come-hither smile.

"You might say that." Her sudden appearance had indeed twisted his composure. She seemed intent on being in the way at every opportunity. What was she about with all the batting of lashes and sidelong looks? He froze for a moment at a sudden thought. She was too young for such manipulations. Wasn't she? "Did you want something?"

"Why, yes, I do." She squeezed his forearm as she chuckled softly.

She flirted with him. He stiffened, resisting the temptress. He'd promised Reggie he'd steer clear of his daughter and stay keen on the business at hand. No distractions. An easy promise since she was a child. While Flint had met her upon occasion, he hadn't realized the girl had grown into such a pretty young woman. One with a sharp mind and comely ways. One apparently interested in his attentions. She was bound to be disappointed.

Although after his chat with Louis the ghost it was difficult to not start thinking about settling down. Even at Louis' young age, he'd been looking toward his future. Starting a family and all that went with it. Life could be very unpredictable. Perhaps he shouldn't put off marrying as he'd always planned. Who better than him to court Cassie? After all, their parents were friends and Reggie had entrusted his livelihood to Flint.

Annoyed at his own musings, Flint shook off his rationalizations. He'd promised Reggie to keep the womenfolk safe which included keeping his hands off Cassie.

He stared at her hand until she removed it with a flash of her eyes and a smirk. Firming his resolve to keep his distance, he gazed at her for a second. He'd have to watch how he phrased things when speaking with her. "What brings you out here?"

"Sheridan has a few items he needs from the mill and the general store in Huntsville." She pursed her lips and then moistened them with a flick of her tongue. "He asked me to see if you'd make the trip into town today or tomorrow."

He nodded and stepped around her to go inside. "I'll go find out what he needs."

An excuse to go to town would give him the opportunity to follow up with the good sheriff as well. Keeping his pace to normal instead of trotting away, he escaped from the temptation staring after him on the porch.

Chapter Six

The posse thundered up the narrow path toward the shack, Sheriff Neal in the lead. Flint had insisted on action from the sheriff and deputies and joined in the assault on the horse thieves. Neal had wanted Flint to wait in town for them to handle the matter. Flint refused. Flat out refused to wait any longer. Then Neal insisted he ride at the back, behind the deputized men, for his protection. Reluctantly, Flint had agreed. But when they arrived, the sheriff proved to be correct in his restrictions upon the innkeeper. Unsurprisingly, the thieves burst out of the door shooting at the ten mounted men in front of the disreputable shack.

Repeated blasts from the many guns surprised the nervous gray under Flint. He clasped his thighs more firmly around the powerful animal and shortened the reins, all to no avail. The terrified horse pirouetted and fled in the opposite direction from the shootout at the shack.

Flashbacks of when he started learning to ride, when his horse had taken off after being stung by a hornet, recalled fear and terror. Terrified, he'd clung to the horse's neck and yelled for help, which only scared the animal into galloping faster. The young horse failed to clear a ditch, stumbled and tumbled him over its shoulder onto the hard ground. Jarring

101

him so that he bit his bottom lip, bleeding all over his new shirt. The horse had come up with a broken leg and his father had been royally outraged when he had to put the horse down to save it from suffering. All because his son hadn't known how to handle a runaway horse.

Flint vowed to not let anything happen to the borrowed horse tearing down the dirt road. He sat deep and sawed the reins, working to loosen the bit from between the teeth of the runaway as it turned sharply to avoid an approaching coach-and-four and race across a flowering meadow. Glancing up, he spotted an immense downed tree in their path and pulled firmly and steadily on the reins. He had no idea whether the animal could jump the three-foot-diameter tree trunk they were approaching at breakneck speed. Literally. The flat panicked gallop hurled them over the trunk, Flint hugging the neck, the horse's front hooves tapping the bark and sending bits and pieces flying up and around them as they sailed over. The reins slipped out of Flint's sweaty hands and he scrambled to catch them before they tripped the horse as it continued across the meadow. Finally, the tiring horse responded to his firm grip on the reins and turned in a slow arc until they slowed to a stop facing the direction they'd come. White foamy sweat dripped from the gray's neck where the leather reins rubbed the hot skin.

"It's okay." Flint soothed the trembling gelding with a shaking hand stroking its wet neck. "I know you're scared but we have to go back and help. Are you with me?"

After a moment, he nudged the gray into a walk and then a trot and they soon were back where the action had all but ended. The two blond men were no match for the sharp shooting of the sheriff and his men. Disabled but not dead, the two men writhed and moaned in the dirt in front of their hideaway. Turkey buzzards gathered overhead, creating a spiraling shaft of black winged birds, their feathers shaggy against the sky.

"Tie them varmints up and haul them to jail." Stephen Neal holstered his gun and aimed his judgmental gaze at the thieves. "You no-good horse thieves will hang."

"We ain't did nothin' wrong." The older of the two men spoke through gritted teeth. "You can't prove we did, neither."

"He has a point." Neal glanced between the men on the ground and Flint. He peered at him, a question in his expression but he didn't challenge Flint on his sweating horse. Finally, he nodded once and lifted one brow at him. "Do you have any proof those horses are yours, son?"

Relieved at not having to explain where he'd been, Flint grinned as he bobbed his head. "I most certainly do."

"Let's see it then." Neal regarded him steadily, waiting for his evidence.

Flint trotted his mount over to the corral and whistled for Buck. The gray lifted its head with a jerk at the shrill sound. The buckskin whinnied and galloped toward him, sliding to a stop in a cloud of dust.

A burst of laughter erupted from the posse riders while Flint greeted the buckskin paint with a pat on his neck over the fence.

"I told you we'd be back." Flint rubbed on Buck as relief and joy surged to overwhelm him. He fought back the press of tears smarting his eyes. He'd not cry in front of the other men.

"Alright. That's enough for me. Take 'em away." Neal pointed to two of his deputies and then motioned to several others. "You guys help Flint wrangle those horses home. The rest are dismissed. All of you make sure to report back to me in town and I'll settle up your pay for this special assignment. Thank you for your assistance."

"Thank you, Sheriff." Flint rode close enough to Neal to briefly shake his strong hand. "I'm glad to know you're willing to punish those who break the law. I realize it's a tough job around these parts."

"I do my best to protect the people of Madison County. Men like you make my job easier. Thanks." With a tilt of his head, Neal spun his horse around and galloped away, several deputies riding hard to catch up to him.

Flint smiled at the three men sitting on their horses nearby. "Alright, men, let's get these ponies moving."

He opened the gate to the fenced enclosure and they rode inside to herd them out and then home. He couldn't wait until he could let his boss know he'd had a hand in recovering his property. Chalk one up for Flint's future.

A fancy coach-and-four rattled to a stop in front of the inn, mud clinging to the wheels as the jangling of harness settled into a murmur of metal. Cassie paused in arranging the flowers in the vase on the table inside the wide open front door of the inn. The extended heat wave finally broke with the rains coming in over the last two days. A welcome relief from the summer sun but the resulting quagmire of the road proved harder to endure.

At least the carriageway had been recently vastly improved by the ingenious concept Flint had learned about from one of the many periodicals he received. He didn't ask for her mother's permission, just made it happen. Which of course didn't win him any points with her ma at first but she'd eventually stopped grumbling about "upstart young men." Still, definitely a fine idea. He'd arranged for some men to break up large rocks harvested from the mountains into much smaller ones and lay them all over the carriageway. Then they added even smaller stones to settle into the gaps between the bigger ones to form a smoother surface. Not only did it lessen the amount of mud and dust, it also made the inn look nicer upon approach. His idea served the customers and the residents well and she held him in high esteem as a result of his clever improvement to the property. Her pa would be very pleased upon his return to see how Flint had smoothly managed the whole project.

The footman opened the door to the coach and helped a handsome couple step down onto the stones. When she spotted the red-haired woman she smiled and hurried to greet the Bakers properly. A more unique couple she couldn't imagine. John Baker had married a woman eight years younger than his forty-eight but the love they shared glowed between them. His reputation for being a stern and shrewd businessman didn't impact the generosity he bestowed on his family and friends. While her plump and friendly person moved easily among those she cared about. Cassie found it very easy to like them both.

"Mrs. Baker, what a surprise." Cassie embraced the older woman as if she were a long lost aunt. "I wasn't expecting to see you today."

Tabitha lifted her brows with a gentle smile. "Mr. Baker had expressed an interest in verifying everything is running along as it should after the theft and return of your horses. And I felt like it was a good day to enjoy some of your cook's fine culinary delights."

John Baker proffered his arm for his wife to lay her hand on. "I trust we're not too late to have dinner?"

"Not at all. Follow me." Cassie pivoted and led them inside to enjoy the coolness after the steamy heat outside. "Sheridan will be pleased you've come especially to enjoy his unique talents."

After seating them at a table near an open window at the rear of the dining room, Cassie went to where Flint worked as barkeep, handsome as ever. Before he noticed her, she studied him silently for several seconds. A new air of confidence surrounded him with his every movement. Tanned arms exposed by rolled up white sleeves, muscles bunching and releasing with each swipe of the rag on the counter. Dark stains under his arms and the glistening on his brow reflected the effort he exerted in keeping the bar surface clean and appealing for customers. She cleared her throat and took a step closer.

"An ale and cider, please." Cassie grinned at Flint as he swiftly pulled the appropriate vessel to fill for each drink.

"For Mr. and Mrs. Baker?"

"Yes. She decided she needed to eat something delicious from Sheridan's menu." She grinned at him as he pulled the tap to fill a tankard with frothy ale.

"I'll go welcome them as soon as I finish here." Setting the mug on the counter, he retrieved a silver cup and dipped it into the cider barrel. Then poured the contents into a porcelain mug and set the beverage beside the other. "Anything else?"

"Not at the moment." She winked as she picked up the two drinks and carried them back to John and Tabitha. "There you are. I'll go retrieve today's repast for you. I'm sure you'll enjoy it."

"I'm sure we will." John regarded her for a moment and then held up a hand to keep her from walking away. "One thing I'd like to know. I've heard from Mr. Hamilton your father intends to be away for an extended period. Are you and your mother satisfied with his presence and abilities?"

She searched his expression for an underlying meaning to his question. What exactly had Flint told him that would make him wonder about his capabilities? She glanced toward the man in question who carefully wiped down the gleaming bar counter with a white cloth. The royal blue vest and black string tie added to his professional aura. To her, though, the sweep of his lush auburn hair against his collar and the intense look on his face made her hungry to touch him. She shouldn't feel so sexually attracted to him, not with him employed by her pa. But she couldn't stop the physical, visceral response any more than stop breathing.

"Miss Fairhope?" John prodded with a querying brow.

She brought her gaze back to meet his and nodded once. "Yes, we've been quite pleased with his efforts now that he's settled into the rhythm." She shrugged lightly with a quick tilt of her head. "He had a few moments but those have passed."

She saw no reason to detail Flint's mistakes nor the animosity her ma felt toward him. How Ma had been hurt by her pa's decision. No point airing their dirty laundry to the neighbors. Most of the rancor had subsided. Maybe not all, but the vast majority seemed to have settled along with the dust out front.

Flint moved around the end of the bar and strode toward her and their guests. "It's good to see you both. And thanks again for the loan of your horses, John."

John stood to shake hands with Flint and then resumed his seat. "I'm glad I was in a position to be of assistance."

Cassie laid her fingertips on the table to draw their attention. "I'll go grab you some food and be right back."

At John's nod, she spun away and sashayed across the room and into the kitchen. Flint's gaze followed her until the door blocked his view and then met John's knowing smirk. Flint swallowed and shrugged one shoulder. Nothing to tell on that front.

"You may want to see if you can settle the palomino mare. She was rather nervous while here." Flint chose to change the subject from speculation on Cassie to a safer subject.

"She is rather on edge in a new place." John lifted the tankard and swallowed several times before setting it back on the table.

"I don't blame her, being surrounded by people she's not familiar with." Tabitha unfolded her napkin and placed it on her lap. "I know I'd feel the same."

"We tried to make sure they were comfortable." Where was this conversation headed? "Was there any problem with your horses when they were returned the other day?"

"Oh no, nothing like that." John waved away Flint's sudden concern. "I'm just being neighborly and ensuring all is well here."

Flint searched his memory of the instructions and insights Reggie had given him prior to his departure. He'd mentioned his neighbors and which might be able to help in what capacity. Nothing about them looking in from time to time to make sure he was doing his job correctly. Perhaps Reggie had written to them after he left with such a request. If so, what did that say about the man's confidence in him? Every time he thought he was making progress in building trust and his reputation for efficient management someone questioned both.

Flint swept a hand to indicate the entire room. "As you can see, everything is in order. I'll make sure it stays that way, too."

"Very good. I'm sure Reggie will be glad to hear of your settling in and conducting business in a manner of which he'd approve." John lifted his drink and saluted Flint with it. "To continued success."

Flint inclined his head with a cautious half smile. More underlay the man's presence than he first intimated. But what? "Are you in communication with Mr. Fairhope?"

"Of course, son." John sat back as Cassie appeared with a tray of steaming plates of beef tips and roasted potatoes to place in front of them. "You don't think he'd walk away without providing independent eyes to oversee his interests, do you?"

Tabitha smiled gently at him. "Don't look so shocked, Mr. Hamilton."

"I wasn't under the impression Mr. Fairhope mistrusted my abilities to such an extent." Shocked was an understatement for the uncertainty and dismay ricocheting through his chest. He steeled his composure and struggled to keep his equilibrium while the revelation weighed on his pride.

Cassie finished putting the plates on the table and then gazed at him. "My father has always provided for contingencies, Flint. Don't take it wrong if he wanted his very savvy business oriented neighbor to check in from time to time. Especially when he'll have a fine report to make about your accomplishments."

"Exactly, son." John winked at him and then picked up his utensils, preparing to dig into the hot meal. "Now if you'll excuse me, I'm dying to taste this."

"Very well, sir." Flint couldn't wait to escape and catch his breath after the surprising conversation. "I'll leave you to your meal. Mrs. Baker." With a brief nod, he turned and strode back to the bar, perplexed and unsure of his reason for remaining at the inn. He blew out a breath. One thing he could be sure of… His own secret contingency plan.

Heat shimmered in the air around where Cassie kneeled and worked on weeding the rows of asparagus plants poking their heads through the soil, reaching for the sky. In a few more days, it would be July and the heat would become unbearable. But her longing for the next month couldn't be stopped. On Independence Day she'd be eighteen, an age when she intended to declare her own independence and be responsible for herself. Then she would decide her future without requiring her parents' approval. She huffed as she shook her head at the slender stalks marching in a neat row away from her. Who was she fooling? Her mother would never agree with Cassandra becoming independent herself.

The back door slapped shut, drawing her attention to where Flint hesitated at the top of the steps. Tall and straight, and wearing a white shirt with a red bow tie, an almond-brown vest, blue jeans, and polished brown boots, he appeared cool and in charge. His questing gaze found hers and he smiled. Her heart flipped over as she returned the greeting in kind. He seemed to be warming to her flirting. Sending her quick glances filled with secrets and hopes. A smile here and a grin there.

Her ma still didn't want him around and continued to harass him, challenge his every decision, and resent any changes he proposed let alone accomplished. Like the upgrade to the inn's menu. What a shouting match the proposed change had entailed. But Sheridan had finally relented and added the turtle soup and quail dishes to the weekend's offerings. Once Sheridan agreed, then Mercy grudgingly stopped the harangue against the change. The stone on the carriageway took even longer for her to relent and reluctantly admit to the benefits of the change. At least, she had acknowledged the improvement as a good idea.

Cassie focused on pulling weeds until she heard his boots on the steps. A quick flick of a glance confirmed Flint approached with long, firm strides. Let him come to her. She kept her hands busy but her ears listened intently to the swish of his boots through the grass, growing louder as he neared.

"Cassie, can I talk to you for a minute?" He stopped at the closed gate, hands gripping the top board.

"I need to finish the weeding before the rains come." She studied his expression, seeing a hint of sadness in his eyes. "Does it have to be now?"

He bobbed his head twice. "I don't want to put this off any longer. Please?"

"Fine." She rocked back on her heels and pushed to her feet. Wiping her hands on her gardening apron, she walked toward the gate. Secretly, his invitation to chat thrilled her throbbing heart. "I can spare a few minutes."

He pulled the gate open and held it until she'd slipped through then let it close. "Shall we go to the gazebo where it's cooler?"

"That's a fine idea." She pulled a rag from her apron pocket and mopped her damp brow. "I should have started the garden chores this morning before the heat of the day."

"Are you nearly finished or do you want some help?" Flint started walking away from the garden, heading around the end of the residence.

Cassie fell into step with him, noting the flowering rose bushes nestled up to the building needed watering. "I'll manage, but thank you for offering."

He fell silent for several strides and then glanced at her. "You enjoy working out there."

"Yes. It's a quiet, meditative time for me to think." She caught his gaze and held it for a beat. "To plan what I want to do with my life."

"I see." He shoved his hands into his pockets as they neared the gazebo. "You've made plans already?"

She stepped up and into the shade of the lattice-sided platform. Three white metal benches spaced around the interior provided a place to rest and relax. She sank onto one and sat straight, her hands clasped in her lap. Flint took a seat beside her with ample space between them for two men to fill. She sighed silently at the distance separating them.

"I have plans but..." She glanced at the front porch of the inn, deep shade obscuring the furniture she knew stood to the left side of the double doors. Also obscuring anyone relaxing in the coolness of the shade. Cassie blinked and turned to meet his steady regard. She shrugged lightly and pressed her lips together for an instant. "But then I have to consider my ma."

Flint frowned and then his brows shot up as he stared at her. "Oh."

He understood her unspoken conditions for planning her life ahead. She waved one hand, dismissing his concern. "She'd probably stop me from achieving any of my own goals. Unless, of course, they meshed with her idea of what I should do with my life."

"Surely she'd support your plans?"

"I'm reluctant to share with her what they are because if she knows and doesn't approve, then my life would be awful."

"What about your father?"

"What about him? He's not even here." Cassie stared out at the sunny carriageway busy with vehicles and people coming and going. Business really had increased under Flint's management. Her father would be pleased. If he could ever see the changes wrought by Flint. "What if I never see him again? What if something happens to him on the long, difficult journey from Georgia?"

She hadn't fully acknowledged her fear—privately or out loud—that her father might not make it safely home. What would become of them if the patriarch failed to reach the haven of the inn? Sadness and worry speared her heart as she stared at the brick structure, her pa's dream.

Flint nodded as he glanced at her and then to watch the arrival of a coach-and-four rattling up the long road to the inn. "I'm sure he'll take the proper measures to ensure his safety as well as the cargo he'll be bringing with him. But you're right, it is a difficult trip. Easier now, though, than when my grandparents made a similar journey."

"I thought you were born here in this area." Cassie turned to level her gaze at him. He continued to study the coach as it drew to a halt and began to unload passengers.

"I was born in a house near the old trading post in the wilderness in what is now north-western Alabama. But Grandpa Nat and Grandma Lyn left Charleston, South Carolina, in 1783. My father was an infant when they traveled by wagon over the hundreds of miles of Indian trails and footpaths to eventually settle there."

"With a baby?" She gasped and put her hand over her mouth as she shook her head. "That's incredible."

Her memories of the treacherous route from the central to northern part of the state made it difficult to imagine a harder journey. Traveling up river meant they had to use a wagon and carriage to transport their belongings. Crossing marshes and swamps with the mosquitoes and biting flies annoying them every step of the way. Jouncing along in the vehicle was better than walking beside when the going became steep and they had to help push the wagon up the hill, sweating and straining. They wore through their leather shoes about halfway and had to wrap rags around them to hold them together and protect their feet. She'd been grateful to finally arrive in Huntsville and spend a few days at the hotel, where her pa had become fast friends with James Hamilton. They restocked supplies and clothing from the various shops and stores in town and prepared for their next adventure, building the Fury Falls Inn. Without the Hamiltons' friendship, her father's dream may never have become a reality. Flint's voice brought her out of her reveries.

"Grandpa told us stories of their journey. How they had to take apart the wagon in order to carry the pieces a few at a time over the steepest part of the mountains and then put it back together again. They had to lead the horses because the terrain prevented them from using wheels at all. Sometimes they'd have to set up a camp because the rivers were too swift to cross, and they waited for days or often weeks until they could continue. They were fortunate no one became ill like so many others had, burying their loved ones alongside the trail."

By comparison, her family's move definitely went easier. She scanned the clearing where her pa had chosen to build his roadside inn. The red brick hostel offered a comfortable place to rest and refresh for weary travelers. The addition of the excellent fare in the dining room attracted customers who came back for more. The stables and livestock also helped create a homey and comforting setting. For others, certainly, since her view of the place as a prison still knotted her insides.

She looked at Flint's relaxed features. "How long did it take them to find a location for their new home?"

"Eight months, give or take. My father was walking by the time they chose a site for the trading post and cabin." He chuckled as a reminiscent smile spread on his lips. "Grandma always said her hands were kept quite full with him getting into everything."

"I can't fathom traveling so far by wagon. So, what did they do then?"

"Grandpa ran the trading post for decades while Grandma made and sold quilts and such."

"I don't understand. Why did they come all this way?"

"After the Revolution, Grandpa had a dream of starting somewhere new and fresh. Where he could leave his mark." Flint pivoted his head to peer at her. A pulse in his neck beat a steady rhythm. His bright green eyes seemed even brighter in the cool shade surrounding them. "He made his dream reality."

"And your grandmother?" Her own mother hadn't wanted to live in an inn despite it being her pa's dream to operate such a place. How many others sacrificed their desires out of love for another? "Was it her dream as well?"

He shrugged and shook his head. "As far as I know, her desire was to be with Grandpa wherever he went. I never heard her complain about where they lived."

"Where are they now?"

"Grandpa runs the livery stable in Huntsville. He's one of the best blacksmiths in all Alabama. And Grandma is one of the town's matriarchs who helps others through her charity work." He cocked his head and grinned at her. "They're enjoying living in town with all the finer things it has to offer. Quite a step up from the old trading post in Indian territory."

She sighed, a heart-weary sound. "I want to live in town as well. That's one of my dreams I plan to make come true."

"I hope you find a way to make it happen." He studied her for a long moment and then let his gaze drift away.

His attention turned inward despite his eyes darting from one thing to another. He sat still but she could almost hear the wheels spinning in his thoughts.

"Flint, do you have a dream, too?"

He blinked and then glanced at her. "One day, I want to run a fine tavern or maybe even a grand hotel in a big city. One that will draw people from all across the country to experience the food, the lodgings, and the entertainment."

She stifled a sigh, knowing he had the ability to make his dream into his reality. He desired to do more and better of the same thing. Run a hostel but at least he wanted to do so in a city, not out in the wilds. Her ma would have a fit if she found out where his passions lay, especially if she discovered Cassie's hope and fantasy in addition.

"That's quite a dream." She smiled at him and then shifted closer so she could lay her hand on his arm. "Where would you like to do that?"

He glanced at her hand and then met her gaze, the faraway hopeful look melting into one of determination with a hint of sadness. "Cassie, we can't do this."

She pulled her head back, a light frown tugging on her brows. "What?"

He lifted his arm, making her hand fall away. "We can't be a couple."

"Why not? Don't you think I'm pretty?" She quelled the desire to slap herself at such an inane, stupid comment. It wasn't about her looks. She needed him to see her as more than a pretty face, but a potential wife. Capable, caring, supportive of his goals. Even as she surreptitiously developed her own dreams and goals into reality. To see her as more than the child of a family friend.

"Yes, I think you're pretty…"

She peered at him, locking her gaze to his. "Am I not smart enough for you?"

"It's not that." He glanced away and back to her.

"Then why?"

He raked a hand through his hair and let the luxurious, tempting mix of auburn and golden brown flow across his shoulders. "I'm not willing to break trust with your father."

"My father?"

He nodded and firmed his lips. "I promised him I'd look out for you which doesn't include allowing any attraction to develop between us."

She arched one brow as she stared at him. Hope sprouting in her heart at his revelation. "*Are* you attracted to me, Flint?"

He blew out a breath. "Yes, but I mustn't be."

"Stop saying that." A flash of ire warmed her insides. "If we're attracted to each other, then why shouldn't we let nature take its course?"

"I gave him my word I would not accost his daughter." He dragged in a deep breath and let it out slowly. "You know me, Cassie. I won't go back on my promise."

"You haven't touched me. Not once. I've invited your attention but you've denied me." She crossed her arms and tapped the fingers of one hand on an elbow and lifted her nose higher. The move ensured she didn't follow through on her building desire to connect with him, touch him and never let go. "I don't think it's any of Pa's affair who I am attracted to. Who I want to court me. I think that's my choice."

"You're still a girl, Cassie. Your father is in charge of you." He stared at her while a vein pulsed at his temple. "I won't go against his wishes."

"Flint Hamilton, you listen to me." She dropped her arms and spun around to look him square in the eyes. "In about a week I'll turn eighteen and then they can't stop me. I won't let them."

"Don't be getting all het up about it, Miss Fairhope." He shook his head and frowned at her. "It won't do any good anyway."

"What now?" She angled her body toward him, a growing annoyance filling her core. "Are you afraid to admit you have feelings for me?"

He chewed on his lower lip as he regarded her for a minute. "You are indeed a lovely young lady who will one day attract a fine man to come calling on you."

"I would like for you to be that fine man." She studied him, feeling pressure building behind her eyes. She swallowed back her anger and the threat of tears. "We could let this—whatever it is—develop or not naturally instead of cutting it off before it even has a chance."

"You'd have me defy your father?" He arched both brows at her and then shook his head. "I won't do that, Cassie. I can't."

"Think of it as not so much defying him as delaying deciding." She searched for the right reasoning to convince him to allow them to test the waters. She couldn't let him talk himself out of exploring how he might actually care for her. "There's no hurry and we don't have to decide anything right now. We can simply spend time together but wait until Pa comes home to make any kind of decision as to whether we're right for each other."

He searched her expression while she held her breath, hoping against hope he'd agree with her logic. She swallowed the nervous desire to say more, to work to convince him to give them time to explore their feelings for each other, if they in fact had such feelings. She waited, hoping, fearing.

"I won't make any promises to you…" He slowly shook his head and then stared at her. "You have to agree to not push me into something neither of us are ready for. May never be ready for."

She held out her hand and he slowly clasped it with his. "One day at a time, Flint. That's all I'm asking for."

He nodded as he squeezed her fingers. "Then fine."

Flint tugged on her hand until she stood next to him. He led her down the steps of the gazebo and across the yard toward the garden. She paced beside him with a new mantra echoing in her mind and a small smile stuck on her mouth. One day at a time… Then one day, with any luck, he'd be hers.

The shadows blanketing the front porch of the inn hid her presence from the pair sitting under the shade of the gazebo. Groups of merchants, a large, boisterous family, and an older couple milled about in front of the inn where several coaches and saddle horses waited. The nosy dogs investigated the new arrivals. Mercy gripped the arms of the sturdy metal chair as she glared at her nemesis. What was Flint about, sitting out there where anyone could witness his abuse of her daughter? Cassie's reputation would be imperiled by his head leaning toward hers as if some secret exchange occurred between them. The thought froze her insides. What were they talking about?

She stewed over her next steps, not wishing to make a scene in front of the guests. Yet fuming more and more the longer they whispered together. Cassandra should be working in the garden not holding hands with the man. He embodied the exact type of man her daughter should avoid. An innkeeper. What was the chit thinking hanging on his every word like he was worth her time? Bah. Mercy rose and paced to the edge of the porch, tempted to rush out to the gazebo and flay him with her tongue. Tell him exactly how she felt about his taking any notice of Cassie as more than a serving wench under his employ. Mixing the relationship up with anything personal simply couldn't be tolerated. Least of all by her.

She spun and strode to the far end of the porch, staring at the open barn doors where Jericho, one of the young stable hands, raked the aisle while Liam, the other lad, led a pair of horses to the creek for a drink. Chickens pecked in the grass beside the barn, clucking and fluttering their wings as people came too close for their ease. She skipped her gaze across the entire Fury Falls Inn property and huffed out a sharp breath. Dirt and dust or mud and mire. Livestock everywhere she looked. Strangers coming and going. Such was the life of an innkeeper's wife.

Mercy lifted her chin and squared her shoulders. She had chosen to marry Reggie Fairhope because he was an honest, decent man with compassion and passion for life. A good man, a loving husband, a fine and fair father to their five children. Truth be told, a better person than Mercy could hope to be. Given how rancorous she'd become about living so far away from the refinements of the city. Well, she might not like where they lived and how Reggie earned a living. She'd never regret marrying him though. She loved him with her whole heart and soul. She'd follow him anywhere, even to the forsaken wilderness.

Spinning back around, she marched to the steps again and shuddered out a sigh when she spotted the two still whispering. As if they had nothing better to do with their time than make love in plain sight of all the guests coming and going as well as the hands and other employees. The very idea of a conspiracy between her daughter and Flint set her jaw and made her grit her teeth in growing ire and frustration. She must protect her daughter from men like him.

She drew in a deep breath in preparation for stalking down the steps and across the grass to break up their little clandestine affair. But she saw Flint rise and pull on Cassie's hand to lift her to stand beside him. Mercy swallowed the anguish flooding her chest. Not wanting to make a scene, she hesitated. Fought with her inclination to interrupt their discourse and forever forbid any further interaction. She pressed her palm to the base of her throat to keep from crying out in protest of his hand on her daughter. Cassie smiled at him, a small secretive grin that wrenched at Mercy's soul. Her daughter was smitten with him. No! The word reverberated through her head and severed the last shreds of her self-control as she stormed down the front steps to follow them around the end of the residence. Time to put an end to their interest in one another once and for all.

She flung a gruff welcome to a pair of coopers stumping up the steps toward her, blocking her progress. She remained the innkeeper's wife and thus must try to present a welcoming persona even when she felt exactly opposite. "Excuse me, sir." She brushed past them, dragging her skirts out of her way as she continued on her mission.

They stepped aside with a quick doff of their hats and a chuckle. Mercy kept going, dodging around Beau and Pickles as they trotted toward the barn, crossing her path and slowing her down. When Flint and Cassie turned the corner of the building, Mercy quickened her pace. Practically jogging, she reached the rose bushes nestled against the residence and paused to catch her breath. Then gasped when she noticed the couple had paused to talk, face to face and hand in hand.

Their stance reminded her of when she and Reggie had taken their vows of marriage all those years before. They'd stood exactly so, facing each other holding hands, while the minister intoned the traditional words forever binding her to her beloved Reggie. Until death parted them. An eternity to two people so young and naïve. She'd barely turned sixteen when she happily married Reggie in front of her supportive and bemused family in Charleston, South Carolina in 1798.

The thriving port city had survived the American Revolution and gone on to grow and become even more important as a maritime trading town. People from all over the world passed through the wharves and populated the surrounding area. The importation and exportation of goods flowed smoothly through the Old Exchange and ensured a booming economy. Reggie had swept her off her feet not only by treating her like a beautiful princess but with his dreams of a business of his own. She sensed his need to control his destiny and his desire for her to work alongside him in that effort. Her training as a plantation mistress ensured she possessed the hospitality and educational skills to supplement his business acumen and drive. She'd fallen in love with him and given him her heart and five children to love and raise together. Even when he chose to move the family to Montgomery she went along and made sure his home was warm and welcoming when he returned from his position as general manager at a modest hotel in town.

Then he decided he wanted his own place, a roadside inn. An inn! She'd resisted with every argument she could muster. But eventually, she'd reluctantly agreed to his going into business for himself. He'd saved up and had enough ready cash to make a start. When he chose the location, though, she'd objected. Dredged up every logical reason why moving to the wilds of Mississippi Territory, as Alabama was known back then, was a bad idea. The very concept frightened her. Didn't he realize the Indians waged war on white folks? What about their children's education? How would they all survive? He had an answer to every objection. And finally, he sweet-talked his reasons to her until she relented.

She blinked away the memories to stare at her daughter and Flint. Remembered how she'd gazed with love and adoration at her Reggie, trusting he'd take care of her and provide for her. Never realizing the difficulties lying in wait after they married. Mercy pressed her lips together as Cassie gazed up at Flint, batting her lashes and smiling at whatever nonsense he was telling her. He looked down at her upturned features with somber regard and an occasional hint of a smile. History seemed to repeat itself in slow motion. She couldn't permit it. When he leaned down, bringing his mouth closer to hers, Mercy flew into action.

"Stop!" She scurried toward them in a flutter of skirts and indignation burbling in her throat. "Step away, Mr. Hamilton. Right this minute."

Flint dropped Cassie's hands as if struck by lightning and regarded her with shock in his eyes. Cassie turned to confront Mercy, her mouth hanging open at the abrupt interruption. Good. Better they not touch let alone dare to kiss right in front of her and the lord above.

Mercy halted between them, facing Flint with an upraised fist. "Don't you dare ever again touch my daughter. Do you hear me?"

Flint took a half-step backward, away from her shaking fist. Slowly raising both hands beside his shoulders, he glanced at Cassie and then fixed his attention on Mercy. "As you wish."

Cassie huffed and shook her head at him. "We have an agreement, Flint."

Mercy spun around to poke her nose at Cassie's startled expression. "No, you do not."

"But, Ma—"

"Enough, young lady. You have work to do and so does he." She shook her finger in her daughter's face, her fingertip glancing off the upturned end. "Nothing exists between you two except the work to keep this place running. Do you understand me, Cassandra?"

"We were merely talking." She flashed a look at Flint, begging for his help in calming Mercy down. "What's wrong with that?"

Mercy dragged in a breath and let it out in a rush. "Everything. And don't even try to tell me there wasn't more going on here than a simple chit-chat between employer and employee. I have eyes." She pointed toward the garden gate. "Now go while I have a word with Mr. Hamilton."

"Ma, please. I can manage this." Cassie reached out a hand as if to try to stop Mercy from continuing to confront Flint.

Mercy lifted one brow and shook her head. "Go. Now. You have nothing further to say on the matter."

Cassie clamped her mouth shut and pressed her lips into a flat line as she turned to walk away. Casting a last glance over her shoulder, she shook her head and then opened the garden gate and slipped inside.

"Now, Mr. Hamilton." She paused, gathering her anger to her with each breath. "I won't tolerate any attempt to woo Cassie. You're not good enough for her. Let's be crystal clear on that point. Under no circumstances would I ever give my consent for you to court let alone to contemplate marriage with her. So keep your hands to yourself and get back to work. Or feel free to pack your bags and go on home. I'll manage the inn myself until my husband returns. Your choice."

He studied her for several seconds while a hawk circled high above calling out with its piercing cry to its partner. A flock of robins hopped among the rose bushes and the fallen flower petals in search of insects. Annoyance followed quickly by understanding and then acceptance flashed across his expression. He dropped his shoulders into place and inclined his head at her.

"Mrs. Fairhope, I wish I could comply with your desire for my departure but I cannot do so until Mr. Fairhope releases me from his employment." He angled his head to one side and let a slight smile slide onto his lips. "I'll stay and do what I promised to do." He slowly shrugged once. "I can't promise Cassie will agree with your dictate. She has some interesting plans for her future."

"What do you dare to suggest by such a statement?" Say it's not that she's set her cap for the infuriating man smiling fully at her. Anything but such an awful idea. She held her breath, afraid she was too late to stop something she knew would be a tragedy for her beautiful, loving daughter.

"You'll have to ask her." He touched his hand to his forehead. "As you said, I must get back to work." He spun to stride toward the dogtrot and inside the inn.

Leaving Mercy with a heavy heart as she watched Cassie busy among her tomato plants and corn stalks. She couldn't be too late. She'd find a way to end the foolish and ill-considered hope for any kind of a relationship between the two young people. Surely she could talk sense into her stubborn offspring before she made the mistake of committing to the wrong kind of man. Knowing her daughter, she'd pursue her own desires even without parental approval and acceptance. But she had to try to stop her for her own good.

Mercy had sensed a growing dissatisfaction coming from Cassie but hadn't realized how deeply she resented her current situation. Was she anxious to leave like her brothers? Her heavy heart dropped at the thought. If so, then how desperate had she become? She pondered the recent comments her daughter had made about living at the inn versus living in town. Cassie wanted to escape not only her mother's protective wing but also the isolation and deprivation associated with living at the inn.

Suddenly Mercy's own dictate to Cassie that she must marry a good man and have children floated back to haunt her. Was she pursuing Flint in order to marry and thus move away from her mother's influence and supervision? Her throbbing heart threatened to shatter as she mulled over the idea of her daughter seeking ways to escape from Mercy's love and care. And heavy, overly protective hand. Mercy pressed a palm to her mouth to stifle the cry of anguish threatening to erupt.

After a long moment, she let her hand fall to her waist and hold on. Knowing the root of the problem and finding a solution were two very different things. Somehow, Mercy had to convince Cassie marriage to Flint would not solve her problems, only compound them. Nothing would stop her. She simply must find a way of preventing her daughter from making the biggest mistake of her life.

Chapter Seven

$\mathcal{F}$lint strode into the office and collapsed onto the chair at the desk. Stared out the window at the busy yard to let his emotions settle after the unexpected confrontation with Mercy about Cassie. He blew out a breath and dragged his fingers through his hair. What a predicament.

On the one hand, he liked the girl. Most everything about her attracted him. Only the fact that he'd vowed to take care *of* her, not care *for* her, made him hesitate. Her tendency to take charge of the situation revealed a certain stubborn streak in her personality. Used appropriately, such a trait could prove useful for accomplishing her objectives. What would happen when her desires conflicted with someone else's, though? Sparks might well fly as a result.

On the other hand, he didn't want to fight with Mercy and perhaps Reggie. He'd arrived at the inn without any thought of starting a relationship with anyone except the owners and the customers. Intended only to work hard and be inventive as to ways to increase business and improve the offerings and appearance of the business. Now he found himself embroiled in a dispute between his employers and their daughter.

What kind of relationship could he have with Cassie if both her parents forbade it? Without their acceptance of him, he and Cassie had no future. Not with any peace. Not as long as they stayed anywhere nearby. So he'd have to use his contingency plan sooner than he expected. Before he saved up enough money. Possible but not preferable. If he chose to pursue Cassie with any further intentions in mind.

And that was the question.

He picked up the magazine, *Traveler's Rest*, laying open on the desk. A new grand hotel neared completion in Baltimore and the owners had sent out the word looking for competent and dedicated staff. With his experience at his father's establishment coupled with the managerial experience he was acquiring, surely he'd be considered qualified to work at such a fine place. But they likely couldn't wait months for him to be available. He couldn't abruptly abandon his current job without any replacement. His code of honor wouldn't allow such an act on his part. He'd made a promise and he'd keep it no matter what other temptations came down the road.

He flipped the page and scanned an article discussing changes in architecture styles incorporated into elegant new buildings. Then he read it again, absorbing the nuances of the discussion. He had not spent much time considering how the new versus traditional appearance might impact business. His father had once mentioned in passing some debate regarding the front façade of the hotel in town, how choosing brick over stone or clapboard might elevate the respect and esteem by those who came to the hotel. A heated exchange followed until they'd finally settled on a path forward. Flint recalled his surprise the first time he'd ridden with his father out to the Fury Falls Inn and seen the red brick double house. He'd expected something rustic, logs or painted clapboard, not the refined appearance of red bricks and painted trim. Reggie's design indeed enticed more customers who then were delighted when they enjoyed their experience enough to schedule a return visit.

He turned the page to stare unseeing at a sketch of the landscaping design the hotel intended to install around the base of the building. The structure and its appearance may indeed invite folks to enter the hotel. Might serve as a calling card of sorts, announcing the who and what of the establishment. But it took more than that to encourage customers to return time and again. The hostel had to offer something unique, or delicious, or different. Services or offerings unavailable elsewhere. Perhaps tied to the location. Some local specialty, like his mother's beautiful quilts on the beds or even for sale. Perhaps promote the mineral springs more, tied with a discount on the lodging fee. Cassie could play the beautiful square piano in the dining room on certain days each week. Ideas swirled in his head the more he contemplated ways to make Fury Falls Inn a unique destination.

He jotted the ideas on a slip of paper and then realized exactly what he was doing. Planning to stay for the long haul. When did his intent change from moving on to planting roots? He dropped the pencil on the paper and then flopped back in the chair, nearly toppling it backward. He swiveled the seat so he could gaze out the window at the bustling carriageway. Dogs, men, women, children, chickens and horses all moved about in his view. His very upset view of the location and situation. He didn't want to stay at the inn. Never planned to stay more than a few months. No, he wouldn't change his contingency plan. His escape route.

Cassie or no, his heart longed to travel, see the country, maybe even the world at some point. Not settle down. Not yet. Plenty of time for such roots after he'd experienced more of living. Gathered more ideas for creating his own unique destination somewhere other than Alabama.

He turned back to the desk and grabbed the paper to scrunch it into a ball and toss it into the wastepaper basket. Feeling freer, he picked up the periodical and turned the page.

The next morning, rain ushered in the dawn. Solid sheets of gray water fell from the heavens, removing color from the view out the rear window where Cassie stood brushing her hair. The summer thundershower rumbled and flashed above the foothills, turning the merry falls up the hill into a torrent. After staring at the sight for a few more strokes of her brush, she swung around and laid the brush on her dresser. Paused when the distinctive sound of sturdy boots in the hall met her ears. The length of time between footfalls suggested a man's stride. Her breath caught as her pulse sped up. Could it be Flint heading downstairs to begin the day?

With a new sense of urgency, she finished buttoning up her dress, then clipped on her ear bobs and fastened a simple gold chain around her neck. Pleased with her appearance, and hopeful of attracting Flint's attention, she scurried through the door and down the stairs. Despite her mother's cautionary attitude, or perhaps because of it, Cassie held ideas and dreams of her own. She'd pursue them whether her ma approved or not.

After all, it was her mother she longed to be free from. So why would Cassie willingly submit to her ma's unreasonable demand to avoid the very man she hoped would rescue her?

Falling into the usual routine instead of following her heart to seek out Flint, she made herself turn and go into the kitchen to see what Sheridan needed her to handle. The hustle and bustle carried on with calm deliberation. Meg and Myrtle worked at the side table mixing cornmeal batter for flapjacks. Steam rose from the black kettle hanging over the fire. The aroma of boiling coffee blended with the delicious sweet smell of fresh bread baking in the brick oven made her mouth water. Sheridan tossed her a grin as he cracked eggs into a large bowl, preparing to poach them in the boiling water.

"What do you need me to do?" She tied on an apron and hurried to the work table.

"Good morning to you, too." Sheridan shook his head at her but maintained the wide grin.

Abashed, she shrugged once. "Good morning. Now, what can I do?"

With a chuckle, Sheridan pointed to lumps from a broken up cone of refined sugar in a metal bowl. A stack of small white porcelain bowls and a small steel sugar nipper waited beside it. "You can finish nipping the sugar into those bowls to set out on the tables."

Mindless task but necessary. A task reserved for the mistress of the property because of needing to guard the expensive luxury of cone sugar. So where was her ma? Perhaps Cassie qualified as an adequate substitute having nearly reached eighteen years of age. Pleased by the thought whether right or wrong, she lifted the scissor-like tool and started nipping the large chunks broken off the large cone by a mallet into smaller lumps as asked. She worked silently, dying to ask about Flint but afraid of Sheridan's answer. Feared her ma had poisoned the information well against her. Her ma likely warned Sheridan to discourage Cassie's interest in Flint. She'd probably told everyone on the property. Which made Cassie reluctant to ask but anxious to know. After half filling a bowl—no need to tempt people to use more than necessary of the luxury—she set it aside and pulled the next one closer. Glanced at her friend and mentor and decided to take the chance.

"Sheridan, have you seen Flint this morning?" She kept her eyes on the sugar nippers instead of peering at the cook.

"He's been in. Why?" He cracked an egg on the edge of the bowl and dropped the contents into the bowl.

"I thought I heard him come down earlier but didn't see him." She flashed a glance at Sheridan and then back to her task. "Just curious what he's doing today."

"Now, listen here." Sheridan pressed his palms onto the wooden table to lean toward her as she lifted her gaze to meet his. "I told you before your father doesn't want you getting involved with Flint Hamilton. Told him that, too."

"But why?" She heard the near whine in her voice and swallowed. No point acting like a child when she longed to be treated as an adult. "What possible reason would my father have to say such a thing?"

"I can't say since he didn't confide his reasoning to me." Sheridan went back to cracking eggs, hitting each on the rim hard enough to nearly break the entire egg into two halves. "But he said it and seems enough for me."

She nipped another small lump of sugar into a bowl and then set the bowl aside to start the next. "But not enough for me. I don't understand."

Finished with his chore, Sheridan regarded her for a moment. "You can ask him either by letter or wait until he comes home."

"I don't want to wait so long." She wanted to take action, act upon her plan and intention. Not sit idly by until someone else gave her permission to fall in love or marry, or both. But writing to her pa might be her best option. If he'd take time to answer. "I'm not getting anywhere this way."

"Maybe not. In the meantime, you have to obey your father's wishes. That's all you need to know."

The constant in her life. Her pa's wishes she had to obey. She'd always been a good, obedient daughter. Minding her manners and listening to her parents. Ha. Not for much longer if she had anything to say about it. Rebellion swelled in her core. The sensation sloshed in her stomach like rancid cider, bitter and cold. Pulsed in her head like a hunger-induced headache. She had her own mind but the harsh realization she'd be forced to defy both parents made her ill. Feeling rather faint, she laid the nippers on the work table.

"I feel a headache coming on. I think I'll go lie down for a spell."

Sheridan peered at her, concern clouding his eyes. "You look pale. Go on with you. I'll send your mother up to check on you."

Perfect. Like she would help. With a weak nod, she spun slowly and eased out of the kitchen to retreat to her room.

She lay dozing on her bed, eyes closed, half listening to the piercing cries from the hawks circling in the sky outside. Wishing for the freedom to seek out her own future rather than having it inflicted upon her. Forced by her loving but misguided parents. She inhaled and let out a long sigh. They meant well. Their idea of how she should live her life simply didn't agree with hers.

A tap on the door preceded her mother marching in to stand beside the bed. A familiar cool hand pressed to Cassie's forehead. "Feeling any better?"

How many times in her life had her mother done the exact same thing when Cassie wasn't feeling well? Hurried to her side to see for herself, to inquire as to how she felt? Tested her forehead for any hint of heat from a worrisome fever. A wave of regret washed through Cassie. Her mother deserved more respect from her daughter than she'd been receiving of late.

Cassie opened her eyes and nodded once. "Some."

Mercy sank down on the edge of the bed and took hold of Cassie's closer hand. "Sheridan said you became upset about your father exacting Flint's promise."

Her mother had always been the most direct person she'd ever met. "Why did he do so?"

"For your protection, my dear." She squeezed Cassie's hand and held fast. "Having a young man such as Flint on the premises for an extended stay would surely lend itself to the two of you young people feeling drawn to one another. Even if it's not a good idea."

Cassie bit her lower lip as much to prevent the cry of objection as to give her time to think about the underlying concerns brought to light in her mother's statement. Her pa didn't trust her to make an informed choice when it came to choosing a husband. Or he wouldn't have held the belief the two of them would automatically want to be together merely because they existed in the same place. Her ma had already expressed similar worry Cassie had dismissed as absurd. But to have both parents in agreement even without having a chance to converse on the matter gave her pause.

Perhaps her escape plan didn't make as much sense as she once thought. Even if she and Flint ended up attracted to one another, as she believed possible, did she want to spend the rest of her life answering to him? Required to obey his every dictate forever, until death parted them? A slight shiver wiggled down her spine. Forever could be a very long time.

"Do you love Pa?" Cassie laid her other hand on top of her mother's, still clasping hers.

"I shall always love your father. Even when I disagree with him." Mercy's mouth curved upwards at the corners. "Why do you ask?"

Cassie searched her mother's expression, seeking confirmation of something she couldn't quite define. Tiny lines spread from the outer corners of her eyes. Her skin remained smooth and clear, maintaining her youthful beauty despite the years of worry and work. From what Cassie had witnessed during her lifetime her mother's life had never been easy. Always some concern or hardship loomed which she and Pa had to overcome. Finances.

Flood. Drought. Lack of employment, even. Starting a risky venture such as the very inn in which they lived and worked. If it failed, they'd be destitute. Where would they go then? At least they'd have each other and together they'd devise a plan, a path forward.

"You'd follow him anywhere, wouldn't you? I mean, you did when we moved here." Amazing concept when she stopped and thought about it. Especially, knowing how much her mother resented living in the inn. "Why did you fall in love with Pa?"

Mercy's smile broadened, making her entire face glow and her eyes sparkle. "His laugh, mainly. More than that, though. He made me feel beautiful and respected for a change. Did you know he actually wanted my opinion on his attire? He said I had a better fashion sense than himself."

"I can see that. You've always seemed to pull together pretty outfits from different bits and pieces than I'd have thought to join together."

"Of course, your father proved himself to me when he shared his hopes and dreams for the future. How he wanted a big family and to support us to the very best of his abilities. Which I know he is doing, and I'm proud of him for that."

"Even if you wish things were different?" How did one reconcile the difference between what you want and what you have? Settling rather than striving for better must be hard to accept.

"I've loved your father too long to lose faith in him when life throws an obstacle in our path to happiness." She sighed as her smile wilted into a straight line again. "I need to find a way to let my love for him be enough no matter where we're living or working. That's the hard part for me."

The tender expression in her eyes stirred compassion in Cassie's heart for her mother. They'd never talked so openly, like one adult to another. A rare and wondrous moment to savor and recall with fondness. Perhaps she could ask the question nagging at her for so long while her mother's defenses had relaxed.

"Why don't you and Pa like Flint? What do you have against him?" There, she'd done it and could only wait and see if her mother would finally tell her the truth. Not the surface bit about his chosen career. There must be something more egregious about him to set them both denouncing him.

"Back to him, are we?" Mercy squeezed Cassie's hand and then released it to smooth her hands down her skirts as she sat on the edge of the bed. "Flint is a nice man, dear heart. I have nothing against him as a person. He's our friends' son, after all."

Cassie huffed as she pushed up to lean against the headboard. "Then why don't you want me to even see if there might be some level of attraction between us? He's smart and handsome and comes from a good family. I don't understand."

Mercy sighed heavily as she shook her head. "He's not the man we would choose for you. It's simple. He's not right for you."

"Because he wants to run an inn of his own like Pa does? That bucket doesn't hold water, Ma." She crossed her arms over her stomach as she regarded her mother's troubled expression. "Has he done something you're not telling me about?"

Mercy shifted her position on the bed, gripping her knees with both hands. Another long breath and a sigh escaped before she spoke again. All the while, Cassie sensed her mother's reluctance and ultimate decision to share her guarded opinion of the man. Cassie steeled herself against whatever terrible secret her mother prepared to reveal.

"Bless his heart, he is a bit touched in the head." Mercy's expression turned sorrowful as she studied Cassie's surprised features. "Even my dear friend won't admit to the fact, but it's clear as day."

Frowning, Cassie blinked several times as she tried to fathom her mother's meaning. Flint seemed perfectly fine to her. He'd never acted out or strangely in her presence. Always composed and in control of himself. He'd made impressive strides in growing the business and improving the appearance of the inn. Other than not having experience with wild animals and thieves, his performance as innkeeper couldn't be better.

"How do you mean, touched? I don't understand."

Mercy leaned closer to whisper, "He says he can see ghosts. Only a crazy person would make such a claim."

She couldn't squelch the chuckled bursting from her mouth. "Ma, if he thinks he can see ghosts, who are we to say otherwise? I don't believe in ghosts, mind. But surely such a belief is harmless."

Mercy straightened her back and then stood, peering down at Cassie with a haughty expression back in her eyes. "You may think it's harmless, but I warrant otherwise. Beliefs such as those could only lead to trouble down the road and that's why you are forbidden to even contemplate for one more minute having any kind of personal relationship with him. Have I made myself clear?"

Cassie continued to stare at her mother, rebellion stewing in her core. Firing up the headache into a throbbing weight. "Perfectly." She pressed her palm to her forehead as she slid back down to rest her head on her pillow. "I won't mention it again."

She closed her eyes so she no longer saw the stern expression on her mother's features. After a moment, her ma walked away and softly closed the door behind her. Cassie sighed as tears leaked from her eyes. What other choice did she have?

"I told you, I didn't order all of those things." Flint brushed a hand through his loose hair as he glared at the burly and persistent wagon driver.

"Not my place to say what you ordered, mister. Just to deliver what my boss told me to and collect payment. That's two hundred, if you please." The man held out a gnarly hand, creased and streaked brown from holding the leather traces most every day for years.

Behind the insistent man, another wagon fully loaded with barrels and crates of who knew what, waited with horses stamping away black biting flies from their legs. Flint felt like stamping his feet as well but drew in a deep, calming breath instead.

"I'm not paying for pickles and produce and whatever else you've got on this here wagon. I only ordered a small cask of molasses and some stationary."

"Flint! I need to speak to you this minute."

Mercy's voice interrupted the lengthy debate he'd been having with the driver. Irritation simmered beneath her tone. When she had spoken with his mother in the dining room, her voice sounded sweet and melodic. Not when she spoke to him, though. Harsh and prickly tones for him. Annoyance shuddered through him, rocking his shoulders as he turned to confront her.

"We're not done, mister." The driver called out from behind Flint.

Flint turned back to the man with a scowl. "I'm aware. Just give me a moment."

The man shrugged and grunted but otherwise relented. One problem at a time. Flint spun around to see Mercy stop in front of him, hands on her hips like some fishmonger's wife. Her scowl did not bode well for whatever petty complaint she harbored.

"What do you need, Mrs. Fairhope?" He kept his voice steady despite the inner qualms her stance sent through him.

"I've told my daughter and I'm giving you fair warning." Mercy angled her upper body to position her nose closer to Flint's face. She stood so close he could make out itty-bitty lines at the corners of her mouth, a pale dusting of freckles across her nose, and a tiny curved scar at her left temple. Her eyes glittered as she stared at him.

He remained in place with a force of will, not wanting to show any sign of weakness or giving way to the upset woman. He must maintain respect for him in his official capacity as manager of the overall business which meant commanding the esteem of those who worked under him. Including the innkeeper's wife no matter how much she balked at the idea.

"Warning about what, exactly?"

"Mr. Fairhope and I will not tolerate you having anything to do with our daughter." She lifted her chin to look down her nose at him. "Stay away from her. Mind your business and keep out of hers. Understood?"

The woman infuriated him. She must have better things to do than to worry about whether or not he paid his attentions on Cassie. The girl wanted his attention even if he himself wavered on whether to adhere to his promise or not. He always told the truth and kept his word. He stood by that as a matter of pride and honor. Yet Cassie had other ideas. He had no control over her and apparently neither did her parents. Interesting.

"Mrs. Fairhope, I can assure you I will not do anything Cassie would object to. But I have no control over her actions nor her desires. She's made it clear to me she would welcome my affections."

"B-but you gave your word to my husband!" Mercy's cheeks flared red as anger emanated from her. "I'm holding you to our vow, young man. Or I'll be in touch with your father myself."

She did have a point. He dragged in a ragged breath and blew it out, pushing out his own frustration along with it. He walked a fine line indeed. "I understand. I have tried to keep my distance, dissuade her from pursuing her aims. However, I see no reason to deny the existence of a certain level of attraction between us. It's only natural I'd find your lovely daughter interesting and intriguing."

Her hand shook as she slowly dropped it back to her hip. "I will not say it again. This is your final warning."

With any luck, the matter would drop like a rock. He would not actively pursue the girl but he couldn't deny he had feelings for her either. How strong those feelings might become he also couldn't say. Perhaps nothing would come of them, in which case he had nothing to worry about.

"Anything else?" Flint itched to turn away but out of respect he inquired before doing so.

She flicked an angry glance at the driver and then back to Flint. "Yes. Sort out this new mess you've made. Honestly, your ineptness does not reflect well on your abilities."

"I'll take care of it." He nodded once and then turned to settle the matter with the driver as Mercy's footsteps faded behind him. "Now, let's settle this once and for all."

"With you paying me. That's the only way we can resolve this." The driver held out his broad hand, palm open.

"I didn't order all of this so I'm not going to pay you." Flint heaved a sigh. The day was not going well and he had much else to do. "I'll pay for what I did order, and happily. But not all the rest."

The rhythmic thud of horses' hooves sounded from the carriageway, drawing Flint's attention. John Baker cantered his distinctive gray horse up the lane toward him. Flint checked his pocket watch to verify the time. Arriving for his weekly supper at the inn. And of course to check in on how well Flint was managing. Great timing.

"I can't take all this back. It's got to stay here but you've got to pay me or my boss will have my hide." The driver slowly climbed down from the wagon seat, dropping the last few inches onto the stone drive to stand beside Flint. "Where do you want it put?"

John dismounted and led his horse over to join the conversation. "What's going on, Flint?"

"A huge mix up, apparently." Flint shrugged and shook his head, his shoulder length hair brushing his shirt collar. With the summer heat swinging upward, he'd be pulling it back into its queue before much longer. Or perhaps the heated exchange with the merchant made him hot. "Somehow my order got mixed together with someone else's and this man insists I pay for all of it."

"He's refusing to pay me is what's going on." The driver rubbed the back of one hand under his nose and then reached out to shake John's hand. "Name's McIntosh. Jerry McIntosh."

John didn't even blink but accepted the hand in a friendly greeting. "John Baker. What is all this?" He motioned to the two heavily laden wagons.

"Molasses. Lumber. Nails. Bolts of cloth, I think. You name it. It's quite a lot." Flint shook his head and shrugged. "I only ordered some molasses and stationery—ledgers, writing paper, pens. That sort of thing. But he's insisting I pay for all of the items." He swept an arm to indicate the entirety of merchandise.

John handed the reins to Flint and then strode around each wagon, peering at everything with a practiced and assessing eye. After several minutes of his perusal, he returned and took the reins of his horse back. Addressing the driver, he smiled. "It so happens I can make good use of most of the items you have here. How about if I pay you for what Flint doesn't need?"

The driver scratched his head for a moment and then shrugged. "As long as I get the money my boss is expecting, I guess it doesn't matter where the stuff ends up."

"That's mighty generous of you." Flint glanced between John and Jerry. "If you'll put my things on the porch, I'll carry them inside."

Jerry waved at the second driver to come help him. Then smiled at Flint. "So that'll be twenty dollars for your items."

Flint fished his wallet out of his pocket and counted off the bills. Handing them to Jerry, he smiled with relief. "Thank you. I'm glad we could settle the dispute so readily."

"Me, too." Jerry looked at John and smiled. "Where do you want the rest delivered, sir?"

"Take everything up the road to Riverwood plantation. You can ask at the house for the main barn to unload everything. I'll be along in a little while to pay you."

"I can't wait long, I've got other stops to make to pick up items heading back south." The frown on the driver's face suggested he suspected a trick.

"Never fear, my good man. Give me an hour and you'll be on your way." John slapped the man on the back and chuckled. "I came here for a hot meal and I'm going to enjoy it before I ride any farther."

"We'll be on our way." Jerry motioned to the second driver to resume his seat and then followed suit. He tipped his cap to Flint and John. "Pleasure doing business with you, gentlemen."

Slapping the leather traces on the horses' haunches, Jerry started singing Yankee Doodle to the horses as the wagons rattled away. The merry tune lifted Flint's mood as much as the handy resolution to the problem the man had presented him.

Flint heaved a sigh as he smiled at John. "Thank you for your help. I'll buy your meal as a thank you."

"You don't have to, son. But if you want to..." He laughed as they strode up the stone steps to the porch.

Flint halted suddenly when he noticed Mercy standing before the double doors open to allow the breeze to cool the interior of the inn. She frowned at him, yet again. Rarely did he see the woman smile. Never at him.

"Is something wrong, Mrs. Fairhope?" Flint dreaded her response, given her posture and expression.

"You not only messed up the purchase but then add insult to injury by giving away our food? Despite Mr. Baker being a close family friend, surely you, an outsider, have better business sense than to do such an irresponsible thing."

Flint blinked at her for several seconds, trying to frame a response which wouldn't incite her further. After all the man had done for him, personally, he owed the neighbor a debt of gratitude if not of financial compensation. "Mr. Baker's generosity in solving the problem earned him my thanks and his meal. Since I'm in charge, I'm within my rights and authority to repay him in such a fashion. Now, if you'll excuse us…"

He brushed past her, holding his breath in anticipation of her sputtering response, as a quietly chuckling John followed him inside. He steeled himself for the aftermath of his actions. He'd likely pay for more than his friend's meal given the affronted features of the woman he had just left behind. And yet a small smile hovered on his lips after finally managing to put her in her place.

Chapter Eight

"Cassie, I have a little something for you." Sheridan held one hand behind his back as he grinned at her from the open door to the parlor.

Her birthday had been a huge let down to her. She had not expected anything big. Not like the rich girls in town would have demanded. No gifts or special dinners with friends and family doting on her. Not even her favorite breakfast of pancakes with berries on top. But nothing? Nobody seemed to remember it and she felt silly bringing it up. Now that she'd reached adulthood it seemed beneath her to feel let down. Obviously, nobody really cared she'd lived another year. It was only another day to them.

She laid the large men's trousers she'd been mending on the side table in the family's parlor. At least she'd earn some pin money toward her plan. Another two dollars to squirrel away for her private fund. "What is it?"

Footsteps behind him sounded as her ma and Hannah followed Sheridan farther into the room as he drew closer. Sheridan showed all his yellowish teeth against his dark skin as he smiled at her. His golden eyes seemed to glow with suppressed…what? Humor or a secret? He glanced behind him and nodded to the grinning women, then faced Cassie and slowly brought his hidden hand around in front of him.

Cassie clapped her hands in delight at the sight of a small square white iced cake with what she assumed would be eighteen unlit candles. "You made that for me? Oh, Sheridan, it's lovely."

"It's all yours." Sheridan bobbed his head as he crossed to the small table with the cake balanced on his large open palm. "For your special day, my dear."

The warmth of his smile filled her heart with happiness, a feeling akin to the hum of the honey bees in the flowering laurel trees at the edge of the forest. Her birthday did mean something to her family and friends. A cake all her own, a very special gift to mark her special day. The day she intended to become responsible for her own actions and no longer be dictated to by her parents. Or anyone. She swallowed the rising lump in her throat. Her eyes pricked but she wouldn't ruin the moment by permitting the pressing tears to fall. She blinked to dry the moisture and pushed a smile onto her face.

"Baking a cake for my birthday is so sweet." Cassie snatched her sewing off the wood surface and dropped it in her lap. "You really didn't have to go to such trouble."

"No trouble at all." Sheridan set the cake on the table and then hurried to light a taper from the fireplace. Soon the candles glowed with tiny yellow flames.

"Okay, my darling daughter, time to make a wish before wax ruins the frosting." Mercy motioned to Cassie to hurry up and state her wish for all to hear. "I hope you enjoy your treat."

"I'm sure I will, but…" Cassie glanced at the door and then back to her mother. "Where's Flint? He should be here."

His presence would be like having one more special gift. He must have some urgent business to take care of or surely he'd have accompanied the rest of them with the cake to wish her well. A flash of annoyance swept across her mother's features. Cassie angled her head, squinting at the distress on her mother's face. At Cassie's insistence on asking for the handsome man or something else?

"No, he's doing what he came here to do." Mercy pointed to the burning candles with an imperious forefinger. "Make your wish and blow them out, child. We've not all day to stand around here waiting."

"I wish he was here." She stared at her mother's stern expectant expression. Pondered the use of the word "child" in her last directive. Noted the pressing together of her lips and could tell her ma grew more exasperated with each passing second. But why? "He may come yet, right?"

"Well, he's not." Mercy clasped each hip with tense hands and indicated the cake with a bob of her head. "Blow them out. Now."

Cassie stared at her mother and her obstinate stance. A position which only meant her mother would not relent, would not give in, and would not accept anything other than compliance. Like the time when Cassandra was six and wanted to climb the tree with her brothers. Sure, she wore a dress but she had her petticoats on. Yes, it might mess up her dress but it looked like such fun. Nothing she said worked to convince her mother to let her try to be like her brothers. She never had climbed a tree and now probably never would. She sighed to herself, presenting a calm she would soon lose.

Sheridan sidled between Cassie and Mercy and nodded. "Your mother has a point. Those candles won't last much longer. Go on before they melt the icing."

Cassie cast a hopeful glance at the doorway, pausing for several seconds, and then relented on a barely concealed huff. "Fine."

Now to come up with a proper wish. One worthy of all those flickering candles and the pretty icing on the cake. One which maybe would cause her mother some discomfort for a change. Not exactly what she'd hope her loving daughter would want. Ah, the perfect idea floated through her mind.

Closing her eyes, she pictured a fine home with lots of healthy children. Flint standing on the front porch surrounding the two-story house. She imagined the kinds of flowering bushes and flowers she'd put in the gardens at the front as well as the vegetable garden she'd tend at the back of the property. The clear glass windows and painted shutters. A stone driveway in front like the one in front of the inn. But mainly, Flint waiting for her with open arms. Turning eighteen presented new opportunities and possibilities for her future.

She opened her eyes and drew in a breath, blowing out all but two of the candles. Another quick breath saw the rest of them out and fine wisps of smoke rising into the air.

"There. Happy now, Ma?" She turned to glare at her mother. "What is it with you and Flint?"

"You know my feelings for the man." Mercy pressed her lips together and annoyance flashed in her aqua eyes. Her ash-blond hair was pulled into a severe knot on the back of her head. "I don't understand why on earth you'd want him in the same room with you."

"I like him." Cassie rose to her feet so her mother wasn't towering over her any longer. "You may as well get used to him being around."

Her mother frowned as she squinted at her and pursed her lips. "Why is that?"

Cassie glanced at Hannah's glinting bright blue eyes, aware the other woman tried to hint she'd do better to not push her ma. But Cassie had grown tired of being told what to do, when to do it, and with whom. She squared her shoulders as she nodded once to Hannah, indicating she understood the silent caution. Then she lifted her chin as she swiveled her head to address her mother.

"He and I came to an agreement regarding spending some time getting to know each other better." She crossed her arms, as much a protective barrier as a means of keeping her hands quiet. Although she'd promised to not mention Flint to her mother again, she'd decided to follow her own guidance and not her overly protective mother's. "That's why."

"You'll not be seen spending time alone with that man. Or any man." Mercy angled her torso toward Cassie and shook her finger in her face. "I'll not have it."

"Stop with shaking your finger in my face, Ma." Cassie lifted her chin and glared at her mother. "You don't have any say in the matter any longer. I've reached an age where I feel I can be responsible for my actions."

"You're still living under this roof and will obey me." Mercy straightened and shook her head. "You must obey me."

Huffing out a bark of a chuckle, Cassie arched her brows and smiled. "Perhaps where it concerns the running of the inn, but not with regard to my heart and my life."

Sheridan cleared his throat and raised both hands to separate the two quarreling women. "Now, ladies, let's not be getting so upset."

"Why not?" Cassie whirled on her friend. "She's always trying to run my life. I won't take it any longer."

Sheridan patted her arm and nodded once. "Your father has already told the man to stay clear of you. I've told you that but you don't want to hear. But you need to."

"You too?" Cassie glared at him and then spun to cross the red-and-blue painted floor boards, put some distance between them. She stopped by the front brocade curtained window and turned back to pin each of them with her frown. "Why do you think Pa would have said such a thing about the son of his best friend? I do not fathom his reasoning."

"It's not your place to try to second-guess your father's orders." Mercy moved to the settle and took a seat, hands gripping her knees through the brown-and-cream cotton dress she wore. "I've told you before to follow his orders without question like I do."

"Ha! You question his orders every time you gripe about Flint's presence. Wasn't that one of Pa's orders, too?"

Mercy jumped to her feet and stomped over to Cassie, grabbing her shoulder with one hand to shake her. "Stop. Just stop this. You claim you're an adult and responsible for your actions but look at this childish tantrum you're throwing. Over what? Having some common sense and decency?"

Cassie jerked away from her mother and opened her mouth to object to the rough handling when Flint burst into the room, all smiles and fresh air. Relief flooded her for an instant as his happy gaze connected with hers.

"What are you doing here?" Mercy bit out angrily. "I thought I told you to mind the business while we had some family time."

Anger flashed hot and white in Cassie's chest. Her mother had the nerve to tell Flint to stay away from her birthday celebration. She'd obviously do anything to break them apart, to keep Cassie from enjoying the man's company and attentions. With that thought, the anger toward her mother's actions mobilized her.

"You didn't…" Cassie raised a hand to slap her mother but Flint reached her before she could draw it back completely.

Annoyance with her mother metamorphosed into deep-seated anger and disgust. She dared to banish the one person in her life she wanted to be present for her birthday. Especially during such a momentous and rare occasion as to be presented with the extraordinary gift of a beautifully decorated cake with wishing candles. The one and only time in her life she'd received such a sweet present. What did her mother do? Ruined the memory. Her mother disliked Flint, she understood as much. But to have intentionally tried to prevent her dearest desire and in so doing to thwart Flint's sharing in her birthday gift rankled deep in her very core. She focused her anger on her mother's countenance as it shifted from startled to wary.

"Don't." Flint pressed on her raised arm until she slowly and reluctantly dropped it back to her side. His gentle smile indicated he understood her instinctive reaction but also knew it wouldn't help the situation. "You've a mysterious delivery, Cassie. Shall I have it brought in?"

She glared at her mother for a moment longer, sending her a silent warning, and then slowly turned to look at Flint. "A gift? Yes, please."

"Will you be okay here for a minute?" He waited for her slight smile and then glanced at Mercy and Sheridan, who stepped forward to take Flint's place separating mother from daughter. Flint nodded once to him and then slipped out of the room.

Cassie aimed a long frown at her mother and shook her head when she opened her mouth to say something. "Drop it, Ma. You've made your position perfectly plain."

"You two shouldn't fight so." Sheridan stayed between them, ready to intervene if necessary. "It's not seemly."

Cassie chuckled and strode over to take her seat again. Picking up her sewing, she stared at it for a moment then looked at the others watching her. She had acted rather childishly but for a very good reason to her mind. She must stand up for herself against the oppression from her own mother. She simply wouldn't tolerate her mother's harsh thumb pushing her down day after day.

Grunting drew her attention to the doorway where Liam and Jericho in smudged jeans and tan work shirts scuffled into the room struggling with a huge crate. Flint directed them to set the slatted crate covered with stamps from foreign ports on the floor between the front windows. She gaped at the stamps from France and Barbados. The crate had traveled far more than she dared dream. The stable boys eased it down and then let it drop the last couple of inches to the floor with a thud.

"Careful, boys." Flint strode over to inspect the box, leaning over to test the slats to ensure they were still attached. Satisfied, he gave the closer boy a pat on the shoulder. "Thanks again."

The two young men nodded to Flint and then left to return to their endless stable chores.

Cassie stood and crossed to read the pale blue label pasted on the top of the crate. "Whatever it is, it's been all over. This label says Charleston." She met Flint's smiling eyes. Was it a gift from him?

"Let's open it and see if you like what's inside." He hefted the crow bar he'd carried in upon his return to the parlor. "Stand back a little, please."

She took three steps backward and leaned forward to peek over his shoulder. He pried open the top of the crate one slat at a time. Then dropped each side in turn, saving the side closest to her for last. Sheridan quickly lifted each side and stacked them in the corner. The suspense ended when she realized what was nestled in the protective sawdust as Flint carefully swept it away. Hannah appeared with a dust pan and broom and began collecting the sawdust in a small barrel to reuse later.

"A doll's house." Cassie eased closer to peer at the finely crafted front of a miniature house that mysteriously matched her wish from a few minutes earlier. She'd longed for such a fine gift ever since a young girl, but her pa had never seen fit to give her the magnificent and extravagant present. Making her way around to the back, her smile grew with each discovery of the detailed design and craftsmanship. The interior rooms held no furniture or furnishings but the walls were painted in popular shades and the floors were ready for carpets or painted carpets. The windows boasted glass panes and shutters on the exterior. When she opened the hinged back of the house, the steps from the first to second floors gleamed in the lamplight from the family parlor. She met Flint's expectant smile. "It's perfect."

He'd given her the best gift. A subtle message of his intentions to provide her with the home of her dreams. Start a family with her in a loving home he'd build for them to live in and love each other for the rest of their lives. Without a word, he'd shown her where his heart lay. The future he planned with her.

"It's lovely." He shifted to move around the house, bending over to peer inside as he side-stepped around each side. "Such attention to detail, too."

"Thank you, Flint. I love it." She beamed at him as he glanced at her and then back at the miniature bedroom he was inspecting.

"I'm glad." Straightening, he shook his head and shrugged. "But it's not from me, Cassie."

"Then who sent it?" Puzzled, she approached the sides of the crate Sheridan had stacked to one side. "Does it say?"

"Oh, wait, I forgot." Flint retrieved the folded paper and held it out to her. "There was a note attached to one of the slats."

She opened the paper and read the brief note.

My dear daughter, I hope you enjoy decorating this house I've ordered from France and populating it with whatever dolls you choose. I wanted to give you something to treasure as you turn eighteen. Love always, Dad

"It's from my father." She lifted her gaze to look at her mother. "I don't understand."

Mercy smirked at her and shrugged. "I guess he still thinks of you as his little girl."

Of all the words possible to spill from her mother's mouth, none other could have hurt as much. She glanced at Flint, tears pressing and welling at the corners of her eyes. She wouldn't cry. Not on her birthday of all days. His perplexed shrug and quiet smile suggested his compassion for her in that moment. But since the house came not from the man she wanted a life with but from the father who still thought of her as a child, the forbidden tears cascaded down her cheeks.

With a stifled gasp, she fled across the parlor, up the stairs, and into her bedroom where she flung herself on her bed and sobbed.

The afternoon heat slapped him in the face as Flint left the shade of the front porch to hurry down the steps into the sunshine. He nodded a greeting to a pair of coopers heading inside for a cool pint on their way home after their daily labor constructing barrels, to be used at various distilleries to age their spirits. Striding across the carriageway, he approached the serious merchant and his burdened wagon pulled by two chestnut draft horses.

"Mr. Davis, I'm sorry to keep you waiting in this hot sun." He stopped next to the high-sided wagon and reached up to shake hands with the cheerful, sweating man.

"I've got your flour and cornmeal order." Bradley Davis perched on the seat, his dusty khaki trousers and black boots evidence of the dry spell the area had suffered through for the past week. Sweat stains discolored his red work shirt beneath a black open vest. But the heat and dust couldn't hide the pleasant grin on his leathery face. "Do you have my money?"

"I do. Thanks for bringing it out to me on your way to Nashville." Flint fished in his jeans pocket and withdrew the required payment. "I hope it wasn't too inconvenient."

"If it was, I'd charge you double." Bradley chuckled as he pocketed the bills. Suddenly his hand froze and his brows arched. "Oh, wait. I forgot."

"What's wrong?" The surprise and concern in the man's eyes made Flint wary.

"I stopped at the Post Office and when the postmaster discovered I was coming your way, he asked me to bring you these letters marked urgent." Bradley handed him some folded paper with the required postage marked on it. "He said you'd picked up your mail the other day and wouldn't be back for a while, so…"

Flint hesitated to take the letters. What could be so important it couldn't wait until he made his bi-weekly ride to the nearest post office to pick up the mail?

"Who's that pretty girl?" Bradley focused on something behind Flint, eyes sparkling as he smiled.

Flint glanced over his shoulder and spotted Cassie strolling in front of the inn. Her plain green dress emphasized her long blonde locks swaying with each step. She tilted her head and bestowed a half smile upon him. Then she turned and walked up the porch steps and through the dogtrot toward the rear of the building. He heard a few notes of a tune she hummed as she disappeared into the shadows on her way out back to work in the garden, no doubt. The gentle sway of her hips, the invitation of her lush hair to run his fingers through, even the sound of her voice calling to him through the tune of a cheerful song. He stared after her but refrained with an effort from following. Temptress.

"The boss's daughter." Flint turned back to face Bradley and the contents of the mysterious letters in his hands.

"Man, I'd be in so much trouble if I worked here." Bradley shook his head with one last glance toward the shadows of the dogtrot. "But lucky you, right? Seeing such a beauty every day."

"You'd think so, wouldn't you?" He sighed as he addressed the man grinning from the wagon seat. "Thanks again."

Bradley lifted the traces in each hand, fingers automatically wrapping around the leather reins. "Don't do anything I wouldn't do." With a wink, he slapped the horses' backs and they trundled forward. He waved one hand in farewell as Flint watched them trot down the drive.

The postmark read Savannah. Flint's stomach fell as he pivoted and made his way inside to the office. He shuffled the letters, one addressed to him, one to Cassie, and the other to Mercy. Plopping down on the chair by the desk, he stared at the paper addressed to him. What did Reggie Fairhope want to tell him? Hopefully, he was returning sooner than anticipated. Then Flint could extricate himself from this uncomfortable and tenuous situation in which he'd found himself.

The word "urgent" glared at him, implying the news might prove distressing. He didn't need more angst in his life. He'd never had to face such troubling and uncomfortable situations prior to working at the inn. Working in the city proved far easier to manage than the events and disruptions he'd experienced in this part of the state. He'd given his word, though, and so he had little choice as to his next steps. All of which did nothing to settle the anxiety worming in his chest.

Between Mercy's constant disapproving eye and Cassie's constant come-hither glances, he felt torn in two. Damned if he did and damned if he didn't acknowledge, let alone encourage, his attraction toward a certain pretty young woman. She most definitely attracted him. He could deny it to everyone and himself, but that didn't make it less true. She drew him to her every time she entered a room, or came within fifty yards, or merely glanced at him with those heavenly blue eyes. He dragged in a deep breath and let it out to the count of three.

Perhaps he should not keep his word. Break his promise to Reggie and go home, back to the hotel and his father's smug welcome. At least he'd be away from the barrage of emotions threatening his composure each and every single day. Ever since Cassie's birthday, she'd renewed her efforts to attract his attention. To defy her mother's overly protective stance, as far as Cassie was concerned.

The white paper on the desk glared at him, taunted him for his reluctance to open it and find out what his boss had to say. What more could he demand than what he'd already agreed to? He fingered the corner of the paper, but left it on the wooden surface. He rose to his feet and paced to the window, seeking a distraction, anything to help him procrastinate the task he wanted to avoid.

As luck would have it, Cassie happened to be carrying a basket of cut flowers on her arm, snippers in hand, as she sashayed toward the inn. Must be refreshing the vases in the foyer and dining room. The swing of her supple hips propelled her curls across her shoulders. She moved like he imagined a princess, or even a queen. No wonder her mother found him lacking by comparison. She deserved someone better, more refined than him.

Perhaps his idea of going home held more merit than he'd first thought. He spun away from the window and his gaze landed on the damned letter again. He should write to Reggie and tell him he'd made up his mind to return home. To separate himself from the girl before their feelings for each other grew to the point of no return. Absence would diminish his desire. Rather than having it flare each time she walked by and risk further recriminations from her mother. Removing himself from the scene should ultimately please Reggie. Then Flint could focus entirely on his aim to establish his reputation in the hotel business and ignore any other personal entanglements.

He strode back to the desk and sat down, grabbing up the letter as he settled. First, he'd see what further instructions the man wanted him to address, and then he'd tell him why he couldn't possibly do any more. He ripped open the letter and laid it flat before him, pressing both palms to the edges as he skimmed the contents. Then read it again in disbelief.

Dear Flint,

I trust you're managing as well as your father said you might. Please remember your oath to me regarding both the management of the inn in my absence and the discreet care of my family as if they were your own. I'm trusting you to keep your word as I must from so far away. I must also extend our agreement for another few months as things here are not going as smoothly as I'd expected. I will return before the snow flies, but it might be Halloween before I can return.

I also have grand news! I've convinced Senator Percy Graham to spend the month of November at the inn. His son suffers from dropsy and the Senator hopes the mineral waters will relieve his symptoms. You surely can fathom how important the Senator's visit is for my business, Flint. I need for you to ensure all is in readiness for his arrival the first week of November. I should be back in Alabama by then, but the burden of preparing for his visit, and hopefully a positive recommendation to his friends and compatriots, falls on your shoulders. I know I can trust you to do me proud. Therefore, I'm promising you a bonus of $500—a year's wages—when all is said and done.

Send me word of your progress and any issues you run into. I'm happy to advise from here as well as I may. I'll write separately to my wife and inform her of my desire that she work with you to maintain the smooth operation of the inn. Also please give Cassie my note in response to her recent letter.

Thank you again my dear sir for your prolonged efforts on my behalf. I'll reward you commensurately upon my return. Until then, you have my undying gratitude.
Kind regards,
Reggie Fairhope

Five hundred dollars! Enough to allow him to start his own tavern on his own terms. He flopped back in the chair, rocking the front legs off the floor and then thumping back down. He stared at the man's ill-timed request. No, not a request. An expectation. One he'd agreed to in the first instance and now…what?

Dragging his fingers through his hair, he shook his head at the letter. He grabbed his nape and squeezed until a headache threatened. How could he stay for three more months? Without losing his patience or his sanity? Without succumbing to the temptress?

How could he *not* stay? He'd given Reggie his vow to represent the man and his interests to the best of his ability. He'd promised to manage everything, apparently including Mercy and Cassie, until Reggie's return. Just because the return had been delayed didn't absolve him of his word. The additional money would go a long way to ease the pain of dealing with Mercy and trying to manage Cassie. He squared his shoulders and thumped the desk with his fist.

No matter Mercy's opinion, or Cassie's attempt to seduce him, he'd stay and do the job. He swallowed the knot of disquiet and pressed his lips together. He'd keep his word no matter what might happen.

Cassie stepped into the shade of the gazebo and settled on one of the metal benches. She glanced around, ensuring her privacy, before breaking the wax seal and unfolding the page from her pa. She didn't hold out much hope he could help when she'd written to him about Sheridan's wife and sons, even less after the insulting gift for her birthday. She'd thought he'd have more depth of feeling, of understanding, about the cook's grief over his family. But how could her pa have such an understanding and then think a child's gift appropriate for his eighteen-year-old daughter? Shaking her head slowly with disappointment, she perused the letter.

Dear Cassandra,

By now you should have received my gift for your birthday. I do hope you like it! I contemplated several ideas before settling upon what I think is the perfect present for my sweet girl as she turns another year older and wiser.

As for Sheridan's family, I fathom your concern but I cannot promise anything to alleviate his situation. I'm aware of many difficulties on that front but not nearly as many possible solutions. Give me time to make some inquiries as to his wife, Pansy. Sheridan's sons are another matter I'll need time to make inquiries about them as they may or may not still be in Louisiana where they'd originally been sent.

Keep in mind that even if I locate these people, there is no guarantee of reuniting them with Sheridan. I'd suggest keeping your own counsel on this matter and not raising his hopes, as a result.

I've tasked young Flint with a very important job and I hope you and your mother will do all in your power to assist him as necessary.

I expect now that it will be months before I see you again. I'm looking forward to seeing how you decorate your doll's house when I return. Enjoy!

Love,

Pa

Cassie sighed and folded the letter then laid it on her lap as she gazed out over the inn and surrounding buildings and livestock, the people and dogs coming and going. The families and individuals all free to move about where they liked without concern. Slaves could also move about, with a written pass, but not free to go where and when they'd prefer and definitely not without worrying about being falsely accused of some crime or trespass. Punishment for such infractions ranged from scolding to beating to hanging. She shivered at the idea of people treating each other like livestock to be bought, sold, herded, and even slaughtered.

Why did people treat each other as though others didn't matter? Or if they looked or acted or sounded different, they should be feared? Weren't all people just that—people? She couldn't control how others felt or how they viewed the world, but she could try to influence how they treated each other. The people in her life. One person at a time.

Cassie shoved the letter into her apron pocket and rose to her feet. If wishes were horses, then beggars would ride. Sitting and hoping for things to be different, for people to treat each other as the Golden Rule commanded, would never make it come to pass. She had to do more than simply wish for change. Even if her pa never located Sheridan's family, Cassie could make sure Sheridan felt wanted in her life as a friend, or better as an adopted uncle, so he wouldn't feel alone and, worse, lonely.

She hurried back toward the inn to find Sheridan and let him know she cared about him. But the rest of her mission must remain a secret from him. Until the right moment came. If it came. She crossed her fingers and trotted up the front steps and inside to seek out her friend.

The two sheets of paper fluttered in her trembling fingers. Mercy held onto them like the life line they represented. Reggie's penmanship surpassed her own. But more than the fluidity of his lettering, his way with words and imagery left her breathless with longing for his touch. Knowing he had handled the pages—laid his hand on them to drag the pen tip across the linen paper to share his thoughts and desires with her, pressed the pads of his clever fingers around the edges to seal in his love with his words—all created a tenuous link to him over the miles separating them. Hot tears pressed for release but she blinked them back. Her love for him didn't need sadness associated with it.

She perused the lines he'd sent her for the third time. She wanted to honor his request but how could she?

My dearest heart,

I delayed writing in hopes of having better news to share but alas it is futile. My sweetest, I fear I must linger here to directly supervise the craftsmen and ensure they do what I picture in my mind. I know you'd agree with me were you here to see for yourself how poorly they'd executed my vision. I also know you are in good hands with the young man I left to manage the inn and property. I have done so because I do not want you to worry about all the day-to-day details. You're my treasure and I do not want you to work so hard, not when there is an alternative. Flint Hamilton is a steady worker, an honest man. He's promised to stay until I return and I have written him under separate cover about the need for me to extend my journey for three months. Also, please assist him as he might request in order to prepare for a November visit from a senator and his family. I've written Flint with the details.

My darling wife, know that if I can possibly conclude things here sooner and return to your loving side then I will.

I hope that Cassandra received the fine doll's house I sent for her birthday. I couldn't be there but I wanted her to know I was thinking of her. I thought it would give her the opportunity to begin contemplating what her own future home would be like. Now that she's reached eighteen years, we'll need to find her a husband ere long. So she might as well begin with a little playful yet helpful way to plan for her own home. What kinds of furniture and furnishings she'd like to collect. That sort of thing. What did she think of it? Please write and tell me.

My time to write this letter to you—one that will try to contain all of the deep-felt thanks that you are my stalwart wife and love of my life—grows short. One last thing, my dear heart. Trust Flint to know what's best and enjoy the free time his presence allows for. I realize my departure must have shocked and surprised you but that couldn't be helped either. I didn't want to interrupt your trip with Cassandra. I hope you rediscover some of the pastimes you once delighted in. Now that the inn is doing well, we can afford for you to have some leisure in your days.

All my deepest love,
Reggie

Mercy pressed her head to the back of the rocking chair and gazed out over the foothills in the distance. The constant undulating shades of green mixed with the cloud shadows fascinated her even as she pondered her husband's letter. She set the chair rocking to and fro, her thoughts shifting and swirling in her head.

He asked too much of her when he insisted she trust Flint. Not when the lad seemed far too interested in Cassie. The very idea she'd not watch him like a hawk raised her hackles. On the other hand, her husband's sweet consideration to try to ease her work load brought a smile to her lips. But three long months seemed forever. It had only been one month since they'd returned from Nashville, excited to share their pretty frocks and hats with him. Only to find him gone without a word.

He had his reasons. She understood as much. Which didn't mean she had to like them. And she didn't like the fact that he remained so far away. Anything could happen to him and she wouldn't hear for weeks. A simple letter took more than ten days to cross the rough terrain from Washington to Nashville. Even with the post roads in place, such a trip proved difficult and filled with uncertainties. Dangers such as highwaymen and wild animals and thunderstorms. Pondering the logistics necessary to bring back the many dining tables, chairs, sideboards, and bedsteads he'd gone to procure made her head and her heart ache. The trip alone would take weeks if not a month.

Folding the letter, she tucked it into her apron pocket. Movement drew her attention to where Cassie came out of the residence and skipped down the back steps to her garden. Dressed in a plain work dress and gardening apron, with a wide-brimmed straw hat to protect her fair skin from the afternoon sun. Reggie believed the time had arrived to begin the search for an appropriate husband. Cassie breezed through the garden gate, letting it slap closed behind her. She sauntered into the row of pole beans, checking the ties holding the vines to the slender poles. Pretty and smart and great with animals and plants alike. She'd make someone a fine wife and a better mother to their children than Mercy had been herself. Her daughter's compassion and loving heart would ensure a peaceful, friendly place to live and grow. Unlike the one Mercy had allowed to bloom around her because of her own annoyance. She recognized how she'd changed over the years but couldn't stop the disappointment and resulting bitterness from poisoning her best intentions.

Flint strode out the back door and down the steps, heading for the garden. His auburn hair glinted with hints of gold. His profile featured a strong nose and chin. Trim and neat in a yellow dress shirt, black vest, and black trousers, it was no wonder Cassie found him easy to look at. But pretty is as pretty does and she definitely didn't like what he was doing.

Mercy sat up straight, then slowly rose to her feet to take one slow step after another toward the steps. Her muscles tensed, preparing to hurry to her daughter's defense. Flint paused at the gate and called out Cassie's name. Grinning, she wiped her hands on her apron and moved to meet him from the other side. The smiles, the angling of their heads, the focus on each other as they talked and laughed for several minutes only served to increase the spooling tension in her gut.

When Cassie gazed up into Flint's face with an adoring expression glowing on her face, Mercy's heart caught and then raced. Flint nodded and then turned to stride back inside without looking up at the back porch where Mercy glared at him from the shadows until he disappeared through the door with a thump.

As much as she wanted to run to her daughter to warn her away from that man, the last time they'd spoken about him they'd ended up in a fight. Yelling wouldn't help Cassie hear the message. A calm approach might work far better. If she could remain calm. Mercy drew in a breath and marched down the steps. She was going to have her say nonetheless.

"Cassandra, can we talk, please?" Mercy opened the garden gate and waited until her daughter stood beside her outside.

"Yes, Ma?" The smile she'd bestowed on Flint had long fled her pert mouth.

"I saw you with Flint just now." She searched for the calm, the balance, and the right words to make her understand. "My darling, he's not for you."

Cassie's eyes widened and then her brows crashed down as she crossed her arms. "Must we do this again?"

Obviously, not the right words. She searched for other ways to convey her convictions about a relationship between the two young people. Perhaps if she shared her own experiences then her daughter would grasp her meaning. "Cassie, when I married your father it was not just because he was fine-looking and clever and I loved him with all my heart."

Cassie lifted one brow but remained silent, waiting.

"Your father showed me he had ambition, dreams, and what's more the skills and talent necessary to makes those dreams come true." Mercy shook her head and pursed her lips. "Flint doesn't. Whoever marries him will have a very difficult life. Worse than the one you're currently living."

"You don't know that." Cassie dropped her arms to make fists at her sides. "Flint is kind and smart and handsome."

"Yes, I know. But it's not enough to provide you with the kind of life you deserve." She waved one hand as if shooing away an annoying yellow jacket hovering over a mug of apple cider. "He'd try but he wouldn't succeed."

"Working together, we could make his dreams reality like you say Pa is doing." Cassie frowned at Mercy and then sighed. "You'll never accept him, will you?"

"No, because I can't."

"Or won't."

"That's also true. But it's for your own good, not mine." Mercy strove to contain the frustration and worry snaking in her core. She'd do anything to protect her fair daughter from a difficult life. From the clutches of a man who couldn't possibly provide for her in the manner Mercy hoped. "Please, listen to me."

"What would he have to do to prove to you that he is the right man for me?" Cassie angled her head to regard Mercy with a quizzical expression.

Her heart fell with her daughter's question. She intended to persist with the undesirable relationship. Somehow, someway Mercy had to show her the difficulty of the path she wanted to follow despite all the cautions she threw at her.

"I don't believe he can, dear." She studied her daughter's crestfallen expression. "Without having some ambition other than to serve the public, he'll never be capable of providing for you in the manner I believe you deserve. Servants do not create wealth or any kind of legacy to pass on for their children. I want more for you."

Cassie huffed and shook her head once. "I would think that's my choice to make, Ma. I think I'm capable of determining my own future."

Indeed, Cassandra had grown into a rational, loving, intelligent woman. With every passing year, she displayed an increasing awareness and sensitivity to those around her. She listened when people spoke, helped where possible, and anticipated what others needed before even they had formed the thought. Small, personal gestures and gifts to show them her consideration went a long way to impress the guests. Still, she had only reached eighteen years and had much to learn about the ways of the world and of men.

"I think eventually you'll be able to make wise decisions." Mercy smoothed a wisp of Cassie's long hair back behind her ear, a caring gesture she'd made all her daughter's life. "But know this. I will never stop protecting you from others as long as I draw breath."

Chapter Nine

_W_ater dripped slowly from a cluster of stalactites, the minerals forming small mounds on the cave floor. An oil lantern flickered where it perched precariously on a rough ledge, casting light on the bull's eye propped against the cave wall. Flint had asked Deputy Barney Parker to teach him how to shoot straight and true. They'd chosen one of the many caves in the area as a safe and private place to practice firing a pistol. Flint didn't want to risk somebody wandering around the foothills stumbling into their practice range. Besides, the steady coolness of the cave offered welcome relief from the hot summer sun.

Flint stared at the shiny pistol in his hand, weighing the heavy wood-handled weapon, then glanced at Parker. The deputy rubbed a cloth on the barrel of a gun, an open, lined case on a stalagmite in the center of the cavern, and then shoved the rag into the waistband of dark blue jeans. Even while off duty in civilian clothing, his bulk and brute strength made him formidable. When he smiled, some of the edge softened but not by much. He acted as though the world owed him respect but hadn't been forthcoming in offering it. An imaginary chip sat squarely on the man's shoulder, making him both overconfident and on the verge of being obnoxious. Which made him the perfect instructor for Flint's purposes.

"Careful with that thing." Parker waved a hand toward the flintlock pistol in Flint's hand. "You said you're not so good with it."

Flint pointed the muzzle away from the deputy with a smirk. "That's why you're here. So teach me how to handle it and shoot straight."

"First you need to load it properly." The deputy held out his hand until Flint handed him the weapon. "Do you know how?"

He seemed to recall it took some special steps, and if you fouled them up then the contraption could explode in your hand. His father had tried to teach him how to handle a pistol years ago. After several near catastrophic missteps, he'd decided Flint would be safer using a rifle or even a musket. They weren't quite as tricky as the smaller weapon, at least for Flint. But now Flint wanted something smaller he could carry with him instead of the larger, bulkier guns. Still, he approached the weapon with extreme caution.

"It's been a while. Remind me." Flint folded his arms while Parker talked him through the process. He forced himself to pay attention as the deputy explained and demonstrated each step, making the entire process look easy. Flint knew better.

Half-cock the hammer to pour in some gunpowder down the barrel. Wrap a lead ball with a bit of cloth and ram it down the barrel on top of the gunpowder. Add some gunpowder to the pan and snap the frizzen on as a cover. Fully cock the hammer and then squeeze the trigger to fire the gun. For each shot of the pistol, he had to do every step. With any luck, he wouldn't need to do it at all. But he must be prepared.

"Your turn." Parker handed him the gun. "Let's see what you've got. Shoot the bull's eye. Or try, anyway."

With a grunt, Flint clumsily loaded the pistol. He raised the gun to point at the target, then steadied his shaking hand by briefly supporting it with his other one. Dropping the second hand, he aimed at the center red circle and jerked on the trigger. The blast of sound rang in the confines of the cavern, slowly echoing into silence. The odor of gunpowder lingered longer. Parker strode to the paper target and examined it. He spun around to smirk at Flint.

"You missed the entire target." The deputy cleared his throat as he sauntered back to Flint. "First off, you don't want to use two hands to hold the gun. What if you're on horseback or in close quarters? You can't use two hands in either situation, so practice using one hand."

"You think I'll need to shoot while riding?" The man had to be daft. Aiming while both feet remained planted on the ground challenged him enough. "I sure hope not."

"Yeah, but you don't know what circumstances may require you to pull your gun. So..." Parker lifted his gun and demonstrated the proper technique for aiming. "Do what I do."

Except the lawman seemed far more comfortable with the idea of shooting another human being. He'd already been in those situations where he'd been forced to shoot while riding or in confined places. Flint truly hoped he'd never need to shoot another man. At the same time, he needed to protect those he cared about as well as his and their property. The horse theft episode taught him a valuable lesson.

Flint dragged in a deep breath and let it out slowly before mimicking the other man's position. "Like this?"

"Right. Now when you want to shoot, smoothly squeeze the trigger until it fires." He peered closer at Flint, nodding as the student did as instructed. The gun fired with a loud bang and the smell of exploded gunpowder filled the air. Parker holstered his gun and hurried to the target to study it. "Nicely done. Not a bull's eye but just off center. Much better."

Better but not perfect. His reluctance to shoot another extended to not wanting to shoot the wrong somebody. When he fired a gun, he wanted the confidence of knowing he'd hit what or who he aimed at. "Teach me to hit the bull's eye."

Barney finished securing a fresh target in place and then pinned his gaze on Flint. "You're very serious about this. Is this shooting lesson because of the horse theft?"

"Partly. I've also heard tell of some guys causing mischief out our way." Flint glanced at the gun in his hand and then back to the deputy. "It's my responsibility to protect what is mine and my employer's."

"Just don't be acting like you're some kind of deputy, you hear?" Parker crossed his arms over his muscular chest. "If you have more trouble out there, you let me know. I'll take care of it for you."

"I appreciate the offer, Deputy." Flint reloaded the pistol carefully, taking his time adding gunpowder and wrapping a ball to shove into the barrel. When he'd finished, he cocked the hammer and peered at his new friend. "Tell me what I need to do."

They spent another hour in the cool cave, firing the pistol until Flint hit the center consistently. Not dead center every time, but close enough for his purpose. Understanding the force of the kick back of the weapon when fired helped him anticipate and counteract the jolt.

"Thanks, Barney." Flint laid the cleaned pistol into the padded case alongside the other matching one. "You've been a big help."

"You're a fast learner." Barney wiped his hands on the rag and then laid it inside the case, closing the lid with a snap. "But I'm serious about staying on the right side of the law."

"Trust me, I have every intention of using a gun only to defend." Flint pressed his lips together as he lifted the lantern. "All of your instruction may be for nothing, but now I'm ready if something happens."

The deputy picked up the case and stack of paper targets. "Let's both hope you don't need to find out just how well trained you are."

With a nod, Flint led Barney out of the cave into the bright sunlight, where he extinguished the lantern. Barney saluted him before walking in the opposite direction from Flint. Trudging along the dusty path back to the main road and on to the inn, Flint hoped he'd never have to fire a gun again.

The bar counter shone in the lamplight and still Flint kept rubbing. He forced his attention to the polished surface, avoiding the tug on his conscience with every ounce of his being. No way would he give in to the temptation to follow her outside. Just to be near her. With no other reason for seeking her out before noon. The last couple of weeks he'd steered away from her as frequently as possible. Tried to ignore the clamor of his heart when she passed by. He sought other distractions, other tasks, other chores. Anything. He rubbed harder, the cloth catching on a corner with a ripping sound.

"Flint, what are you doing?" Hannah paused across the counter, peering at him with raised brows over twinkling blue eyes. "I think it's clean already."

With a huff, he grabbed up the cloth and grunted. "Just making certain."

"Mm-hm." Shaking her head, the chuckling woman sashayed across the dining room toward the kitchen door, a large tray tapping against her leg with each stride.

He must find something else to occupy his attention. He

scanned the room, greeting customers with an inclination of his head as his gaze met theirs. Late morning meant few customers lingered, most having either already had breakfast and departed or not yet arrived for dinner. He sighed at the lack of inside tasks and made his way toward the dogtrot. May as well go to the office in the residence side. Tracking expenses and purchases as well as income from the increasing number of guests proved an ongoing task, a ready excuse for making himself scarce. Only when he pushed through the door and paused on the covered porch he heard her singing from out back in her garden. The sound drew him toward the rear of the building rather than inside where he could safely work.

He stood at the edge of the porch, listening and watching her putter in the enclosed garden. Imagined the dimple on the right side of her pretty mouth appearing and disappearing as she sang a melancholy tune. Imagined her light blue eyes twinkling with pleasure as she pulled weeds and snipped the dried blossoms from the medicinal flowers. Imagined taking her hands, smudged with life giving soil, in his and pulling her close, tasting her lips. The slam of the laundry shack door broke into his musings, making him jump as the laundress carried a basket of folded sheets down the dirt path and inside the inn. Seeing the dust rising around her ankles, he made a mental note to apply the crushed rock like he'd added out front of the inn to the worn groove in the grass. Cassie would benefit from such an improvement and may even thank him. With a kiss.

Rats and hard cheese. He squared his shoulders. Enough. Despite agreeing to let things develop or not on its own, he couldn't in good conscience continue to do so after receiving Reggie's reminder of his vow to protect the man's family, not become part of it. He needed to put an end to this daydreaming about a girl. And her flirtation. If she'd stop that, then he wouldn't think about her so much. He could focus on what he needed to rather than mooning over what couldn't happen between them. He'd put a stop to that, too. Marching down the back steps, he crossed the grassy lawn in long, quick strides. The sooner he informed her of his decision, the better.

"Cassie, I need a word with you." He gripped the top rail of the gate until she gained her feet from where she'd knelt to tug on some weeds.

"Anything you'd like, Flint." Her smile grew wider, flashing the dimple he couldn't forget, as she neared the gate. Another reminder of what he couldn't have. He yanked the gate open and held it until she'd passed outside. "What's on your mind?"

"You." He shut the gate and forced a frown onto his face. "You and your flirting."

She batted her lashes twice and pursed her lips, drawing his gaze to their pink perfection. "What do you mean?"

The slap of the back door to the residence drew his attention up to the porch where Mercy stood with a large wooden bowl propped against one hip. Her stern expression gave him goose-flesh on his skin. He couldn't have this conversation with Cassie under the suspicious woman's intense glare. He grabbed hold of Cassie's hand and led her around the side of the residence.

"Where are we going?" Cassie laughed as she trotted alongside.

"Let's take a little walk so we can talk…in private." He skimmed the front yard, noting the approach of a couple of wagons and several men on horseback. The rush had begun. They'd not find anywhere quiet around the inn and stables. Not for a couple of hours as least. He searched for a suitable place and then snapped his fingers. "Up to the falls. Okay?"

He slowed his pace so she could more easily keep up with his long strides. In short order, they'd crossed to the dirt path leading between the inn and stables and up to the mineral springs and falls beyond. The narrow path wound gently through a copse of trees, a hot breeze meeting them as they sauntered among the pines and oaks, the tang of pine filling the air around them. A pair of white-tailed does paused in their grazing to stare at them before bounding away up the hill. Birds twittered and chirped in the trees, a constant melodic symphony. He drew in a deep breath and let it out slowly, letting the tension inside his gut unwind into the pastoral surroundings.

"What did you want to talk to me about?" Cassie glanced up at him. "About my flirting, I mean."

"You have to stop." He shook his head and glanced away from her and then back. "I can't do this anymore."

"Do what?" She smiled at him, her lashes shadowing her cheeks in the summer sunlight.

He waved a hand between them. "I know we had an agreement to let things develop as they might. But your father and mother object to me even thinking about courting you. I must adhere to their wishes."

There, he'd said it. Put it out there where she would have to agree with him. She couldn't go against her own parents. She was such a good girl, she'd surely fall into line and do what would make them happy. Stay away from him.

His stomach fell when he thought about her with another man. A better man. Batting those lashes at him, inviting his attention. His heart clenched when he imagined the mystical man holding her hand or touching her face. Or more. He swallowed the cry of injustice. He'd made his decision and he'd do all in his power to stick to it.

In time, he'd find another girl to moon over. Perhaps even court. He'd forget… Surely, he'd manage to put the temptress behind him, away from him, and look ahead to his future. If he focused on his plans then everything else would fall away and let him move on. As long as he didn't weaken in his determination and commitment, all would work out.

"You're quite correct that Ma has warned me away from you." Her strides slowed as she stared at the path ahead. "She doesn't think you're the man for me."

"Then I should abide by her wishes in your behalf." Even though the mere thought threatened to choke him, stabbed a spike through his heart. He'd find a way to keep his distance. He must. "I will not bother you again."

"I see no reason for you to do such a silly thing." She stopped and turned to face him. "It's not their decision."

He frowned at her. Her words made no sense. "Of course it is. You're their daughter. Who else could possibly make the decision if not them?"

She pulled her shoulders back and pressed her lips together. A stubborn light gleamed in her beautiful eyes as she gazed at him. She searched his eyes, looking for something she ultimately found, for she nodded once as she cleared her throat.

"I shall make my own decision as to who I will or will not permit to court me." She raised her chin, the dimple winking at him as she regarded him for several moments.

He had no response to such a bold claim. He'd never heard of a mere slip of a girl making such an important choice on her own. By the angle of her chin and the glint in her eyes, he could tell she meant what she said. Did her parents know of her attitude? Did they concur? Surely not. They'd clearly expressed their objections. The girl before him needed a firm guiding hand to keep her safe and secure. Or she'd end up in trouble of one kind or another.

"Do you wish to court me, Flint?" She studied him, her eyes searching his, her dimple making an appearance when she slowly smiled at him.

He opened and then closed his mouth. How should he answer such an impertinent question? He should be asking

Reggie for permission to court her, not the girl herself. Right? When did the rules of courtship change? Or had they? He blinked at her, trying to grasp the right course to follow. Could he be the firm guiding hand she needed?

She wet her lips with a swipe of her tongue and then tilted her head to one side. "It's okay to answer me. I'm waiting."

His little temptress at it again. Mesmerizing blue eyes made him want to stare at her forever. The little dimple winking at him with each smile of her oh-so-tantalizing lips. He moistened his lips in anticipation and then mentally shook his head. He had to get a grip on his composure or he'd be doing things he shouldn't. Things he'd promised to avoid.

"You know I'm attracted to you." He took her hand and held it loosely as he tried to form a coherent response. "I would like to court you. But—"

"No." She laid two fingers on his lips to silence him. Dropping her free hand back to her side, she smiled up at him. "I would like for you to court me. Will you?"

The direct question floored him for a long moment. The light touch of her fingers to his lips spiked desire through his entire frame. The pretty girl intrigued him. The boss's daughter who had been officially declared off limits for him. He should obey the declaration. Yet she had overruled it and made her own. Strong-willed and determined to reign in her personal world. She'd make a fine life companion, someone to help shoulder the daily burdens and joys equally. If he could persuade her parents to accept him as her beau. The longer he contemplated her question, the more sure he became of his preferred course of action. Difficult as it might be, she would be worth the effort.

He slowly nodded as he smiled at her. "If you're sure, then yes."

"Good. I'm glad that's settled." She returned the grin

and continued walking up the path, still holding his hand. "Now we can enjoy the rest of our walk."

He let her lead them up the steepening path and around the curve where they could see the rushing waters cascading from high above into the river winding across the Fury Falls Inn property. Steam drifted up from the sequestered hot springs off to one side, surrounded by boulders and rocks. Steps had been added to make it easier to submerge in the hot water. A log hut with cedar shingled roof hunkered beneath a maple tree, a private place where guests could change their clothes before immersing themselves in the healing waters.

He looked at her studying the flowing water with a half-open mouth and laughing blue eyes. Her long blonde hair fell past her shoulders, shifting in the slight breeze. Standing a little over five feet, her head was even with his shoulder. He imagined she'd fit perfectly into his embrace, her head resting against his chest while he snuggled her close to him. The urge to make his imaginings real flooded his soul. "You're beautiful, Cassie."

She brought her gaze to meet his, the delight lingering in her expression. "Thank you, Flint."

"This isn't going to be easy." He searched her eyes, looking for her response. "You do realize the reality, don't you?"

Her smile widened as she canted her head. "I'm fully aware of my mother's stance."

"I shouldn't agree to let you put yourself in such an awful position." Now that he'd allowed himself to daydream about being with her, he didn't want to go back to denying his attraction to her. He held his breath, praying she wouldn't agree with his half-hearted suggestion of his backing away.

"We will share the blame and the rewards of getting to know each other better." Her smile vanished as she contemplated his serious regard. "How else could we possibly determine if we have a future together?"

He took her hands in his, bringing her a step closer to him with a gentle tug. The feel of her sturdy hands in his sent a jolt of awareness straight through him. "I know I'm fond of you and look forward to knowing you better."

She stared up into his solemn features. "I'm fond of you, too. Maybe with time we'll find out we're not such a great pair but I like what I've seen so far."

"Then I guess we're courting." He liked what he'd seen of her as well. But he wanted…no, needed…to satisfy his heart's desire. He'd become so close to her and simply couldn't walk away without the reward he sought. "Cassie, may I kiss you?"

With her eyes glowing, she glanced at his lips and then met his gaze. "Please."

He lowered his head, watching her lashes fall against her cheeks as he pressed his lips to hers. Sampled the sweetness of her lips and hungered for more. He clasped her arms to draw her closer and to keep his hands from exploring further. Not yet. He wanted to take it slowly and enjoy their time together. Give her the time she needed to learn him, to adjust to being together. He didn't want to scare her away. After a few moments of tasting her sweet offerings, he broke away to witness her rapture as her eyes fluttered open, out of focus from the passion they'd shared. He longed to lay with her and discover together the pleasure awaiting them but he merely smiled and took her hand. If all went well, they'd have plenty of time for such precious moments later. After they married and built their own home, eventually started their family. But for now, he'd be content.

"Thank you, my sweetheart." He smiled at her, pleased when she grinned back at the endearment he'd used. A sense of happiness spun a web inside him. "I hope you enjoyed that as much as I did."

"Oh, yes." She pressed her fingers to her mouth. "I did indeed."

"Good. I'm glad, but we need to go back. They'll be wondering where we've been so long." He squeezed her fingers and she blinked up at him.

She glanced at the sun and nodded. "Yes, it's later than I thought. Ma will worry."

Flint tugged on her hand and they started walking down the path. "What will you tell your mother about us?"

She chuckled for a brief moment and then sobered. "The truth, I guess. She will have to accept our decision."

Flint gazed out over the serene valley as they made their way down the winding path. The very air seemed to shimmer and smile at his new found happiness. The only fly in the ointment remained the reception they'd find at the inn. How would Mercy react when Cassie broke the news to her? He couldn't imagine she'd be happy or even accepting. Irate. Angry. Volatile, sure.

He'd need to write to her father and ask for his understanding and blessing. Not a letter he looked forward to penning, truth be told. But writing was the right thing to do.

Then he'd have to share with Sheridan the new status between Flint and Cassie. As her dear friend, he'd more than once reminded Flint of Reggie's expectations concerning his daughter. Expectations not including Flint. Apparently, Cassie hadn't consulted her family or friends before making her own decisions.

The inn came into view as they rounded the last curve. Such a welcoming sight, bustling with customers and stable boys. With so many witnesses, perhaps Mercy wouldn't make too big a scene. He scoffed at his own musings. Who was he fooling?

The din from the packed crowds in the dining room had

chased her into the relative quiet of the parlor. Mercy busied about the room, straightening and dusting the furniture and decorations. Hannah had dissuaded her—without much difficulty truth be told—from pitching in with serving meals and drinks. Instead, she preferred to work on the private side of the building. She fluffed a pillow Cassie had embroidered flowers on and replaced it in the corner of the long settle. The girl had so much talent. She could do anything with her life. If she'd listen to her mother's guidance she'd have quite a wonderful future ahead. Yet she insisted on having all the answers at the tender age of eighteen years. In years past, marriage at a young age was expected, necessary to raise a brood of children to help around the farm or plantation. But in the current state of society, such a need had lessened. Cassie could wait until she'd matured enough to make sound choices. But would she listen? Mercy shook her head as she picked up the matching pillow at the other end and bounced it between her hands to fluff it.

She dropped the pillow into place and rested her hands on her hips as she perused the remainder of the family's haven. Content, she sighed and moved to the forlorn doll's house standing between the front windows. Leaning down, she peered inside to look at the empty rooms. Barren and in need of populating with furniture, décor, and doll-sized people. Cassie ignored the waiting rooms as if the house didn't exist. Her doting husband had sent the perfect gift to Cassie given his intentions behind the gesture. She dragged in a deep, unsettled breath. Until Mercy had ruined it with her hurtful answer to Cassie's confused question. Reggie didn't think of their daughter as a child. Rather, he saw her clearly, as a young woman on the verge of starting her own life with a husband of her own. She'd make sure to relay Reggie's real intention when Cassie returned from where she and Flint had disappeared to.

She straightened as a flash outside the window caught her eye. Odd to have someone outside the residence when most everyone went to the public side. She hurried to peer out the front window, a coldness seeping through her interior. People coming and going on foot, horseback, and in sundry horse-drawn vehicles met her uneasy gaze. The nosy dogs moved among the flow of traffic while a flock of chickens pecked in the grass beside the stable.

Three burly men dismounted at the hitching rail and started up the steps. The sound of clomping boots on the porch stopped. She couldn't see where they'd gone from her position. The men must have entered the inn. She blew out the breath she'd been holding and turned back to inspect the doll's house again. More clomping on the dogtrot porch jolted her upright as she spun to face the door. When the side door flung open with a bang, she jumped back, knocking the doll's house several inches askew.

Three hulks with floppy hats pulled low and black bandanas over the lower half of their faces surged inside. They were dressed like any other tradesman or merchant who visited the inn for a meal and cold drink. Khaki trousers, dark work shirts damp with sweat, scuffed brown boots. She stood taller, ready to send the intruders back outside and off her property. Defend her own territory as best she could. A quick assessment of their size and movement confirmed she didn't know the men.

"There she is." The lead man pointed at her as he approached, pistol drawn and aimed at her.

Her heart froze, the coldness spreading throughout her, making her tremble. They sought her out. She frowned at them, trying to recognize them. She must have seen them before if they knew her. Why didn't she know them? She quickly examined the leader, noting dark bushy eyebrows over brown eyes. A crooked nose, broken some time ago. Probably in a fight given his current occupation. The man beside him had bright green eyes piercing into her as he glared at her. His light brown eyebrows suggested he might be a blond-headed man but the hat hid his hair. The third man stood behind the others, somewhat taller and thinner but still dangerous. Dark brown brows and golden eyes studied her, but without the overt malice of the others.

"What are you doing in my home?" She swallowed the fear filling her throat. Lifted her chin and pulled back her shoulders. She wouldn't let them see how much they affected her. "I don't know you."

"Let's keep it that way." The second man chuckled, a dark, dangerous sound that sent chills down Mercy's spine.

"What do you want?" She held her ground as the three hulks came closer, one measured stride at a time.

She darted a glance out the window and then to the open door the men had burst through, hoping someone would see her predicament and come to help. The busy yard had cleared. She couldn't see anyone outside. By coincidence or design? Where was everyone? Fear clawed up her throat, choking her.

"We heard tell of your treasure and we've come to get it." The first man's dark eyes narrowed when he stopped within a few feet of her and he lifted the muzzle of the pistol to point at her chest. "Take us to where you've got it hidden and you won't get hurt."

"I don't have anything you'd want." How had he heard of her sentimental treasures? She'd only ever spoken of them in the privacy of her bedchamber. "I have no treasure you'd be interested in."

"I'll be the judge of that, woman." He motioned for his companion to grab her.

The man with hard green eyes moved as fast as a striking snake to grab her arm and spin her around, pinning both arms behind her. She lost her balance and he jolted her upright. The pain in her shoulders drove tears into her eyes as she cried out.

"Hush her up." The dark-eyed man growled out the order and the green-eyed man yanked on her arms harder.

Tears fell as her fear overwhelmed her, froze her in place. She'd never been so afraid. Never been so helpless. She must cooperate or risk losing her life. But she wouldn't give them what they demanded. Her private collection of books and costume jewelry served as a symbol of hope to return to the kind of lifestyle she preferred. They represented a better way of living. Something to pass on to her daughter as she began her own married life and started a family. Mercy searched for some way to talk them out of harming her, physically or emotionally.

"It's upstairs in her bedroom. That's what the chit said." The second man moved to stand in front of Mercy. His golden eyes glared at her with contempt. "Which room is it?"

She shook her head, her voice impaired by the fear wrapped around her vocal cords.

The man holding her pushed her toward the stairs at the other end of the room. She bumped her knee into a table as they roughly shoved her forward. She gasped at the sharp pain and stumbled. He jerked her back upright, wrenching her shoulder with a flash of heat and agony. Forcing her up the stairs, one excruciating step after another, she finally reached the top landing, breathing heavily.

"Take us to your room, wench." The dark-eyed man put the muzzle of the gun to her temple. "Now."

Whimpering, she led them to her bedroom. She wracked her brain for something she could give them as her "treasure" but came up empty. Nothing she owned had any intrinsic value. Merely memories of better times. Books were precious to her, but these most likely illiterate highwaymen wouldn't consider them valuable. Nor would they look on her simple pendants and cameos with anything but disdain.

They weren't worth more than a few dollars each but meant the world to her. Likewise with her furnishings. The fancy mirror her son had bestowed upon her years ago. The bedstead with its quilt sewn by her mother, now deceased. All precious to her but nobody else would pay money for them. Tears coursed down her cheeks. What could she do?

The man shoved her through the door and she stumbled forward, catching herself on the post of the bedstead. Holding onto it with both hands, she cowered as they ransacked the room. She kept quiet, tears drying on her heated face. Let them take whatever they wanted. She would never reveal the true location of her things. Never tell them about the attic where the books and special items were safely locked away. Her gaze dropped to the dressing table and the key ring laying in its dainty glass bowl. If they took the keys, she wouldn't be able to access her treasure. Could she reach the keys and pocket them before they noticed?

She slowly released her death grip on the bedpost and eased around the end of the bed. Sidling toward the table, she kept one eye on the three men tossing pillows and yanking open drawers, the doors to the wardrobe, tearing down the curtains at the window. A few more steps…

"Where you going?" The green-eyed man grabbed her arm and halted her steps. He glanced at the table and then leered at her. "Hey, Joe, grab those keys. They look… pretty."

"Why?" The dark-eyed man crossed to the dressing table and lifted the set of three keys of differing sizes. "What are they for?"

"Nothing." Mercy forced the word out of her mouth. The items secreted behind the attic door were everything to her, but definitely nothing to them.

The one called Joe inspected the three keys and then slipped them in his pocket. "Then you won't miss them, will ya, wench?"

"No, please." She reached toward him, palm up. "They're not worth anything. Honest."

He chortled at her and shook his head. "Like I said, then you won't miss 'em."

Joe took two quick steps to grab hold of her arm and shake her until her teeth clicked together. "Now where's the real treasure?"

When he stopped shaking her, she closed her eyes for a moment to steady herself. Then opened them to address her captors. "I told you I don't have anything of value. There is no treasure." A cold chill crashed through her at the evil emanating from the dark eyes. "It's just what I call my mementos and such."

The front door opened below and she heard Cassie's distant laugh followed by Flint's deep rumble in reply. Help had finally arrived. If they knew of her trouble. Which of course they didn't. Flint's deep voice reverberated downstairs and then faded into silence. They must have left again when they didn't see her in the parlor. No rescue would happen after all. It was up to her. Despair fought with the determination in her chest. She needed some way to escape the nightmare she found herself living second to second. She glanced at the grip the man had on her arm, calculating whether she could break away and run.

Joe put the muzzle to her forehead. "Don't even think about it, wench." He pushed the metal hard into her head, making her wince and try to back away. Only he pulled her closer with a grip on her shoulder.

Desperate and afraid, she jerked away and fell backward against the table, bumping it against the wall behind it. The looking glass rattled as it rocked to and fro and then settled. She didn't dare look to see if it had been damaged as the golden-eyed man aimed his pistol at her. She couldn't afford to take her eyes off of the men.

"What do we do, Joe? There's someone downstairs." The green-eyed man aimed worried and nervous eyes at Mercy.

Joe glared at her. "Last chance, wench. Where's that treasure?"

She gulped and put up both hands and then shook her head. "I don't have any."

"We've got to get out of here." The golden-eyed man cast fearful glances at the other two men.

"Not without that treasure." Joe's finger tightened on the trigger. "Or whatever else we snatch."

Before she could reply, the green-eyed man fired his gun. The impact of the bullet on her forehead cracked her skull and shot searing pain through her. She crumpled to the floor, sprawled across the flowered carpet. She laid there as the men cussed and stomped out of the room and down the stairs. She thought of her lovely daughter, her four sons, and most of all her loving husband so far away. She'd failed them all. She laid there as her life force seeped onto the carpet and the world turned black.

Chapter Ten

$\mathcal{B}$eau trotted up the steps to where Cassie stood dithering on where to look for her ma next. She patted the curly head as Flint crossed the yard from the stable. She smiled at the sight of his easy, confident stride bringing him closer with each passing second. They'd been searching for her mother in order to tell her of their decision as soon as possible. They'd agreed on the walk back to have it over and done with so the tension stopped hanging over their heads like a storm cloud.

"Have you found her yet?" Flint patted Beau's head and glanced toward the residence. "She hasn't come out?"

"No. I don't understand." She pursed her lips with a worried frown tugging on her brows.

"Maybe she's upstairs?"

"If so, then I wouldn't want to interrupt whatever she's doing. What if she was taking a nap or changing clothes or something?"

He chuckled, a rich rumble in his chest. "Take a nap? I highly doubt your mother would do such a decadent thing in the middle of the afternoon."

"You do have a point." She grinned back at him. "I'm not really in any hurry to relay our happy news to her. I know we said we wanted it done, but I don't think she'll take it well."

In fact, she knew they'd probably end up in a war of words again. She didn't want to argue with her mother over her choices. She understood her mother's viewpoint, or most of it, but her ma didn't want to even try to comprehend Cassie's.

"Then we should—" The distant sound of a gunshot stopped him midsentence. "What was that?"

"I don't know. Sounded like it was inside." Cassie frowned at him then glanced toward the residence. "How odd."

Pounding footsteps made him tense. Cassie spun around and then stepped back toward Flint as three masked men ran through the door from the residence and rushed past them. They leapt onto three waiting bay horses and galloped away, trailing a cloud of dust in their wake. Flint patted his side but then frowned when he realized he wasn't wearing his gun holstered on his belt.

"Who are they?" Cassie shot Flint a shocked glance. "What were they doing in there?"

"Damn it all. I don't know but they've gotten away. Let's go find out what on earth they were doing inside." Flint led her back into the residence and they hesitated at the door to scan the room. "Nothing seems amiss in the parlor or dining room."

Skimming her gaze over the familiar family living space, she had to agree with him. Except for one small detail.

"My doll's house has been moved." She hurried over to inspect it for damage. "It looks like someone bumped into it pretty hard."

"Let's find your mother." Flint rushed to the stairs and took them two at a time.

"Wait for me." Her long skirts didn't allow for running up the stairs but she followed him as quickly as possible. Her heart beat thrummed in her ears as she scurried up the steps. Where was her ma? Was she all right?

"Hurry then." He waited for her to catch up, impatient and anxious.

Out of breath by the time she reached his side, she panted as she dropped the handful of skirts. "Come on." Cassie turned right at the top and hurried straight through the ajar door to her mother's bedroom.

She shrieked at the sight of the ransacked room. Cassie paused, quickly evaluating the situation before she surged closer. Her mother lay sprawled across the floor, blood ran from her forehead onto the carpet. She lay perfectly still in an unnatural position. Her clothes lay in piles on the floor and her bits of jewelry and hair brush were in disarray on the dressing table. The pretty little chair had been broken and the pieces scattered. Even the quilt on the bed had been tossed to the floor and the straw mattress slit open.

"Oh lordy, lordy. Ma?" She fell on her knees beside her mother, looked for signs of breathing. Tears smarted behind her eyes, but she refused to let them fall. Not until she knew for certain what she had to deal with. She looked up at Flint. "Oh my God! Help her."

Her mind scrambled for a reason for the senseless violence directed at her mother. Sure, she could be brusque or rude, but such behavior didn't warrant being shot and robbed. In her own private bedroom. In the middle of the day. How could it have happened? Those men killed her mother and escaped. Her stomach roiled and she swallowed the acrid bile rising in her throat.

Flint quickly knelt on the other side of Mercy and felt for a pulse in her neck. He stared at her chest for a few seconds and then slowly shook his head. "I'm sorry, Cassie. There's nothing I can do."

"No!" A dam of pain broke, rushing and cascading before it finally drowned her.

Tears flowed down her cheeks as she wailed, rocking on her knees. She gathered her mother's body to her, clinging to her like she'd never done while her mother lived. She brushed the bloodied blonde hair back from her face, where the bullet hole marred the middle of her forehead. Dismay engulfed her heart when she noticed her hand bore red smears on the fingers. She cried harder at the sight, distraught knowing her mother had been shot in the head. She sensed Flint move away but stayed near to her. She'd loved her ma even though she could be overly protective, overbearing, and harsh. She'd never wanted her to leave her so abruptly. Never wanted her to die. Hot tears washed her cheeks as the pain and grief engulfed her being.

After several minutes, Flint moved to stand behind her. He laid a hand on her trembling shoulder and waited. Sobbing, she eased her mother's body back to the floor. She leaned over and pressed a tender kiss on her mother's cheek, salty tears dripping onto her chin.

"Goodbye, Ma." She swallowed and cleared her throat, wiping her cheeks dry. "I love you."

She should have told her ma how she felt about her more often. She'd thought they had years together. If she'd known this morning how the day would end, she wouldn't have left. Wouldn't have sought ways to avoid her ma out of fear of a repeat of the angry words they'd exchanged. Her entire frame trembled with grief and sadness as she stared down at her mother's dead body.

"Are you okay?" Flint helped her stand, bracing her with a hand on her elbow.

"It feels like someone has ripped my heart out." She cast a tear-drenched glance up at his somber features. "Hold me?"

He wrapped his arms around her from behind and held her tight for several moments. Then he drew in a sharp breath and blew it out. She felt him stiffen, his arms squeezing and releasing in short order.

"What's wrong?" She eased away from him to pivot so she could look into his eyes.

He stared at something over her shoulder so she followed his gaze to scan the bedroom. Dresser, window, dressing table and chair pieces, bed, wardrobe. Everything tumbled and pulled out of drawers and the wardrobe.

Flint blinked and then captured her gaze. "Your ma…"

"Those men. They did this." She ignored the haunted look in his eyes, the one he displayed when he'd hint about haints. Cassie frowned at him as she waved a hand to encompass the trashed room. "What were they looking for?"

"Why only in here?" He shook his head. "What did she have they might have wanted?"

She pondered his question for several heart beats. Her parents were not wealthy but they had invested in some fine furniture and attire. But she couldn't recall anything a bandit would find valuable enough to steal.

"Nothing worth dying over, that's for sure."

He glanced over her shoulder and stared at nothing for a second, then met her gaze again. "Apparently, she thinks differently. Look."

"At what?" Cassie slowly spun around to see what Flint was pointing at.

At first she didn't see anything she hadn't seen before. Then slowly she saw a figure appear wearing an ankle-length tan dress and a mop cap on her blonde hair. A chill washed over Cassie's bare arms and she hugged herself to warm them. Her eyes widened for a beat as her mouth slowly fell open.

Her mother's ghost stood by the window, shimmering as she smiled at Cassie.

Then the room went dark when Cassie fainted into Flint's strong arms.

He'd wanted her in his arms, just not fainted dead away. Flint cradled her head in the crook of his arm as he patted her cheek. "Cassie?"

What a mess. Her mother dead. Cassie frightened into passing out. Mercy's ghost lingering in the shadows. He cast a quick glance about the disheveled room but found no sign of her. At least when Cassie came to, she wouldn't be confronted yet again with the apparition.

"Come back to me, Cassie." He gently shook her, doing whatever he could think of to revive her.

They couldn't stay in Mercy's bedroom. They needed help and to alert the sheriff of the murder and possible theft. Her lashes flickered. He pressed a kiss to her cheek and then pulled back to see if it had the desired effect. Her eyeballs shifted beneath closed lids and then her eyes blinked open.

"Flint? What happened?" She stared at him with confusion in her clouded eyes.

"You fainted. How are you feeling?" He helped her ease up to a sitting position.

She pressed her lips together and fluttered a hand to her forehead. "I don't know." Shaking her head to remove mental cobwebs, she frowned at him. "I think I'm alright."

"Good. Let's get you on your feet." He scrambled to stand and then helped her up beside him. "I need you to do something if you think you can. Will you try?"

She nodded slowly, keeping her gaze locked on his.

"I know this won't be easy for you." He swept an arm outward, indicating the entire room. "Take a look around and tell me if anything is missing."

She dragged in a shaky breath and let it out slowly. Cassie glanced where he pointed and then down where she spotted Mercy's body and froze. After a second, she shuddered and moved to the mess of clothing and shoes strewn across the floor. Then reached the dressing table. Straightening the looking glass, she arranged the brush and perfume bottles. She seemed to be handling the situation with fortitude. He admired her courage and strength as she went through the various small items on the table, inventorying as she went. Then her hand froze in midair in the act of reaching for a small glass bowl beside the mirror. She spun around with horror and anger mixed in her frantic expression.

"They're gone."

He strode toward her, dodging around objects in his way to reach her side as quickly as possible. "What's gone?"

"The keys. She always kept them in this bowl." She glanced back down to the empty dish.

"What were they for?" She seemed unduly upset over the loss of a few keys. He could get replacements without too much problem. "Something important?"

"What Ma called her treasure."

"What kind of treasure?" He hadn't been made aware of anything valuable he needed to protect.

Gold? Jewels? Securities? What had the woman been hiding in her room? For three armed men to force their way in and kill the woman, there must have been something to tempt them. Surely they wouldn't have risked being caught if the reward didn't justify the danger.

She shrugged and lifted her brows in a helpless gesture. "The attic door for one. A small chest where she kept things important to her. I don't know what else."

He raked a hand through his hair and sighed in frustration as he scanned the room with one swift look. "I don't see a chest. Damn. I guess they stole it."

She shook her head quickly. "No, it was locked inside the attic. If they have the keys, though, they could have found it."

"They'd have to know what the keys are for. Would Mercy have told them, do you think?" An anguished cry burst from Cassie and he instinctively pulled her into an embrace. "I know, sweetheart. It's okay to cry."

She sobbed against his chest, dampening the cotton shirt. He held her for several minutes while she cried in short hiccups and low moans. The death of a parent hit the children with a new type of grief. One he imagined would linger for many years if not forever. All of the questions she would have liked to ask her mother, all the new joys she'd want to share with her. Each time he could imagine how the grief over her loss would be compounded. She sniffled and eased away so he could see her tear-streaked flesh.

He offered a hand to hold. "Let me get you out of here. I'll send some of the men up to take care of your mother's body."

"One thing before we go." Cassie regarded him with red-rimmed eyes and then turned to look around the room, ignoring his outstretched hand. After a pause, she brought her gaze back to meet his again. "Did I see Ma's ghost before I fainted?"

"I believe so. Yes." But why had her ghost stayed behind in the room?

"I've never seen a ghost before." She swallowed and shook her head slowly side to side. "Why would she remain?"

"Unfinished business perhaps?" He shrugged and moistened his suddenly dry lips. Did Mercy know about their courtship? Did she want to break them up? Is that why? "I don't know."

She let out an unsteady chuckle. "I guess I can't chide you about seeing haints anymore, huh?"

He smiled as he huffed a laugh. "Right."

He'd thought he'd managed to rid the inn of its ghost but apparently another had taken its place. This one an angry, bitter woman who hated his presence. What mischief would she cause? Damn. He'd have to try to guard against whatever she'd do. But how, he had no clue. One thing he did know. Cassie believed him now which could lead to her true acceptance of him and his ability to converse with haints.

He took her hand and led her from the room, pulling the door closed behind them. No need for anyone else to stumble upon the crime scene. Next steps included having two of the hands move the body to the parlor to prepare her for burial as soon as possible. With the summer heat on the upswing they'd not dawdle on digging the grave nor wait for family to travel in. Such a delay wouldn't be healthy for anyone, physically or mentally.

"You'll need to pick a nice dress to bury your mother in. Or would you rather Hannah prepare her for burial?"

"Hannah?" She lifted her chin and swallowed hard, firming her lips into a harsh line. "No, I'll take care of my mother."

He squeezed her hand then released it as she preceded him down the stairs. "You're a strong woman, Cassandra Fairhope."

At the bottom she turned to meet him when he took the last step down. Her eyes glistened with unshed tears as she gazed solemnly up at him. "I don't feel very strong."

He grasped her hands and pulled her close so he could kiss her sweet lips. "I'm here for you. I will be strong for you."

She stared at him then sighed. "The next days will be difficult but it helps to have you at my side."

He pressed another gentle kiss on her mouth and then nodded once. "Go tell Sheridan and Hannah what has happened. I'll send word to the sheriff and get the hands to help me clean up the room before you go back up. Agreed?"

She nodded, the movement releasing a lone tear to trickle down her cheek. He brushed it away with the pad of his thumb and then leaned his forehead to hers. Closing his eyes, he remained still, willing his strength to support hers. After a long moment, he straightened and searched her eyes. What he saw there broke his heart. The anxiety and grief swamping her usual sparkling and mischievous eyes.

He vowed to catch the men who caused her such pain even if it were the last thing he did. The big question was where to start the search since they'd escaped without him being able to identify them. Even their horses were plain bays with no distinguishing markings he recalled. He sighed as he parted with Cassie, she to head to the kitchen to inform Sheridan and the others about Mercy's demise and he to the stable to begin preparations for a funeral.

One thing he knew for certain. Maybe not that week, or month, or even year, but someday he'd find those men and make them pay.

Was she breathing? Cassie sat up straighter in the upholstered chair beside her mother's velvet-draped casket on display in front of the fireplace in the parlor. The stiff fabric of Cassie's black mourning gown crinkled as she leaned forward and peered closer at her mother's body laid out in the plain pine casket. Sitting vigil on a quiet Sunday evening, alone, left her too much time to imagine her mother hadn't died after all. Perhaps shocked into a deep unconsciousness mimicking death but not actually dead. Or maybe the good lord would see fit to restore her to health. She closed her eyes and sighed. Why did Ma have to die?

Flint had arranged for the Bakers' carpenter to build the hurriedly made coffin. Hannah arranged for the laundress to quickly dye a dress and undergarments black for each of them in the huge dye pot behind the laundry shack. The awful stench lingered in the clearing, drifting through the open windows. Cassie had immediately draped all the mirrors with black material as required and Flint stopped the small clock in her parents' bedroom to prevent the rest of the household from having bad luck. The men handled moving the body downstairs so the group of women from neighboring homes, organized by Tabitha Baker, could prepare her mother for the laying out of the dead and visitation. Thank goodness she ultimately hadn't been allowed to help. She didn't think she'd survive such an intimate handling of her mother's body. Tomorrow she anticipated a steady flow of friends and neighbors stopping in to pay their respects. Now all she had to do was keep watch over her mother's inert form until the actual funeral the next day.

A mix of irritation and regret simmered in her chest as she stared at her ma. The women had dressed her in one of her favorite gowns and arranged her hair, folded her hands over her stomach. Ma looked more peaceful than ever. Cassie sucked in air and held it for a moment before easing it back out through her nose. She needed to restore her composure. Naturally sadness followed her mother's death. But her death also trapped Cassie at the inn with no escape possible for months, if ever.

As the only Fairhope, it fell to her to represent the family in her mother's place. At least until her father returned. Even then, she might not have the courage to leave him on his own. He may need her help and she could never turn her back on her father. He'd done so much for her over her lifetime. The sting from his birthday gift still smarted but he had sent it out of love for her, however misguided.

In addition, they still had the impending visit by the senator and family to prepare for. How on earth could they prepare for such an important event without her mother or father present to guide the effort? If her brothers were around, they'd have a better chance. But they wouldn't likely venture home without a compelling reason. Like her mother's death.

She stifled a cry, a sob, a wail of anguish with a hand over her mouth. How was she supposed to carry on without her parents? What should she do? Flint, of course, would continue to manage the business operations. But taking care of the residence side had been her mother's main function, which just became hers. In addition to the garden and helping Sheridan in the kitchen. And now helping Flint with planning for the most important occurrence in the inn's existence.

A chilling thought made her grip the armrests. Would she have to give up helping in the kitchen in order to manage all the rest? She loved prepping the vegetables and fruits for her friend. Savored every minute spent in the bustling, friendly kitchen. It pulsed with life and activity aimed at helping others with a hearty meal and a refreshing beverage after a hard ride or long day. Working side by side with the older black man with the laughing light brown eyes was the highlight of her day.

One other change resulted from her mother's demise. The courtship and marriage plan had gone out the window. She had no reason to leave but every reason to stay and help her pa. Her ma would want her to do as much in her honor. She blew out a frustrated breath. All her dreams and desires lay dead at her feet.

The door from the dogtrot opened to let Sheridan ease into the room. "Cassie, may I come in?"

"Of course." A shiver wiggled down her spine. She'd been thinking about him and suddenly he appeared? Unable to remain still, she rose and met him in the center of the parlor, accepting his outstretched hand with her own. "She always thought highly of you."

He nodded once, his serious eyes fixed on her gaze. "I'm so sorry for your loss, Cassie. Is there anything…"

She shook her head. Nobody could do anything to assuage the grief and profound sadness filling her. But not sitting vigil by herself might help with the inner distress building with each added awareness about her new reality. "Come sit with me awhile."

She resumed her seat while Sheridan snatched up another

chair and carried it over to position it near hers. Settling onto the hard wooden surface, he crossed his ankles and let his elbows drop to the carved armrests. Her mother had chosen the set of dining chairs when they lived in Montgomery. Mercy loved their high polish and intricate scrollwork on the legs and arms. She'd been proud to successfully barter for the set, exchanging two of her best pastoral paintings for six chairs. Not only did she acquire something beautiful for her home but she also had the pleasure of someone else finding value in her talent. Her mother had given up what she termed the frivolity of painting after they'd moved to the northern wilderness. She'd claimed the additional work necessary to build and sustain the inn kept her too busy. Cassie didn't believe the number of chores the only reason but her ma never said more on the subject. How distressed and depressed had her mother been with her life? She'd never know now. Never be able to ask.

Sheridan whipped out a handkerchief from an inner pocket and handed it to her. She blinked and then realized she'd started crying. Again. She dabbed her eyes with the clean white cloth, trying to stop the flow.

"Thank you." She clutched the handkerchief and attempted but failed to smile at him.

"I imagine you're still in shock after your mother's sudden death." He laced his fingers together over his black vest. "It's a terrible thing."

She blotted the tears from her cheeks, struggling to hold back more of them. "It makes no sense. Why her?"

"We're so far out it does seem unlikely it was mere opportunity." He steepled his fingers as he tilted his head in thought. "Like they knew she had something worth risking their necks to get ahold of."

"She didn't have much easily resold for cash, nor did she have any cash or gold." She rested her head on the back of the high seat and regarded her friend.

"What about her treasure you were bragging about the other day?" He winked at her as he dropped his hands into his lap. "Maybe they were after that."

She pursed her lips and brushed his comment aside with a wave of her hand. "Her treasure? We both know she only had a collection of stuff from when we lived in southern Alabama."

The items carried more than a hundred miles along rough roads, across rivers and swamps. Each must have also carried a wealth of sentimental memories for her mother or she wouldn't have bothered with transporting them under such difficult conditions.

"But you called it her treasure the other day in the dining room." He chuckled lightly. "I thought at first you were serious, but then realized you were joking."

"Of course, I was teasing." She shook her head once and then froze. "Oh my god."

The blood drained from her head to leave her shaking in horror.

She'd never given any thought to her declaration in front of so many people. Strangers who wouldn't, *couldn't* know if she were serious or not. She searched her memory of the moment, the terrible moment when her careless teasing gave someone the idea of money or gold or both hidden in her mother's room. Tried to see again who might have overheard. The men who might have become greedy enough to return and go after the bounty. The nonexistent treasure. Then to kill her mother when she couldn't hand it over.

Her mother's death was all her fault.

"Oh." She covered her face with both hands and keened as guilt spiked in her heart.

Sheridan leapt from his chair and grabbed her shoulders. "Are you alright?"

His strong arm around her shoulders steadied her. She

lowered her hands from her tear-soaked face and stared into Sheridan's worried eyes.

"What's the matter?" Sheridan moved to squat beside her trembling knees. "Tell me what I can do."

"She died because of me." The words echoed in the silent room, lingering in the air like the stench of the black dye.

"No, honey, you didn't kill her. Those bad men did." Sheridan patted her knee with one hand. "Don't blame yourself."

Of course she blamed herself. She'd not given thought to the consequences, the ramifications of stupid comments in the wrong place. Around people she barely knew. Around people whose intentions she couldn't know. How could she trust folks when they acted for their own best interest without a care for how it might impact others?

"You warned me, but too late. If I hadn't mentioned Ma's treasure in front of all those strangers, she wouldn't be dead." She welcomed the warmth of his hand when he clasped hers. Staring at the gentle strength of her friend, a knot formed in her throat the more she pondered her stupid, naïve actions. "I'll never forgive myself, Sheridan."

She'd loved her mother with all her heart. Despite her over-protective stance, she had always worked for Cassie's best interests. She harbored such a deep love for her daughter, she had tried to provide the guidance and education she felt would best serve to make her an intelligent and savvy young woman. She'd done her best. Was it her ma's fault she didn't fully understand what Cassie wanted when Cassie hadn't ever made it clear to her? Never had the nerve to stand up and declare her own intentions for her future? She wasn't worthy of her mother's love.

She wasn't worthy of anyone's love. Not after what she'd done. When Flint found out how she'd caused her mother's death with a few careless words, he likely wouldn't have anything more to do with her. Walk away and not look back. She wouldn't blame him. What if she caused his death with other careless words? The idea of his death choked her like a hand around her throat. She couldn't swallow, couldn't speak. Couldn't bear to contemplate his dying as a result of her actions. She gasped and covered her mouth with trembling fingers.

"Cassie, listen to me." Sheridan patted her knee and then stood up to tower over her. "You didn't pull the trigger."

"It's all a piece. What I said led directly to her death." She hugged herself, holding on tight to try to prevent falling into little bits of desolation and anguish. "I can't forgive myself for being so stupid."

Sheridan paced several strides away and then turned to look at her, gripping the back of his neck with one hand. On a sigh, he strode back to take his seat again. Leaning on his elbows, he peered at her. "One day, my dear, you will see you're wrong."

"I doubt it." She dropped her hands to her lap as her gaze drifted to rest on her dead mother's body. She swallowed the tears clawing for release. Crying wouldn't help her overcome the depth of guilt reverberating in her soul. "Somehow, someway I'll find a way to make it up to her. To my pa, too. To everyone."

Then maybe she'd be earn the right to be loved again.

Chapter Eleven

ew glistened on the grassy rise behind the inn. The sunshine slowly evaporated the moisture, creating a shimmering in the muggy air. Flint contemplated the low hills rising in the distance, varying shades of green mingling with dark shadowy valleys. If he peered close enough, he could detect the difference between the shiny deciduous leaves and the blurry clusters of spiky pine needles. The cloudless sky allowed the sun to illuminate the hillside in a wash of light. A few minutes of quiet allowed him to compose himself. He needed to be strong for Cassie.

A breeze brushed his cheek, lifting his hair to dance around his head. Ere long he'd need to have Hannah snip it shorter but he enjoyed the play of his hair in the wind. Even such a simple thing as leaving his hair loose gave him a tiny sense of freedom and lightness during such a somber period of mourning. He glanced down at the dark blue suit he wore. He didn't have time or money to purchase a complete black mourning suit. As a friend of the family, he wasn't required to wear mourning but he did want to show his respect for Cassie's grief.

Which made him think about the custom of how long she would be in mourning for the death of her parent.

Custom dictated six months of deep mourning followed by six more of half-mourning and then three more of light mourning. If she followed the strictest rules out of love and respect. He watched the two stable hands cross the back yard with spades to finish digging the grave in the small area marked off for the family cemetery. She loved her mother but they fought so often, would she follow the rules? He huffed. She wasn't one to do so. No, she'd mourn in a way as distinct as her person.

The door opened behind him, drawing his attention. He glanced over his shoulder. Sterling and Abigail Nelson strode onto the porch and made their way toward the grouping of chairs and tables at the other end. Nelson had offered his condolences upon Mercy's death and asked to be permitted to attend the poor woman's funeral. Flint had requested and received Cassie's agreement and thus the couple waited for the ceremony to begin.

Light footsteps on the wooden boards on his other side made him turn to see Cassie slowly approaching. Her long unadorned black dress made her look even smaller. Her red-rimmed eyes and pale face reflected her grief. She halted in front of him and aimed sad eyes at him.

"Are you ready for this?" He searched her distraught expression, missing the flash of her dimple as she stared at him in silence. "You are not required to attend if you're not up to it."

She let her gaze slide away to anchor on the two men putting the finishing touches to the roughly rectangular hole in the ground. The ring of metal on an occasional rock reached his ears as he followed the direction of her regard. He rested a finger on her forearm, drawing her attention away from the cemetery.

"Cassie?" He studied her features and suppressed a sigh of his own. She seemed upset and nervous. "What's the matter?"

She looked up at him and shook her head. "It's all my fault."

"What is?" A frown tugged his brows as he tried to make sense of her statement.

Tears trailed down her cheeks, following the curve of her high cheekbones and then down to slide under her jaw. "All of this."

"All of what?"

She pulled a kerchief from a pocket in her skirt and dabbed at her eyes and cheeks. Her shoulders drooped as she looked at the floor. "I killed my mother as surely as if I had pulled the trigger."

"I don't believe you had any part in your mother's death." He lifted her chin so she could see his serious expression. Tears pooled in her eyes until she blinked and then they dripped onto her pallid flesh. "We weren't even in the house when those men did the unthinkable."

She pulled her chin away and cleared her throat. Dabbed at her eyes again as she bit her lip. "They wouldn't have been there if I hadn't foolishly mentioned my mother's treasure. Nobody would have known about it. So yes, it's my fault for opening my mouth when I shouldn't have."

"Sweetheart, don't think that way." He took one of her hands and held it loosely. "You didn't make those men greedy and despicable."

"I acted stupidly and Ma died as a result." She stared at him while tears slowly coursed down her face. "I'm not worthy of being loved by anyone. Including you."

"I care for you, Cassie. Your mother's death doesn't change my feelings for you in the slightest." He pulled on her hand until she nodded once. A slight acknowledgement of his real meaning. "You definitely deserve to be loved, so don't fret. Please?"

"I can't agree." She stepped back and shook her head at him. "Don't press me. I want to get through today and try to find some way to make amends for my previous ill-considered actions."

He opened his mouth to say something, anything to make her feel better, but the residence door opened. Hannah stepped outside and held the door for the pallbearers, husbands and sons of the ladies who had taken charge of washing and dressing her mother's body, to carry the casket across the porch. They solemnly marched past Flint and Cassie and down the back steps to the yard, careful to keep the casket level as they descended the few steps.

Cassie squared her shoulders and drew in a long breath before blowing it out silently. "I guess it's time."

Flint proffered his arm and she clung to it as they followed the procession to the grave. The dew had dried in the growing heat of the summer day, leaving the grass smelling sweet and fresh. Each step brought them closer to the final moment when the casket would be lowered into the ground and covered with rich soil. The Nelsons appeared at his side when he and Cassie stopped beside the grave. The casket rested on a pair of sawhorses beside the opening, waiting for those attending to say a few words about Mercy's life, followed by a scripture passage and prayer.

He scanned the group gathering for the funeral, acknowledging each individual with a tilt of his head. Cassie squeezed his arm, drawing his attention to her.

"Who is that?" She indicated with her head for him to look down the clearing. "By the garden."

He swiveled his head to see what she meant. A child hunkered by the fence, facing the mass of people. Wearing some kind of short-sleeve tan shirt and brown trousers on his thin frame. A floppy hat shaded his features from the sun. "I don't recognize him."

"Me, either, but I don't like that he's there." She lifted her free hand to shade her eyes. "What's he about? I wonder…"

"What?" Flint perused her frowning countenance. "Have you seen him before?"

"No, but I've found the garden gate propped open more than once since the deer incident." She glanced up at him and then back to the boy. "Maybe it's been him all along."

"Do you want me to go chase him off?" He shifted his stance, prepared to jog down to the unknown visitor and ask a few pointed questions.

"There's no time now. We'll deal with him later, I promise. Just keep an eye on him." She glanced back to the grave and then sighed. "Here comes Sheridan."

Reluctantly, Flint focused on the black man approaching as Cassie requested rather than going after the boy. Still, he wondered and worried about the child's presence. He'd never seen the boy—he thought the child was a boy, but wasn't really sure—before. Did any of the neighboring farms have children? A good question. He'd never paid much attention to the composition of the families of the neighbors before. Why would he when he only planned to work at the inn for a brief span of time?

Sheridan strode up wearing a black armband around his upper arm out of respect for his employer and friend's death. The black man's features were somber as he opened a black, leather-bound bible. His light brown eyes met Flint's gaze, a question lurking in their depths.

"Thanks for agreeing to read the passage and lead the prayer." Flint nodded at Sheridan, firming his lips for an instant. "I know she'd want you to."

Sheridan nodded as he turned the pages until he reached the one he sought. "I'm honored to be asked." He glanced at Cassie with a small smile. "Thank you."

She inclined her head but remained silent. She stared at the casket as the crowd slowly grew with the arrival of several more of the long-time customers who happened to hear of Mercy's tragic death and made a point of attending.

Flint believed they came not for Mercy's sake but for Cassie's. She'd always been sweet to the people who enjoyed meals and beverages at the inn. Ensuring they had what they needed all with a friendly smile in place.

Sheridan ambled around the small crowd to stand at the head of the casket and cleared his throat. "Ladies and gentlemen, we're gathered today to say farewell to our friend, Mercy Fairhope. If you'd like to say a few words about her or share your memories of her, please feel free to speak now."

Flint listened as one after another shared a short story, a memory of how much Mercy had done or how much she meant to them. Cassie stood still beside him, silent as she drank in the words of affection and respect regarding her mother. A flash of light caught his attention, followed by a slight breeze to cool his cheeks. He glanced over Cassie's head and nearly gasped when he spotted Mercy's ghost hovering under the trees edging the forest. A smile grew on her lips the longer she stood and listened to the people talk about her life.

How long had she been there without him knowing? Should he tell Cassie? Or did she already know and was trying to ignore the haint? He hadn't seen the woman's spirit since Cassie fainted. After Cassie had asked about whether she'd actually seen her mother's ghost, she hadn't mentioned it again. The struggle between being open and honest about his ability to not only see but to converse with ghosts and keeping his secret to himself raged in his chest as he glanced between Cassie and her mother's ghost.

The inner struggle ended when the spirit captured his gaze with a wink and a nod and then vanished. He released the breath he unknowingly held and suppressed the shiver racing down his spine.

Sheridan's voice brought Flint back to the present. "Let us pray."

Flint bowed his head. Yes, please. Prayer was exactly what he needed.

The sticky mass of bread dough shuddered with each pounding. Cassie lifted an edge and folded it over, mashing her hands into the springy substance again and again. Kneading dough helped relieve her self-deprecation and grief. Something had to help release the tension coiled inside her gut.

"Don't try to kill the bread dough." Hannah chuckled from her side of the large work table where she shredded a roasted chicken into bite-size pieces. "It can't fight back."

"Ha, ha." Cassie folded the dough and punched it down. Then divided it into pieces to shape into several small round loaves. Leave it to Hannah to poke the sore spot in her heart.

Cassie glanced over to the Marple sisters, their plain hickory brown dresses and white aprons displaying the amount of effort they put into their work, busily scrubbing potatoes and carrots. She appreciated the hard-working older sisters who lived down the road and showed up every morning at dawn to help ready the fruits and vegetables for the day's menu. A large black kettle hung over the fire, steam rising in a steady column up the chimney. The chicken chowder had become a favorite for the midday repast. Sheridan would arrive before long to combine the ingredients with his signature touch of herbs and spices.

Hannah pinned her with a slight frown pulling on her brows. "I was joking. I'm sorry if you thought otherwise."

Cassie patted a piece of dough into a slightly flattened ball and then pulled on the top to make a knob which would serve as a handle for the lid of the bread bowl. Pressing her lips together to prevent saying something she'd regret, she placed the loaf on the wooden paddle in preparation to slide the dough into the heated brick oven. Even with the windows open, the heat from both the cook fire and the hot bread oven had everyone glistening with perspiration.

Snagging another lump of dough, she shot a quelling glance at Hannah. "It's been a difficult day."

Only that morning they'd buried her mother in a hole in the ground. Right out back of the residence. Nice words had been said over her before shovels were used to throw dirt on the casket. The resulting thuds reverberating in her chest like thunder rolling across a stormy sky. She'd hoped for a lightning strike sent by the heavens to end her misery. None came. Afterward, she'd sought something to do with her hands rather than sit and brood on her actions and their effect. Rather than dwell on her guilt and grief. Better to keep her thoughts to herself and remain silent.

Hannah nodded once and then focused on her task. "Yes, it has been a tough day for everyone."

Cassie finished shaping the loaves and then lugged the heavy paddle over to the oven. Resting the edge of the paddle on the work table, she grabbed a handful of her skirt to open the hot metal oven door. Then she slid the loaves off the wooden surface and onto the brick floor of the oven. She let the paddle drop out of the hot oven and then closed the door with a clang of metal against brick. She wiped the sweat from her brow with the back of one hand as she crossed back to the table to start the next batch of dough.

She started to scoop flour into a large wooden bowl when a flash of light caught her attention. She glanced toward the end of the table nearest the kitchen door and then stilled, her mouth dropping open as she swallowed a scream. Her mother stood at the end of the table, a frown marring her pretty features. Wearing her favorite dress Cassie had selected for her to be buried in. Her hair cascaded down, shifting as by a light breeze to dance around her shoulders.

"What's wrong with you?" Hannah paused in chopping chicken with a sharp knife to aim quizzical eyes at Cassie.

Cassie inclined her head toward her mother's ghost and arched her brows. Hannah bit her lip as she turned to follow the direction of Cassie's gaze. Then the scream stalled in Cassie's throat erupted from Hannah's. Eyes wide, the terrified woman raced out of the room, the swinging door banging the wall after she left.

"Oh!"

The startled cry made Cassie cut a glance at Meg and Myrtle. The sisters dropped the potatoes they'd been scrubbing, leaving them to roll across the floor. Wide-eyed and trembling, they sidled quickly across the kitchen and out the door, brown leather boots pounding on the hard floor. The distant slam of the front door reverberated in the silence left after their sudden departure.

Cassie couldn't leave without passing close to the ghost and she really didn't want to do such a daring thing. She longed for Flint to come give her some support. After all, he claimed to be able to see ghosts, too. Which meant he'd been telling the truth all along.

"Cassie…" Mercy stretched a hand toward her daughter. Her voice emerged raspy and harsh, unlike her normal melodious if harsh tones.

Great. Cassie could not only see but hear ghosts, too. How had such an ability escaped her notice until her mother's ghost stood feet away, calling to her?

"Ma, what are you doing here?" She wrapped her arms around her waist, trying to still the trembling shaking her to the core. She silently chanted "she won't hurt me" to keep from following the other three women. Alone, she faced Mercy and hoped she hadn't put her faith in the wrong hands.

Mercy dropped her hand to her side. "You must… avenge…my death."

"Do you know who killed you?" Cassie's teeth chattered in the chill invading the kitchen.

Mercy shook her head as she glared at Cassie. "No. But they…came to the…inn."

Speech seemed difficult for her ma. Had the men strangled her and she hadn't noticed? She frowned at the idea of missing a detail of such importance. But she'd figured the men must have frequented the inn or they couldn't have known about the treasure. Wouldn't have plotted to steal it. To kill her mother. Who stood in the kitchen as a translucent version of herself. The shivers increased until she feared she'd fall.

The kitchen door burst open and Sheridan hurried into the room, a worried frown creasing his forehead. Then he stopped when he spotted Mercy. Cassie saw the fear suddenly blanket the dark-skinned man. Saw it in his wide eyes and shaking shoulders, the ashen complexion beneath his dark skin. He'd already said he didn't want to hear anything about ghosts and then to meet one. No wonder he'd reacted strongly to such an occasion. Mercy shot him a stern look and waved a hand to shoo him out of the room. Sheridan darted a hopeful glance at Cassie and she nodded. Relief replacing the worry, he spun and marched out of the room, the door swinging wildly.

Alone again with her mother, Cassie forced a deep breath and relaxed her shoulders. Her mother, in life or after, wouldn't hurt her. She needn't fear the haint. She only needed to adjust to the concept of conversing with a ghost. Easy. She mentally shook herself and squared her shoulders.

"Flint has told Sheriff Neal of your murder and the theft of the keys." Cassie pressed her palms to the work table, puffs of flour rising around her fingers. "I don't know what I can do."

"I saw…them." Mercy leaned forward to bring her glimmering face closer. "Tell him…I can help…identify the…three men even…though I don't…know names."

Having her mother near to talk with provided a small measure of comfort. She wasn't gone entirely from her life. Cassie could still ask for her advice, her guidance, if she wanted. Her mother would be around. Whether Cassie wanted her or not. A kindness or a curse?

"Ma, I'm so sorry." Cassie blinked back a tear pressing for release. "I didn't mean to…"

Mercy frowned at her, quirking her mouth to one side for an instant. "What?"

The moment of truth. "I told Sheridan about your 'treasure' and those men must have thought it gold or something else valuable. That's why they killed you. Because of my stupidity."

She dragged in a breath and blew it out, guilt swamping her heart. She had to tell Ma what had happened and why she felt so bad about all of it. Yet forcing the admission from her lips proved more difficult than she'd imagined. If her mother were alive, she'd probably kill her for being so stupid and naïve.

"If I'd kept my mouth shut…" She breathed heavily for a short span, struggling to maintain her composure while breaking apart inside. "None of this would have happened. You'd still be alive."

Mercy studied her in silence and then shook her head. "I don't…blame you…my dear."

"Perhaps not, but I blame myself. I'm such an idiot."

Mercy shook her head harder and drifted closer to where Cassie gripped the edge of the table with both hands. "Don't…You didn't…put a…bullet…in my head."

She tasted salt and realized she'd started crying. "My casual comment had the same ultimate conclusion. I don't know if I can ever forgive myself."

Mercy opened her arms and smiled at Cassie. "I forgive…you. I…love you…. I only…ever wanted…the best for…you, my…darling."

Sobbing, Cassie covered her face with her hands. The weight of guilt and grief lifted a fraction from her shoulders. After a moment, she wiped her face with her fingers and attempted a weak smile at her mother.

Only, she was gone.

Frantically, she searched the kitchen. She had more questions. Needed answers. Flint would need answers. She glanced around the kitchen, remembering her mother's words. Her mother could help identify the men. Once they found them. But how would they start such a search and how would they know when they'd located the right three men?

At least her mother forgave her. In time, maybe Cassie could forgive herself. One thing remained certain. She wanted to find the culprits and retrieve the stolen keys. Keys which opened important locks in her mother's life and which had become Cassie's destiny. She wouldn't fail her mother again.

Chapter Twelve

The ride back to the inn passed far too quickly for his peace of mind. Flint trotted the sturdy buckskin gelding up the road leading toward the welcoming structure feeling depressed and defeated. According to Sheriff Neal, unless Flint could determine who the culprits were they would likely get away with the murder. How on earth was he to figure out the identity of the strangers when he had little idea of their description?

The description he had could fit most of the men in the entire region. Tall, strong, swaggered from riding horses all their lives. Riding bay horses. But hair color or eye color? Anything distinguishing? He had nothing.

While in town, he'd scrawled a letter to Reggie Fairhope informing him of his wife's death and urging him to return at his earliest convenience. He didn't expect the man to drop everything and race home. He couldn't do anything to reverse the death. She'd already been properly buried. Flint would stay and continue to manage the daily operations. Cassie and the others would pitch in to keep things running smoothly as they cleaned and primped for the senator's visit in a few months. Most likely, Reggie wouldn't arrive until the end of October as planned. Whenever he started for home, the combination of distance, rugged mountains, and pitiful roads meant a long and arduous journey. Made even more so if he brought a quantity of furniture with him.

He slowed Buck to a walk as they turned onto the carriageway leading to the stone steps of the inn. The sun slowly sank toward its bed for the night. Beau and Pickles rose to their feet in greeting when he halted in front of the inn and dismounted. Jericho hustled out of the barn to jog over to take the horse's reins and lead him back to the stable.

With a sigh, Flint climbed the steps, his new flintlock pistol bumping against his hip. Until those men were caught, he'd stay vigilant and ready to defend the people who lived, worked, and visited at the inn. But he dreaded having to tell Cassie his news. Pausing at the edge of the dogtrot he heard raised voices coming from the family parlor through the open windows. Changing direction, he strode to the door and pushed inside. Cassie paced quickly from one end of the parlor to the other and back again. Sheridan, arms crossed, stood by the doll's house, a frown of concern creasing his forehead. They both turned to stare at Flint as he closed the door behind him.

"What's wrong?" Flint moved to the middle of the room and addressed Cassie who seemed more agitated than the cook. "What's all the shouting about?"

"We have a major problem." Sheridan stepped closer to shake his head at Cassie. "The Marple sisters and Hannah have run away because we saw a haint, Mercy's to be exact, in the kitchen. We don't have enough hands in the kitchen without them."

The frightened man appeared to want to follow the ladies' lead and leave the premises. Sheridan had already stated his opinion on the subject of ghosts and now seemed on the verge of quitting as a result of the possibility.

"You're sure?" Flint held his breath in anticipation of the

man's reaction. Not everyone liked the idea of spirits hovering about. "You saw her, too?"

"Yes. I warned you about my stance on ghosts around here." Sheridan's brows drew together and he pursed his lips for a beat. "I'm not staying if that be so, Mr. Hamilton. The idea is unnerving."

"Sheridan, my man, you're a strong guy and you understand the way of the world." He nodded encouragingly, seeking the man's agreement.

Sheridan nodded once but his eyes turned wary as he continued to glance between Flint and Cassie. "Go on."

"So you know we can't always explain everything we experience." Flint shrugged and forced a smile in place. "Sometimes we have to accept facts."

"Especially since I talked to her." Cassie grabbed Flint's upper arms with both her hands and peered up at him. "She's here to help."

"Who?" But he knew from Cassie's pale cheeks and overly bright eyes.

"Ma. Or rather—" She fluttered a hand in the air as she spun away and resumed her pacing. "Her ghost."

Flint flung a glance at Sheridan who shook his head slowly back and forth. "Really?"

"She said she's seen the men before. They'd dined here." Cassie's firm steps slowed until she stopped in front of him again. "She wants me to, and I quote, avenge her death."

He stifled the surprise at her revelation. It made perfect sense for her mother to linger and seek vengeance for her murder. For her to appear to her daughter to ask for her help. He studied Cassie's flushed face and glittery eyes and relaxed. She'd accepted the presence of her mother's ghost far easier than he had accepted his ability to see spirits. Mercy's demand, though, might not ever come to pass.

"I wish it were possible." Flint sighed and dragged a hand through his hair. "The sheriff needs names."

"Then we'll have to get them." Cassie laid a hand on his crossed arm and searched his expression with serious eyes. "Ma said she'd help."

He raised his brows as his heart thundered in his chest. "How might she be able to help?

What kind of help, exactly? She'd actively worked against him while alive. She most likely hadn't changed her opinion of him after death. Especially after Mercy discovered Cassie asked him to court her the same day the woman died. Maybe they shouldn't reveal their agreement for the present time. Conflicting emotions and thoughts warred in his mind as he studied Cassie and Sheridan.

Sheridan huffed and folded his arms over his chest. "You two are making no sense whatsoever."

Flint addressed the upset man, searching for words to help him accept and understand the situation. "Don't be afraid, Sheridan. Mercy won't harm you or anyone else."

Sheridan's ebony skin blanched two shades lighter as his brows dropped over scared eyes. "You're telling me you're content to have her haunting this place?"

Flint had to convince Sheridan to stay and help. Not only because he needed the cook's expertise in order to impress the senator and to continue to draw customers but also because Cassie relied upon the other man's friendship and guidance. Someone she'd lean on even more now her mother lay dead and her father hundreds of miles away. Brothers, too, stayed far away and only reachable by letters.

"I imagine her sudden death left her with unfinished business she wants to deal with before she can rest in peace." Flint studied the man ready to bolt out of the room. "Come on, man, you've nothing to fear from her ghost. She liked you, you know that."

His slow nod gave Flint hope. "I liked her, too, when she wasn't trying to run everything her way."

Flint chuckled to alleviate the serious discussion. "Right. So now you can run the kitchen however you see fit without her interference. Or at least mostly."

"What do you mean?" Sheridan tilted his head to one side to look askance at Flint.

"I still have some say in the menu and such." Flint raised a hand to ward off Sheridan's bristling countenance. "But you manage the kitchen as you see fit."

"Without Hannah." Cassie shrugged. "I went after her but she'd packed her stuff and fled anyway. Said she couldn't stay at a haunted inn, especially with it being Mercy's ghost."

"She quit?" Flint peered at Cassie's grin and twinkling eyes. "I'd counted on her to help us keep the place running smoothly after…"

Cassie shrugged and chuckled. "Nah. We'll be fine without her. I'm sure we can find another serving wench who won't flirt quite so much with the menfolk."

"What about Myrtle and Meg?" He hoped they hadn't been scared off as well. He couldn't manage without the scullery maids to maintain the flow of foodstuffs from the kitchen to the dining tables for the many customers who frequented the inn.

"I saw them flee, too." Sheridan shook his head again. "Don't know if they're coming back."

"I'll have to go talk to them, I guess." Flint raked his hand through his hair again. "Try to convince them to stay."

Sheridan nodded and dropped his hands to his sides. "They have been a big help in the kitchen. If not them, you'll need to hire someone else to take their place. I can't be doing everything all by myself."

Flint smiled at the burly man as relief flowed into his soul. Sheridan was staying. "I'll see what I can do. In the meantime, we need to get back to work."

Sheridan sighed and started out of the room. "I'll go see what's going on over there."

"Right behind you. Cassie?" Flint detained her with a hand on her upper arm.

She stopped beside him to gaze up at him. "Yes?"

"I sent a letter to your dad while I was in town, telling him about Mercy's death and suggesting he come home." He relished seeing the touch of color return to her cheeks from all the excitement. "Perhaps you should write your brothers as well?"

"I've been thinking about what I'd say to them. We could use their help and expertise. Their connections." She moistened her lips with a swipe of her tongue. "I don't know if they'll heed my call for their return. It's not like they're very close to her after all she said and did."

"Do I want to know?"

She shook her head. "It's not very important at this point."

Maybe not but he had one other concern on his mind.

"My dear, do you still care for me?" He searched her eyes, looking for her truth. Looking for her continued affection and attention after her doubts and depression.

She studied him as she dragged in a shaky breath and released it slowly. "I can't help feeling fond of you. I'm glad you're here with me."

He smiled as relief and hope flooded his core. "Then our courtship may continue as planned."

The light in her eyes dimmed as her dimple disappeared. "I don't know how you could still want me after my stupidity. I feel I've lost the right to invite your attention."

He pivoted to face her, take her hands and tug her closer. He pressed a kiss to her cool lips and then pulled back a space to regard her serious countenance. She still held back from being fully in a relationship with him. Needed time and distance from the untimely death of her mother in order to come to terms with the many ways her life had changed as a result. He'd give as much to her, wait patiently. Or as patiently as he could when what he really wanted was to protect her from ever feeling such pain again.

"I don't know how to stop wanting to be with you, sweetheart." As her eyes overflowed with tears, he embraced her, holding her as she wept against his heart.

Morning sunshine streamed into the kitchen where Cassie scrubbed carrots. With only herself and Sheridan to prepare everything, she'd risen earlier than usual to begin the day's chores. Dropping the bunch of carrots onto the work table beside the cluster of celery stalks, she dried her hands on her apron and then picked up a sharp knife. Deftly, she trimmed and cut up the vegetables and added them to a large ceramic bowl of chopped parsnips.

Sheridan hurried through the swinging door carrying a burlap wrapped haunch of meat—ham from the shape of it—and grinned at her. "Good morning. I see you're up with the sun."

"Before, actually." Cassie finished the last stalk of celery and laid down the knife. "What do you think about adding some yellow squash for color to the dish you're making?"

"I hadn't considered that, but yeah. Let's try it." Sheridan placed the meat on the table and began unwrapping the salted shroud.

"I'll be right back." Cassie scurried outside to retrieve some ripe squash from the garden.

She strode onto the back porch and glanced across the grassy expanse as she started down the steps. She halted briefly when she noticed the young boy, dressed in the same outfit as the last time she saw him, arms full, walking through the open gate. His youthful arms struggled to juggle several ears of corn and some squash. After the funeral, he'd disappeared, but she'd found the gate propped open again a day or two later with a child's footprint in the damp earth.

But this? The little thief dared to steal her hard work in broad daylight? Not if she could help it.

"Hey!" She raced down the steps and ran toward him. "Stop!"

Her shout startled the boy. He spun to aim wide eyes at her before hugging his bounty to his chest and running in the opposite direction. A yellow squash dropped to the ground and he swiftly turned and snatched it up and then ran on.

She raced after him, holding her skirts as she struggled to close the distance. He may be a young boy, but he sure could run. A stitch in her side made her gasp and slow her pace, but she persisted in chasing after him. Suddenly, Flint appeared on a young black gelding at the far end of the clearing. She waved a hand wildly in the air to attract his attention.

"Flint, stop him!"

Flint nodded and urged his horse toward the boy who suddenly veered away to dash between several trees, dropping the produce as Flint swiftly caught him up. Flint leaned down as the horse crashed through the underbrush and disappeared into the forest after the thief. Cassie slowed to a fast walk, pressing a hand to the sharp pain in her side. When she reached the discarded vegetables she picked them up and cradled them in her apron. Thrashing and shouts drifted to her ears from the forest and then stopped. She waited, scanning the trees for any sign of Flint's return. With or without the boy. She hoped for *with* so she could give the child a piece of her upset mind.

After several minutes, Flint emerged from the shadows with the boy on the saddle in front of him. When he reined to a halt, he handed the boy down to Cassie's waiting grasp on his wrist.

"Let me go!" The boy kicked out at her, connecting with her shin.

"Ow! Stop that." The sudden pain made her drop the corn and squash again. They'd be ruined, which made her blood boil. All her hard work left to rot because of some scrawny, scared child. She shook him until he quit squirming. "What's your name, boy?"

"Let me go." He turned wary eyes up at her.

"Your name." She squeezed his wrist and lifted one brow.

"Teddy." He spit it out like he'd eaten a bad grape. "Not that you care."

"Oh, but I do, Teddy. See it's like this…" She motioned to the stolen produce scattered at her feet. "Growing the food we use takes me a lot of time and effort. You're stealing what's mine. I'm going to have to report this to the sheriff. What's your father's name?"

The boy's face paled as his eyes widened. "Please, miss, you can't tell him."

Flint dismounted and dropped the reins to ground tie the horse. He towered over the frightened boy but otherwise made no move toward him. "We most certainly will. Now tell us his name."

"Please…" Teddy cast about for some means of escape but Cassie took hold of his shoulders to make him face her.

"Teddy, you must tell us. Now." She squeezed his shoulders, saw the fear replaced with resentful defeat. "Come on."

He kicked the grass, dirt exploding into the air. "Adam Jacobs."

Flint nodded as he squatted down in front of Teddy. "That's the first step toward making up for what you've done. Why did you steal food?"

"'Cause I'm hungry, why else." The boy heaved a sigh as he put a hand to his stomach. "Ain't had nothing to eat in days."

"I see." Flint silently regarded the boy for several moments. "You know what you've done is wrong, don't you?"

He hung his head for a second and then lifted his gaze to look Flint in the eyes. "I did what I had to and I'd do it again so I don't feel hungry all the time."

The poor child. Cassie regarded the miscreant in silence for a few seconds. A host of questions swirled in her head. "Where's your father? Doesn't he give you anything to eat?"

"He's been away again." Teddy waved at the mountain with a floppy hand. "He goes up in the hills and don't come back sometimes for a week."

Shocked and appalled, Cassie stared at the boy as her mouth fell open. "Who takes care of you while he's away?"

Teddy peered up at her with a defensive glare in his eyes. "Me."

The boy had guts, she'd give him as much. Forced to survive on his own, he'd done what he felt he must to live. Still, stealing couldn't be condoned. He must learn that lesson before she could help him. And she would help him.

"Where do you live?" Flint rose to his full height and took a step closer to the boy. "Not far, I'm guessing."

Another wave at the mountain. "Takes me almost an hour to walk here from over the ridge. I don't know how far it is, though."

The boy walked near an hour in order to fill his belly. Desperate times certainly warranted desperate efforts. Where did the father hie off to for so long? Why would he leave the boy to not only provide for himself but also protect himself? How had he stumbled upon her garden as a means of survival? Questions swirled in her mind but one thing remained clear. The boy mustn't continue on the same path.

"Teddy, if you will promise me to never, ever steal anything again, then I will promise to not report you to the sheriff or your father. Deal?"

He slowly shook his head as he frowned. "I wish I could, miss, but how do I eat if I agree?"

Cassie released his shoulders and took his hand. "You'll come with me and I'll give you something. Give so you won't need to take." She smiled at the incredulous expression spreading across the boy's face.

"In exchange for Miss Fairhope's kindness, young man, you'll work around here." Flint laid a firm hand on the lad's shoulder. "Helping in the stable and the inn where needed. Deal?"

"Yes, sir." His grin revealed crooked white teeth with a gap in the disorderly rows from a lost tooth. He glanced to Cassie and grinned wider. "I can do that."

"Good." She led him toward the rear steps while Flint grabbed the gelding's reins. "I'm sure Mr. Drake, our cook, will have something delicious for you."

"I'll meet you two inside after I take care of Smoky." Flint turned and ambled off toward the stable, the black gelding following behind.

Cassie opened the door to the inn and ushered the boy inside. "Come with me."

She kept hold of the boy's hand as she crossed the foyer to the kitchen. "Sheridan, I have someone I'd like you to meet."

The big black man stopped slicing the ham to sweep an assessing glance over the youth. His arched brows revealed his surprise and curiosity. "Who do you have there?"

She made the introductions and told Sheridan of the plan, inviting the boy to eat at the inn whenever he'd like and he'd help out where needed. Suddenly, Flint burst into the room, worry heavy on his brow.

"Man, it's chaos out there. Customers waiting with no one to wait upon them." Flint raked his hand through his hair as he stared at Cassie. "Get him settled and then get out there. As soon as I can, I'll slip down to the Marples' and do my best to persuade them to come back. We need help."

"Take Teddy out to wash up and then into the dining room and I'll get busy." Cassie gently pushed Teddy toward Flint. "Go on with you, now, and I'll be out with food shortly."

The boy cast a glance over his shoulder before trailing after Flint, the door swinging shut behind him. Cassie smiled at Sheridan. "Forget the squash for now. We'll have to make do as is."

"You'll have to tell me where the child came from after we get everybody taken care of." He hefted the knife and finished slicing the ham with two sure strokes. "Put them vegetables in the pot and get 'em cooked up right quick."

"Yes, sir." Cassie saluted him and then fell to work, glad to have solved the mystery of the open garden gate and started on a solution to the boy's missing father. A temporary one, at best. With a name, though, they had a place to start.

The flickering light from the oil lamp on her desk shone on the stationery. She'd delayed as long as she could in good conscience. After a long day of gardening, helping in the kitchen, and waiting on customers in the dining room, she'd retreated to the quiet privacy of her bedroom. Only to be faced with the necessity of writing to her four brothers and begging them to come back home. Even if only until the senator's impending visit. She'd slowly realized how alone she was. Out in the wilds of the state with only Flint and Sheridan to rely upon. Neither of the men being family but good, reliable friends. Still, it was inappropriate. She needed one of her brothers, if not all of them, to come home. She missed them all. More importantly, they should come and pay their respects to their mother. And their unique abilities would be a godsend.

She dipped her quill pen in the iron gall ink and then

started a letter to her youngest brother, Silas. A year older than her, he also proved to be the most unreliable and irresponsible. But he'd found his calling as a reporter in Boston. His ability with words, of composing a compelling story, would help advertise the inn's amenities to the public. Her pen scratched across the linen page as she strove to convince him to make the hazardous trip back to the inn. For her sake, for Pa's sake, if not his. With a sigh, she laid her quill pen down and picked up the tin sander to cast sand over the ink to dry. After a minute, she lifted the page carefully to funnel the sand back into the tin sand container. Setting the letter aside, she pulled another sheet of paper from the stack inside the desk drawer.

Next Daniel. From his infrequent letters she gathered his job as a professor in Knoxville kept him very busy. She dipped the quill and began a quick, pleading letter to her twenty-year-old brother. His good nature and willingness to help others could work in her favor to bring him back home and would prove useful to ensuring the inn's guests enjoyed their stay to the utmost. She finished a few lines to him and then dried the ink and set the page aside, only to pull another sheet out of the drawer.

She tapped the end of the pen on the desk as she contemplated her second-oldest brother, Abram. Dashing and handsome verging on vain, she didn't hold out much hope he'd forego his responsibilities in the nation's capitol in order to come to her rescue. Although, his need to maintain a good reputation might work in her favor if she could persuade him to see his coming home as an altruistic endeavor. He likely knew the senator in question and would best be able to anticipate his needs and desires, further ensuring the success of the distinguished man's journey to the inn. She dashed off several urgent sentences begging for him to return to what he considered to be the savage wilderness.

Finally, her oldest brother, Giles. She'd stayed in closer contact with him over the years he'd been away in Mobile building up a reputable import and export business. He'd remained rather protective of her even from so far away. His approach to safeguarding her safety and reputation proved far gentler than their mother had used. All of which made him her favorite brother. His need to protect and serve might well help with discovering her mother's killers and bringing them to justice. She dipped the quill and quickly worded her desire for him to make the trip north from the Gulf of Mexico. Sanding the letter, she sighed at the subtle ways she'd been trying to manipulate their reaction to her requests. She had no choice but to bring them back to her. She needed them not only to assist at the inn but also to say their farewells to their mother.

A knock on the door drew her attention from the stack of letters. "Come in."

Flint stepped into her room but stayed near the open door. He glanced at the short stack of paper and nodded once. "Writing your brothers?"

"Just finished." She rose from the chair to cross the room to where Flint hesitated. "Do you need something?"

"You." He grinned as he lowered his head to steal a quick kiss.

She smiled against his lips, enjoying the thrill of his mouth on hers. The feel of his strong, capable hands grasping hers. When he pulled away, she felt bereft for an instant at the loss of his warm lips. In time she may even forgive herself enough to permit her feelings for him to grow into love. But not yet. Her heart and soul believed she'd caused her mother's death. Only finding the murderers and making amends for her actions could heal such a deep wound. She'd do what she could to enable her ma to finish whatever unfinished business she had and finally rest in peace. She peered into his open expression.

"What brings you in search of me?" She held onto his hands as she waited for his reply.

"I slipped down to speak with the Marple sisters after the dinner rush."

"What did they say?" She hoped they had agreed to continue working at the inn. Myrtle and Meg had become dependable and ultimately indispensable as far as she was concerned.

He wiggled his head side to side and then shrugged. "I think I managed to talk them into coming back. I guess we'll see tomorrow if they show up as usual."

"With Hannah gone, you might want to put the word out we're looking for servers and house maids. We'll need some extra hands with the increased business you've been generating."

"A good problem to have, I suppose." He grinned at her and tilted his head to one side for an instant. "Needing more hired help to wait upon our many guests."

"And before the senator and his entourage arrive."

"Indeed."

She chuckled as she regarded him, noticing how tiny lines fanned from the corners of his eyes when he smiled. The playful smirk lifting his lips. Her heart soared the longer she searched his laughing eyes. Despite everything her mother had said about him, about *them*, she'd never stop caring about the man holding her hands.

Yet, she had to ask him for one huge favor.

"Flint, I—" She hesitated and then cleared her throat.

She'd pondered for the last day what her path forward should be. How to help her mother with closure so she could indeed move on and rest in peace and not be wandering around scaring people. She'd finally made her decision but hadn't figured out how to ask Flint for his agreement to her intention. She sucked in a steadying breath and smiled at him, infusing it with all the fondness she could muster. Surely he'd understand.

"What is it, sweetheart?" Flint squeezed her hands, encouraging her to continue.

"I need to ask you to do me a favor. A really big one." She arched a brow at him as he nodded.

"Anything. What do you need?" He regarded her with a small, expectant smile.

A sharp stab of regret went through her heart as she prepared to say her next necessary words.

"I can't agree to anything more between us than courting until and unless my father returns home and can give his blessing." She searched the surprise in Flint's eyes, looking for his understanding. "I'm sure I'll be able to sway him to my side."

"You can't agree to what exactly?" Flint swallowed hard, his Adam's apple sliding swiftly up and back down.

"I need my father to agree you're the right man for me."

Flint shook his head as if to clear it. "I'm not following."

"I can't start a relationship of such far-reaching magnitude without knowing my pa will give his blessing. It wouldn't be fair to any of us to begin a life together with anger or disapproval hovering over our love like a storm cloud."

He bit his lip for a moment and then squeezed her hands. "I believe you've a good point, sweetheart. I wouldn't want your father to resent me seeing you let alone marrying you. Which, by the way, is the direction I hope our relationship will go."

He understood and accepted her stance. She smiled up at the man who made her feel special and beautiful.

"Me, too." She reached up to kiss his mouth, a slow press of her lips to his. "Just not yet."

He gazed at her in silence for four beats of her heart. "Know this, sweetheart. I am willing to wait. On one condition."

Her pulse sped up as a slow, sexy grin lifted the corners of his mouth. His green eyes sparkled as they reflected an inner happiness while he leaned in to kiss her. She closed her eyes as he lingered, sampling her lips and then slipping his tongue inside to explore and taste. A jolt akin to the sizzle in the air after a lightning strike nearby flashed through her. She inhaled his unique manly scent and felt slightly dizzy with the affection they shared. Slowly, he withdrew to smile into her eyes.

"Wh-what condition?" She licked her tender lips and his gaze shifted to watch the tip of her tongue glide across her lower lip, then lifted back to meet hers.

He held up one finger to point at the ceiling. "Under no circumstances will you rebuff my attentions for the duration. I want to be able to show you how much I care for and about you."

The thought of not letting him kiss her again had never crossed her mind. Indeed, she might literally die if she never had another of his tender kisses. She moistened her lips, pleased when his gaze dropped again before meeting hers. She loved being with him.

"That's a deal." She sealed their bargain with a kiss. "I can't wait for Pa to come home."

"Neither can I." He squeezed her hands and smiled. "But as long as I have you at my side, we can face whatever comes our way."

"Yes, we can." Cassie gazed into his loving eyes. "Together."

The End

Thanks so much for reading *The Haunting of Fury Falls Inn*! The adventure is just beginning for Cassie and Flint, so stay tuned for more to come in this six-book series.

To find out about new releases and upcoming appearances, please sign up for my newsletter via my website at www.bettybolte.com. I send out a monthly newsletter with book news to share with my readers, upcoming events and signings, and even a few favorite recipes, puzzles, and other doings!

I'd love to hear from you! Feel free to send me an email at betty@bettybolte.com, find me on Facebook at www.facebook.com/AuthorBettyBolte, follow me on BookBub, or connect with me on Twitter @BettyBolte.

You can always find an updated list of the titles in this series, as well as all of my other books on my website, at www.bettybolte.com/books/.

Thanks again for reading!